G. COUCHMAN

D0324925

THE VENGEANCE

ALSO BY ROBERT C. SLOANE

A Nice Place to Live

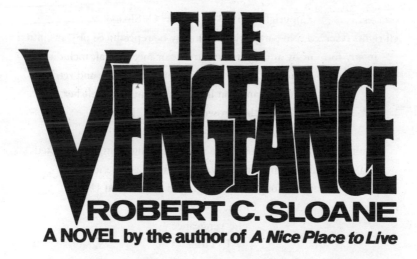

THE VENGEANCE

ROBERT C. SLOANE

A NOVEL by the author of *A Nice Place to Live*

CROWN PUBLISHERS, INC.   NEW YORK

Copyright © 1983 by Robert C. Sloane
All rights reserved. No part of this book may be reproduced or transmitted
in any form or by any means, electronic or mechanical, including
photocopying, recording, or by any information storage and retrieval
system, without permission in writing from the publisher.
Published by Crown Publishers, Inc.,
One Park Avenue, New York, New York 10016, and
simultaneously in Canada by General Publishing Company Limited
Manufactured in the United States of America
Library of Congress Cataloging in Publication Data
Sloane, Robert C.
The vengeance.
I. Title.
PS3569.L594V4   1983   813'.54   83-2013
ISBN 0-517-55064-4
10 9 8 7 6 5 4 3 2 1
First Edition

To my wife,

Joan,

with love

There are more things in heaven and earth, Horatio,
Than are dreamt of in your philosophy.

Hamlet, act I, scene v

Beware the dark forest, O ye mortals,
The sweetness of the night pines.

Ancient Nordic ballad

Norway
Spring, Present

1

THE SHIP GLIDED swiftly through the black waters of the fjord. The waves at its prow bubbled white with foam and then hissed away into stillness. Stillness pervaded the night. It flowed across the water to the shadowed pines on the shore, swept up the ice-rimed cliffs, and muted the high, silver cataracts, misting them into silence as they fell.

The woman stood with her hands resting lightly on the railing. Her upturned face was cast in moonlight as she watched the towering stone escarpments pass darkly through the star-filled sky. Their stark lineaments filled her thoughts with memories, remnants of nightmare.

The first radiant beams of the northern lights that streamed across her vision turned her gaze upward. She watched raptly as shaft after shaft of pure light ran the firmament, slowly bursting the midnight like the rays of an alien sun, until the entire horizon was encased in a dome of gold.

Beautiful land, she thought. Land of gold and ice. Perhaps here I shall find what I am terrified to find. Perhaps here is the horror that I seek, the horror that shattered my life, the horror that shall kill me with sadness. Dear God, let me find it. Dear God, lend me strength when I do. The fearful tenor of her thoughts seemed to transform the gilded crags above her. Unwillingly she watched as the polar brilliance turned them into bronzed monoliths, primeval ruins, great golden-hued halls filled with trumpeted terrors.

Abruptly, the ship's horn blasted the quiet. The woman's whole body recoiled in fright as the sound reverberated through the burnished air and up into the mountains beyond.

The creature stood on the flat rock above the now iridescent water. His body was thrust forward, a silhouette of menace. His eyes were riveted on the caribou stag grazing beneath him. He felt no hunger. The impending struggle was a need within him, a desire that could be assuaged only in blood. Suddenly, the horn of the ship far beneath him keened through the night, rending the still air like the call of a mournful leviathan. The stag bolted so quickly that he was running before he raised his head. The creature turned toward the sound with reptilian quickness, his flared eyes and open mouth forming a mask of utter savagery. A low growl started in his throat. When the horn sounded again, he stepped forward to the edge of the rock, raised his head to the beamed sky, and bellowed into the night. It was an answer, an exultation, a challenge to the stars. As the volume of his voice grew, he moved his head from side to side and roared with a wild and primal ecstasy. From the surrounding mountains other cries came—some of them abominable howlings, others breaching the air like claps of thunder, until the walls of the fjord echoed and reechoed with sound.

As the unearthly clangor came racing across the water through the bright air, the woman released the railing, one hand going to her mouth. Her eyes searched the illumined precipices around her, darting in fear, uncontrollable. Her perfect features crumpled with an inner, unbearable pain. She shook her head several times as if in denial and drew her coat more securely around her. In another moment she was gone, walking quickly toward lighted doors and the voices within.

Unhurriedly, the night winds carried the bestial calls down the fjord toward the sea. The night returned once again to silence. Bathed in the strange light, the ship turned gracefully in toward the glowing harbor. High above it, the creature watched its path with the gleaming, intent eyes of a predator. A hideous smile parted his lips. He had seen these ships before. Tomorrow his forest would be full of prey, laughing and unafraid. Tomorrow the hunting would be good, very good. Only his eyes moved as they followed the gliding ship. His body remained immobile, a part of the rock, a part of the night, the essence of the night. The feral smile grew wider, the eyes glowed redly in terrific anticipation.

BOOK ONE

Long Island
1974

2

A CHILL SEPTEMBER fog covered Mill Harbor, shrouding the dawn with a quiet beauty. The moist trees shone in the pale light, their branches still dripping from the night rain. The tall reeds along the shore bowed their feathery tops under the crystal weight of droplets. The inlet was calm and flat, pressed by the heavy mist into quiescence. Like silver specters, a pair of swans winged their way across the cove toward the Sound, melding into the gray enchantment, disappearing in silence.

The tall man stood by the charred ruins of the house, one hand resting on the stone chimney. His body, even at rest, had the tensed, charged look of immense power, his back and shoulders so heavily muscled that he seemed to crouch rather than stand. The large head was framed in thick silver hair that fell to his shoulders. The wide face had large-boned, Nordic features that were marred by a wild and ravaging harshness that showed in the thin, cruel lips and in the arctic eyes, cold and blue as moonstruck glaciers, merciless as the stars.

As he stood above the burned timbers, he lifted his face to the mist. A terrible rage clenched his hands, contorted his features. Slowly, his head began to move from side to side. As these movements quickened, he became no longer man but apparition. A black wolf's head appeared above his left shoulder, its yellow-gleaming eyes bright with feral hatred, its lips rippling in a malevolent growl. Another head appeared above the right shoulder. It was an abomination. It came from the polar reaches that rim the edge of the world, the hair and beard of ice surrounding a face of madness. Out of the black squared mouth issued the screeching sounds of tundra winds that hurl across barrens without suns.

The sound of a branch cracking came through the damp air. In an instant the two demonic heads had disappeared. The tall man turned toward the noise. On the path that followed the shoreline of the cove a man appeared. He was jogging slowly, a wool cap covering his graying hair, breathing deeply and evenly in the cool air. The tall man watched him approach. One ear moved imperceptibly. His nostrils flared. His eyes became alert, eager. He almost smiled. As the jogger passed below him, he drew his arm back across his chest and struck the chimney with his fist. The force of the blow cleaved the structure in half, the stones and cement falling as if in slow motion onto the blackened wood below. The jogger stopped, frozen in his tracks, as the sound rumbled toward him out of the fog.

That evening, seated at a table in a motel room, the tall man stared down at the paper before him. He began to write.

Sister,
   Our premonitions were correct. Mama is dead. Jotunn, our brother, is dead. When the police told me he died by fire, I had to leave without further details. You know my nature. You know my temper. But I shall get details. All details. Something is not right here. Jotunn would never allow fire anywhere near his house. Someone caused that fire. There are responsibil-

ities here. I feel it. Retribution fills the night. Vengeance and death are all around me. I inhale vengeance, my sister, I exhale death. How my blood sings!

The tall man paused, staring down at a fleck of dried blood that clung to the hairs on the back of his huge hand. He hunched forward, licked at it, then straightened up and continued.

Of course, Thagnar, I have made an appropriate sacrifice and placed it properly. A small gesture. There are larger ones to follow.

I shall write again. I need information. I need names. Details, then havoc. That is my way.

HYRMGAR

3

NICK MARINO STARED at his wife, not quite believing what he saw. The three days of Florida sun had served her well, emphasizing her prominent cheekbones and lightening her long blond hair.

"You look like a vision tonight, pal o' mine," he said. "It's amazing what skillful application of expensive makeup can do for a person."

Christine Marino stuck her tongue out at her husband and looked down at the boy seated between them. "Joey, your father never *could* stand the fact that I am prettier than he is." She looked back at her husband, at the blue eyes, the curling black hair, the too-pretty mouth. "Not by much," she said softly, placing her hand lightly on his.

Their mood was interrupted by a loud voice from across the table. "You two are positively pornographic. It's like watching an old, badly directed movie. Visions? Holding hands? That stuff went out with Guy Lombardo."

Nick's eyes never left his wife's. "Did you hear somebody wheeze, darling?" he said.

"No"—Christine shook her head— "it was more like a rasping sound, wasn't it, dear?"

"No, no, sweetheart, I really think it was a definite garrulous wheezing."

"You may be right, my sweet. It's really so hard to tell when a person's bridge doesn't fit, isn't it."

The voice spoke again, trying not to laugh. "Sure, make fun of my sixty-seven-year-old gums. Let nothing be sacred. Look, did we come to this fancy restaurant to rejuvenate your tiresome libidos, or did we come here to eat? And, lest we forget, drink."

Christine and Nick turned toward the speaker. Henrietta Knapp, Christine's spinster aunt, was staring at them through glasses that threatened to fall off her nose. She was dressed in a bright yellow blouse with matching pants. Both were covered with black rosettes. Inside each rosette was a pair of red lips. Her right arm and shoulder were encased in a plaster cast held in a sling. On each ear was a large circular earring with a plastic YES swinging freely within it. A necklace with a huge pendant YES lay atop a rippling black feather boa. On her head was a blond wig with thick bangs and two long braids in back. The severe anachronism of the wrinkled face and the girlish wig was further emphasized by the fact that it was slightly askew, giving her an odd, unbalanced look.

Christine glanced down at her aunt's cast and then at the similar heavy cast on Nick's right hand. She tried to smile. "What a bunch of wrecks," she said quietly.

Henrietta shook her head. "Not according to your husband's eyes, dearie. You needn't stare at me in that hungry Neapolitan fashion, Nicholas. It cannot be. Forget me if you can. This body shall never be yours."

Nick raised his eyes to the ceiling. "God is good," he said quietly.

Henrietta fixed him with a hard stare over her glasses. She looked around the table. "Say, why is everybody so dressed up, anyway? You'd think it was somebody's birthday or something."

"You know it's mine," Joey Marino said, smiling.

Henrietta looked down at the blue eyes, the sunburned nose. Her face softened. "Yes, I know, handsome." She touched the thick black hair for a moment. "Nine big ones, hmmm? I've got a liver spot that's nine years old. Ah me." She sighed. "Nicholas, isn't it about time you bought some wine?"

"Yes, it is, my dear," Nick answered.

The wine steward was at their table a moment after Nick had summoned him. He was a small, immaculately dressed man with a deep tan and white hair. "*Monsieur?*" he said.

Although her eyes never left Nick's, Henrietta's demeanor became suddenly alert. "Nicholas," she breathed. "How very sweet. I forgive you your dark thoughts, *mon pauvre.*" Her hand went to her necklace. The YES began to twirl slowly.

"I think we'll have the Châteauneuf," Nick said after a moment. "Not too cold."

When the steward returned, Nick inspected the label briefly and nodded toward Henrietta. A small amount of wine was poured into her glass.

"Ah," she said. "I am to be *tasteuse.*" She inspected the dark wine in front of the candlelight and then drained the glass.

"Satisfactory, *madame?*" The steward waited.

Henrietta's expression was worldly, patient. She chose her words like someone crossing a stream on slippery stones. "I think, *après tout*, that there can be no such thing as a satisfactory wine. Does this approach it? Yes. I am amused by its indelicacy. And yet, and yet, it hides. One little grape foot thrust forward, and then quickly withdrawn." She closed her eyes. "Yes, yes. It becomes suddenly clear," she said after a moment. "Wicked, wicked little wine. Its insouciance flirts with the salacious. A coquette. She must be very careful. Or she must be served very cold."

Nick watched the stoic wine steward stare down at Henrietta steadily. He turned to Christine. "I am going to break into little pieces at any moment," he whispered, his shoulders shaking with laughter. "Please dance with me. Now."

"All right," Christine said softly. "If you'll promise not to step on my little grape foot."

Nick groaned and looked upward. As they walked toward the dance floor, one hand was covering his face.

Christine gave her body to the warm morning sun. Her glance rested on Henrietta, who sat crumpled in her beach chair, the brim of her wide hat flopping down around her face. Christine smiled affectionately. "Henrietta, I say this regretfully, but you really look as if someone left you out here overnight."

"I feel like it," Henrietta replied. "I can't lift my tongue up, my whole body won't talk to me. That was some birthday party last night. What, may I ask, in hell was I drinking?"

"Ask rather, auntie dear, what did you not."

"That is nice. That's wonderful. What I need right now is a sarcastic niece. If you're so incredibly clever, tell me why my knees hurt."

"That most probably comes—I'm just guessing, mind you—from dancing in high heels with only one shoe on."

"I danced?" Henrietta almost smiled. "With whom?"

"Yourself."

The other woman nodded. "Of course. It figures."

"Now, now, auntie, don't feel bad. You were the center of attention. Why, just about everybody was watching you. I think you started a new dance craze. I really do. It most probably will be called Going in Circles While Pivoting on One Foot and Waving Your Napkin. Nick and I are certainly very proud of you."

The two women sat looking at each other, slow smiles spreading across their faces. After a long moment, Henrietta's face softened. "Look at you," she said. "I mean, just look at you. If I'm a potential alcoholic it's strictly your fault."

"Potential! Ye gods! And what do you mean, *my* fault? What on earth are you talking about?"

"I mean, dearie, that you're too much. You're too perfect, too beautiful. I don't suffer enough, I have to suffer by comparison, too? I mean, why does the brim of your hat stay up so perfectly, and why did mine fall down? Hmmm? Who says you have to have such a perfect nose *and* green eyes *and* skin like that? Where is it written that you had to have the legs of a beauty queen, the ass of a goddess?"

Christine stared at her. "The . . . ass . . . of . . . a . . . goddess?" she repeated.

"You heard me, sweetie." Henrietta shook her head moodily. She reached into her sling, withdrew a Bloody Mary, and sipped at it.

Christine gazed at Henrietta. Her smile slowly faded as her eyes roamed up and down the heavy cast that covered her aunt's arm and shoulder. She remembered seeing Henrietta bound to that broad, flat stone in the Anderson boathouse. She remembered seeing the bone protruding from that frail, shattered shoulder. She remembered the blood dripping in the darkness. She remembered. Tenderly, with infinite care, she reached out and adjusted the stiff golden braids of the wig toward the back. As if she could read the younger woman's thoughts, Henrietta looked up at Christine. They did not speak.

"Does it hurt, Hen?" Christine asked finally.

Henrietta ran her fingers lightly over her shoulder. "Yes," she said. "It hurts." After a pause, she spoke again. "I'm glad you killed them, Chris. I'm so proud of you and Nick. They were going to murder us all. Murderers! Both of them, mother and son. Murderers, giants, unearthly bastards, whatever they were."

Christine looked down at the sand, her face rigid. She did not answer.

Henrietta reached carefully for her drink again. She sipped it, staring out over the water. "I had a dream the other night," she said. "You want to hear it?"

"No," Christine replied.

"It was horrible. There was this terrible pounding on my bedroom door. Then this huge, ugly creature comes roaring through it, grabs me by the shoulder and starts shaking me until . . ." She stopped.

Christine looked up. "What is it, Hen?" She watched as her aunt finished the drink quickly.

"What is what?" Henrietta said.

"You look funny. What are you thinking about?"

"Nothing. I just stopped talking, that's all."

"You never stop talking. What's on your mind?"

Henrietta's head turned. She looked seriously into Christine's eyes. "Thought for the day, niece. Supposing . . . supposing there are more of them out there. Supposing those murderers had relatives out there, somebody's Uncle Igor or something. Supposing they didn't like what we did. Supposing they found out about it and . . ." Henrietta stopped speaking. She did not like what she saw in Christine's face. She bit her lip. "Forget it, honey," she said softly. "That was very stupid of me." She tilted her head toward Christine, who seemed not to hear her. Pain etched her features as she watched Christine's glance darting about, looking at nothing. "Oh, Chris, baby. I'm sorry. It was just a bad dream, a bad joke, I . . ." She shook her head. Her free hand went up to her forehead. "Dammit," she said quietly

The hot sun glared down on the two women, who sat, silent and unmoving now, surrounded by glimmering waves of heat. High overhead, a bird shrieked, then plunged toward the water to kill.

4

THE TALL MAN rose early. He glanced at himself in the mirror. His hair had come out just as he had wished. Brown, with just a hint of gray areas along the sides. He shaved carefully, dressed in a gray pin-striped suit, and stood before the mirror once again. Staring at his face in total concentration, he furrowed his brow and wrinkled the lines around his eyes. When he relaxed his face several seconds later, the deep furrows and lines remained. After making several further adjustments to his face, he put on a pair of sunglasses and picked up a briefcase and raincoat from a chair. The man who emerged from the motel room a moment later appeared to have aged twenty years. His stomach protruded outward, and he walked with a slow, heavy gait.

An hour later the tall man emerged from a barbershop, his hair neatly cut. He walked into a small printing shop, picked up the business cards he had ordered, and inserted several of them in his inside jacket pocket. He threw the rest of the cards away in a nearby trash can.

Later that morning he stood in front of the desk sergeant at the Mill Harbor police station. He handed the sergeant one of the cards.

"I'd like to speak to someone in connection with the Anderson fire. Insurance investigation." His voice sounded bored, tired.

The sergeant flipped a switch. "Lieutenant Broderick, someone here to see you about the fire at the Anderson place. Insurance."

It was several minutes before a slim man in a brown, vested suit appeared at the desk. His red moustache was precisely clipped. The hard, green eyes read the card the sergeant gave him and then snapped up toward the tall man. "How can I help you, Mr. Kronberg?"

"Well, it's a little involved." The tall man spoke apologetically. "I wonder if we could sit down somewhere. My feet are killing me."

The detective turned toward an office off the main hall. The tall man followed, smiling his thanks to the desk sergeant.

After they were seated, the detective stared into the sunglasses. "Yes?" he said.

The tall man fumbled with his briefcase, did not open it. "Yes. Well, as the sergeant told you, I'm here about the Anderson fire. I have been to the fire marshal's office. He was very helpful. He suggested that I might check with your office. Have you any idea why he would say that?"

"I might. May I inquire who the insurance beneficiaries are? Relatives, perhaps?" Broderick's voice was casual. His face was not.

The other man crossed his legs and flicked at something on the knee of his trousers. "No. No relatives," he said. "As a matter of fact, Mr. Anderson left his money to charitable organizations. Needy children and all that. It's a considerable sum, or I wouldn't be here."

"Precisely why are you here, Mr. Kronberg?"

"I told you. The fire marshal thought it might prove helpful. My impression is that there is more here than simple accidental fire. Was this fire a police matter, Lieutenant? If it was deliberately set by the Andersons, I cannot authorize payment. We do not pay in such cases."

The detective shook his head slightly. His cool gaze never left the other man's face. "We have ourselves a situation here, Mr. Kronberg." After a pause, he continued. "That fire was deliberately set. But it was not set by the Andersons."

The other man's fingers spread slowly out over his briefcase. "Ah," he said. "You are right, Lieutenant. We do have a situation." His voice lowered to a whisper. "Who set it, Detective?"

"Is that really important?" Broderick's eyes studied the face before him.

"So important," the tall man exhaled. He took a deep breath and settled his features. "You force me to repeat myself, sir. I cannot authorize payment unless I have the details, Lieutenant. I must have the details."

Broderick stared at the other man. He pressed his fingertips together and tapped them several times. After a long moment, he rose and went to a file cabinet. When he returned, he placed a thick green folder on his desk. "Mr. Kronberg," he said. "Because of the highly unusual circumstances involved in this case, I am going to let you read a transcript of a tape I recorded on the day after the fire. I am going to have to ask you to keep this confidential until this matter has been officially resolved."

"Of course. And I cannot tell you how much I appreciate your help, Lieutenant." The hand that reached for the folder moved with the power and directness of a large constrictor.

Statement made to Lieutenant Clifford Broderick, 1:00 P.M., September 7, 1974.

My name is Christine Marino. I live at 45 Kensington

Road, Mill Harbor, Long Island. I am thirty years old. I am giving this statement to Lieutenant Detective Broderick of the Mill Harbor Police Department.

It is very difficult for me to talk about this, Lieutenant. These people, these monsters kidnapped my son. They were going to kill him. I'm glad we killed both of them. I'm glad we burned Anderson and destroyed his mother. I would do it again.

The tall man closed his eyes, adjusted his sunglasses delicately against his nose, then continued to read.

You told me to begin at the beginning, Lieutenant, so I'll try. It began almost as soon as we moved in. We had a dog, the worst-looking thing. We loved him. Something killed him, tore his head off his shoulders. We bought a Great Dane and something ripped *him* to pieces. You saw what happened, Lieutenant. I can still remember your face. Bowen Stirner knew what was happening. He let you read his paper on giants and their bastard troll offspring—leave it in, Lieutenant—and because he knew them for the murderous beasts that they were, Anderson killed him. Karl Anderson, troll, beast, bastard, killed him—I'm sorry, Lieutenant, I'll be all right in a moment. And his mother. A murderess, Lieutenant.

Kronberg's breathing became labored. He looked up at the ceiling. He seemed to be searching for something. After several seconds, he continued.

Karl Anderson told me everything before he died. He and his murderess mother. Killing and slaughtering in Mill Harbor. And do you know why, Lieutenant? Do you want to know why? They were in love. In love,

Lieutenant. Anderson with me, his mother with my husband. They lusted after us, Lieutenant. And in their impatience and jealousy, they murdered, they slaughtered, they drank blood, troll beasts and bastards. It's all in Bowen's report, Lieutenant. You read it. You have it on file. Read it again, Lieutenant. Believe it. Believe it.

The tall man looked up at Broderick. "Trolls, Lieutenant? Giants? Is this a police deposition or a fairy tale? This is a report from an unbalanced witness. I cannot take this back to my supervisor. Impossible."

Lieutenant Broderick drummed his fingers on his desk. "Unbalanced, Mr. Kronberg? No. Distraught? Definitely. This deposition was taped at Mrs. Marino's house the day after all this happened. I believe she was still somewhat in a state of shock. She has gone away for several weeks to rest. We intend to get a finalized version when she returns. If you continue to read, you will understand the reasons for her mental state."

The tall man shook his head unbelievingly. His breathing was regular now, but very deep.

Trolls can change their shapes, Lieutenant, the way they look. Murderess Anderson changed herself into a beautiful young blond siren. She enchanted my husband with her evil magic. She almost turned him into a troll. It was horrible. She made him take Joey over to their house. When I went over there to get him, Anderson threatened Joey. That's what saved us all. Anderson's threats broke the spell over Nick. It was Nick's love for Joey that made him set that house on fire so we could escape.

The tall man's lips parted. It was not a smile. He looked up. "A truly close-knit family. Ideal. Enough parental devotion here to burn down a house. A house with occupants. Splendid people."

Broderick glanced at the other man quickly, then looked away, his face unreadable.

"I asked for details," the tall man continued, "and I am getting details. My cup, in fact, runneth over." His eyes returned to the deposition.

> Karl Anderson was burned in that fire. That's how he died. His mother ran after our car. I don't know whether you're going to believe this, Lieutenant, but she was over eight feet tall, she had tusks, she was a horror. She caught us at fifty-five miles per hour and jumped on our station wagon, holding on, pounding on the roof. Then, just as we came to a railroad bridge, she leaned over on the driver's side, trying to get at me. I swerved the car along the bridge's foundation, knocking her off, killing her. She was trying to kill my son.

The tall man closed the folder gently. He looked up at the detective. When he spoke it was a controlled whisper. "The Marinos. They do protect their own, don't they. Burning. Burning and killing. For son Joey."

This time Broderick stared at the other man coldly. "I am not sure I understand your tone, Mr. Kronberg. As far as we can determine, the Marinos were acting out of self-defense. We have no reason to doubt their story."

"Doubt, Lieutenant Broderick. Enter into doubt." The tall man's face contorted suddenly. Behind the dark glasses, the eyes hardened. "It is not pleasant to die by fire." His voice became a low hiss. "Consider, Lieutenant, who are the monsters here. Meditate upon who is a murderess. Do your work, Lieutenant. Let justice be done." The tall man became suddenly aware of Broderick's calculating stare. His mouth twitched once, clicking his anger off. He stood up and placed the folder on the desk in front of him. "I cannot accept this information, Lieutenant. I came here for facts. You give me fables. Eight-foot women? Witchcraft and sorcery?" His voice rose. "Tusks, Lieutenant? Unacceptable. I shall have to wait for a final, more sane statement when Mrs. Marino comes back from . . . where did you say she had gone?"

Broderick's eyes had never left the other man's face. After a moment he said quietly, "Away."

"Ah, yes. Well, thank you for your attempted cooperation. I shall return, you may be assured." The tall man rose and walked toward the door. Without seeming to hurry, Broderick was there ahead of him.

"I'm curious, Mr. Kronberg," he said. "You wear sunglasses indoors. Is that habit or affliction?"

The tall man glared down at Broderick, his huge shoulders hulking over the detective. He removed the glasses with deliberate care, the eyes of ice glittering malevolently. He cracked the frame with the fingers of one hand and dropped the glasses to the floor. "Neither," he said. He brushed past the other man, opened the door, and walked out.

Lieutenant Broderick stood looking at the door. He put a cigarette in his mouth and began absently to pat his pockets in search of his lighter. His right hand flicked the flame to his cigarette while his left hand continued to search. He walked to the telephone and dialed the number on the card Kronberg had given him. It was not in service at this time. He dialed it again, carefully. It was still, the machine informed him, not in service. He hung up. He inhaled deeply and nodded his head. His hunch had been right. He had sensed it from the beginning. The man was not an insurance investigator. The man was an Anderson. The huge physique, the aura of physical power, the facial resemblance. He had proved it by getting a look at those glacial Anderson eyes. Terrible eyes. Predator eyes. Inhuman. His gaze rose to the ceiling, squinting through the cigarette smoke. Hell, he thought. Damn it to hell. What have I got here? Another murderous Anderson troll?

Broderick stared at the ceiling, seeing nothing. He was remembering how he had sat in the Marinos' living room a month ago and listened to Bowen Stirner accuse Karl Anderson of murder. He remembered the professor's insistence that Anderson was a beast, a troll, a supernatural being, the result of giant-human intercourse throughout the ages. He remembered his own disbelief and then reading Stirner's paper on the former existence of giants. It had not convinced him, but it had come close. He remembered the report on trolls found on Stirner's desk after his disappearance. He had described them as murderous monsters who live in human societies today. Beast-humans whose titanic forebears gave them sexual lusts that involved dismemberment and the drinking of blood. They could, according to the professor, change their faces and forms to seduce their human sexual prey, or enchant them into becoming trolls themselves.

And then Broderick remembered the night they had found Bowen Stirner's body. He remembered the winches lifting up the cement floor of the boathouse. It had been like lifting up the lid of hell. The few small human skeletons. The decapitated, shriveled body of Stirner, drained of blood. And he remembered the snakes. The long black snakes that slid through the bones, that interlaced themselves over the professor's body possessively. The snakes that were unafraid of the screeching cables, that raised their heads in the bright light, hissing in immobile, archaic readiness.

The detective replaced his cigarette. That had been a bad

night, he thought. Very bad. Despite himself, the sight had shaken something inside him.

Smoke curled up in front of him once again. And agent Kronberg, he meditated. What have we got there? Another murdering Anderson? Another troll, bent on revenge for the killing of his clan members? Stop it, Clifford. Training, Clifford, training. Suspicion is not proof. Don't touch him until he does something. But I'm going to have you watched, you cold-eyed bastard. Believe it.

The detective thought about the Marinos and what they had already gone through. And then he thought about their return home, into the vengeful arms of Kronberg and who knows who else. His face hardened. Suddenly, his fist shot out and struck the top of his desk viciously. The force of the blow sent the ashtray to the floor, spilling half-smoked cigarettes on the worn green carpet. Broderick did not notice. He was thinking about Kronberg's eyes. An absence there, of . . . what? He took out his revolver and methodically rotated the cylinder on the desk in front of him.

5

THE TALL MAN stood at the motel window staring up at the moon in an ancient enchantment. The light reflected off the harsh planes of his face, giving it a white, fierce beauty.

Havoc is coming, he thought. Mayhem is near. Blood is upon the midnight, dark and delicious hour of rapture. Poor detective. The detective as victim. Thin, plodding, suspecting man. What did you see, Lieutenant, what did you see? It does not matter. Your knowledge is your nemesis, your cleverness is your doom.

An alien smile parted his lips. He listened to the secret nightsong that streamed toward him out of the darkness. His uplifted features received the moonbeams as caress. The blue glittering eyes made love to the bright orb above him.

A heavy knocking on the door behind him interrupted his thoughts. Unhurriedly, he turned his head toward the sound. The knock was repeated, louder, more insistent. The tall man glided toward the door and opened it. Standing in the brightly lit corridor was a woman whose glacial eyes matched his own. Her tall body was firm and supple, but she was not attractive. Her features were correctly proportioned, but she was not beautiful. The fault lay somewhere within her, in the cast of her mouth, in what emanated from her eyes.

"Sister!" The tall man spoke harshly. "You are not needed here." He stood, blocking the doorway.

The woman pushed her way past him into the room. She turned and spoke, her mouth contorted in disdain. "As ever, Hyrmgar, you are selfish." Her voice was harsh, unearthly. "You are secretive. You hide things from your sister. I know what you will do here. You stink of vengeance. Why was I not invited to participate?"

"These people are mine." The tall man's voice rumbled like approaching thunder. "They killed my mother. They are *mine*. You are not needed here."

"They killed *our* beloved mother!" The woman's voice rose. Scarlet fires ignited deep within her eyes. "I shall have them, I shall *have* them."

The tall man pointed a huge finger at her. "Go home, Thagnar. You are a blunderer. You will overdo. You will arouse suspicions. Go home!"

The woman whispered, "Unfair. You are selfish. Unfair." Suddenly, like a striking snake, her neck extended, her teeth clenched on the finger in front of her.

The tall man recoiled, shaking his hand. "Evil woman!" he shouted. "Biter!"

The woman's head reared back; her body was rigid. Slowly, the hair about her head began to move. As her anger increased, it divided into strands, writhing and coiling above her like a pit of restless vipers. "Unfair!" she whispered. "Unfair!" Her eyes glowed red, the movement above them frenetic now.

The tall man stared at the malevolent Medusa before him, his eyes matching hers in crimson intensity, his mouth opened in a silent howl of rage. The malignancy in the room seemed to bulge the walls outward, threatening to burst them. They stood motionless for several moments. It was the man who spoke first. His eyes glinted murderously.

"Someday, Thagnar, I shall have to chastise you. Properly." A menacing sibilance issued from the woman's open mouth. "But not now," the tall man continued. "Not here. It would be imprudent." He paused. "All right," he said finally. "You may have *one*. No more."

"And how many shall you have, brother?"

"One only. Let us not be uncivilized, Thagnar. There is a detective here. Suspicious, meddling, knowing. He shall be mine. A joy that is also a necessity."

"And mine? And mine?"

"A man named Maynard Drogin, my impatient sister. He lives in an old mill at the end of the inlet. A real-estate agent. Buy something from him tonight. Purchase his soul, my sister. It was he who told me only this afternoon that our brother and our precious mother got only what they deserved."

"Ah-h-h," the woman exhaled. It was a long, sexual sigh.

"Yes, Agent Drogin is a talkative man. It was he who told me where the killers are, where the people who burned our brother are at this very moment." The woman's face became animated with hate, hideous in its eagerness. "Sit down, sister, and I shall tell you a story. About a family who burns and murders. And why, after making the appropriate offerings tonight, we are flying to Fort Lauderdale, Florida, tomorrow. A land of milk and honey, sister, where Marinos play in the cursed sunshine. Oh, yes. But we shall bring the darkness, sweet sister. Vengeance. Vengeance and justice. Murder to the murderers."

The moon silvered the Mill Harbor night. It illumined small patches of fog above the marshes, vapor ghosts that danced beside the still, shimmering water and whitened the willow leaves that fluttered in the shore breezes.

Detective Clifford Broderick ran along the dark road, his feet pounding rhythmically on the blacktop. His legs were surprisingly thick for a man of his weight. He ran at a fast pace with little effort.

Usually when the detective ran, the tensions of the day drained out of him with the perspiration. Tonight it was no good. He couldn't get Kronberg out of his mind. Kronberg, the returning Marinos. Something bad was coming down. He could feel it. Hell, he thought. Damn job. Can't even run in peace. He tried to shadowbox his frustration away, his arms flashing in the moonlight, but it was no good, no good at all.

As Broderick passed a side road to his right, another runner appeared out of the darkness, tall, powerfully built, running smoothly. Several seconds later Broderick heard footsteps behind him, and then the big man was abreast of him, slowing his pace to that of the detective. Broderick glanced up at the huge shoulders that loomed beside him. The detective could see, he could even feel, the immense power of the man next to him. A thrill of fear coursed through him. The man's face reminded him of Karl Anderson.

After a moment, the runner spoke. "I feel exhilarated. Truly exhilarated."

Broderick increased his pace. The man stayed with him effortlessly. His body bumped into the detective's lightly, then again and again.

Without turning around, Broderick spoke, his voice steadier than his emotions. "What do you say, buddy. What do you say you knock it off."

The tall man smiled, crowded still closer. "Buddy," he repeated, savoring the word. "How compatible. We are friends of the road, are we not?"

Broderick did not answer. They continued on in silence. The huge man jarred him once again, knocking him off his stride. Despite himself, Broderick was frightened, but his face showed nothing.

In another minute the man spoke again. "Do you believe, my buddy, that anticipation holds more joy than fulfillment?" He raised his eyes. "And did you know, my companion, that the moon makes lovers of us all. The blood tides run and we are helpless in that red current."

Broderick stopped. He turned and faced the tall man, who had halted beside him. "Say, fella"—he tried to keep his voice even— "what the hell can I do for you?" He looked up, not prepared for what he saw. He had seen bad eyes before, plenty of them, but none like these. Never. Cold and blue, with a wild eagerness, a savage lust that went beyond human desires. Bowen Stirner's report flashed through his mind. This was a troll in front of him. He knew it. This was a killer of men. His hand went automatically behind him. His gun was not there.

The tall man's glance caught Broderick's movement. His smile broadened. "Say, pal," he said quietly. "What can I do to you?" His right hand slowly rose until it was even with Broderick's mouth. The forefinger slowly unfolded and went forward until it pressed against the detective's lips. Broderick clenched his teeth, too stunned to do anything else. Without effort the huge man thrust his finger forward. Shock and pain shot through Broderick as he heard his front teeth crack and break. Acting out of pure reflex, he swung a vicious karate blow at the throat above him. Moving with incredible quickness, the other hand of the man was there to block the incoming blow. Searing pain jolted through the detective's arm. It had been like hitting a cement wall. The detective's reaction was pure survival now. He could not fight the man who towered above him. There was something unnatural here, something that made combat unthinkable, useless.

He wheeled and hurdled a ditch at the side of the road. He stumbled, slid down the embankment a few feet, and then clambered back up, entering a sparsely wooded area above him. He ran as fast as he could, dodging the trees and the thick vines attached to them. His mouth was filled with blood and his right hand hung numbly at his side, but he felt nothing, his mounting fear driving him forward. Hearing no one behind him, he glanced backward toward the road. What he saw through the pale trees stopped him in his tracks. Below him, still standing on the road, the man stood staring at him, his body tensed, motionless. But Broderick saw only his eyes. Red windows into Chaos itself, glaring through the night like beams from the maelstrom.

The two men looked at each other for a long moment, frozen in the most ancient of dramas. And then the detective heard what the archaic depths of his being knew he had to hear. A low growl rolled toward him through the stillness. The panther in the dead of night, the feral sound of total menace. Broderick's face became ashen.

He turned and sprinted through the woods, his heart pounding, his mind numb with the terror that only prey can know. When he reached the edge of the forest, he glanced back over his shoulder again. His eyes widened in horror. His pursuer was running through the trees now, racing at an incredible speed, with unbelievably long, lunging strides.

The detective ran across the narrow meadow in front of him, his eyes resembling those of a madman, searching for cover, for a place to hide. Before him stretched the moonlit cove of Mill Harbor. Desperately, he darted toward it, seeking sanctuary in its dark waters. As he ran past the tall clumps of salt-marsh grass, the ground beneath him became increasingly soft. Before he realized what was happening, his feet were buried in mud and the water was up to his knees. Blindly, he struggled forward, each step agonizingly slow, until at last he was buried to his hips in the black ooze, unable to move. He stood there trembling, a trapped deer awaiting the spring of the tiger. He did not look around as the sound of thudding feet pounded toward him. He did not look around when the thing behind him reached the shoreline. He heard the great sucking noises of feet being pulled effortlessly from the enveloping mud, but still he did not turn. His trembling ceased. Shock flooded his brain. A huge hand grasped him at the base of the spine, sinking deeply into his flesh. Near death, he barely felt himself being lifted up into the night, the vicious shaking that snapped his neck, the teeth that clamped on his throat beneath the uncaring stars.

The mill stood on an ancient cement dam at the end of the cove. Dark tidewater spilled through a gateway at one end of the thick wall, awakening the still waters into shifting moonlit patterns. The weather-scarred structure thrust itself into the night, stark and square, obstructing the stars.

Seated at the bar in his small den, Maynard Drogin stared into the mirror in front of him with satisfaction. The dark hair above the thin, pale face was neatly parted. He checked both sides of his new moustache. It was coming in nicely. He sipped his martini, his eyes never leaving the mirror. He liked his new black smoking jacket, the white ascot. He liked everything he saw. There was a certain flair here, he decided. The small perfections that led to elegance. And why not? It had been rather an elegant day. The contract on the Kellner place had gone smoothly. And the binder on the Armquist mansion looked solid, very solid. He'd already worked out the water rights in his mind. Foxy Maynard. Maynard in the halls of affluence. He smiled and took another drink. He turned and glanced up along the high, stained walls that rose to his bedroom and the rafters above it. Lonesome halls, he thought. Halls without a woman. He stirred his drink slowly with his finger, listening to the crackling of the ice. Should have gotten married a long time ago, he mused, then shook his head. Bad idea. He looked around at the dark leather furniture, the tall, bare windows, the strange pictures on the wall, his special collection of the macabre. He shook his head again. A wife would want to redo. Frills, bits of chintz, that ilk. His mother wouldn't set foot in the mill. Said it terrified her. If it did, it would be the only thing in her life that ever had. Stay lonesome, old fox. Doom yourself to the good life. He stroked his budding moustache and raised the glass to his lips.

The sound of the heavy metal knocker on his front door reverberated suddenly throughout the house. A puzzled look flitted across Drogin's face. He patted his hair and hurried across the huge living room, carrying his glass. When he opened the door, his eyes widened. Standing before him was a tall, striking woman. A Viking maiden, he thought. Incredible blue eyes, blond hair flowing down below her shoulders. An amazon, a woman of dreams.

Drogin tried to adjust his face. "My dear," he said in his real-estate telephone voice. "How may I help you?"

The woman looked down shyly. "This is most probably the rudest thing I have ever done. Well, anyway. My name is Katherine Towers, Mr. Drogin. I stopped at your office this afternoon, but you had already gone. Someone in town told me that you lived in this wonderful old place, and because I am in desperate need of a house and, I admit it, I wanted to see the mill that gave this town its name, I . . . well . . . here I am. It was just an impulse. Have I interrupted you? Am I very bad?"

Drogin lifted his glass gallantly. "One can only hope so, dear lady." Beautiful, he thought. A beautiful retort. The woman's thin blouse fluttered in the night breeze. She was not wearing a bra. Drogin was sure of it.

The woman smiled at him in mock disapproval. "What a naughty thing to say. Now I shall never come in. I'll see you at your office tomorrow morning." She turned to go.

Drogin's hand went up. "No, wait, Miss Towers, please. I am harmless. Every woman in Mill Harbor can vouch for that. Please come in and look around. I insist."

The woman hesitated. Finally, she turned around. "Well, I *am* dying to take one quick peek inside. But I'll never believe you're harmless, Mr. Drogin, not for a minute." She stepped past him into the dimly lit living room. Maynard Drogin stroked his thin moustache. He closed the door softly behind them.

Twenty minutes later, seated on a leather couch, drink in hand, the woman's eyes stared levelly into Drogin's. "I love it," she said. "It's dark and it's weird, and it looks like there should be bats way up there somewhere, but I love it. Why don't you just sell this place to me?"

Drogin smiled happily. Those blue eyes, he thought. They sort of reach right into you. He drained his glass. "Dear Miss Towers," he said. "At this moment you can freely have anything I own. My mill, my Mercedes, my heart." He held up his empty glass. "We shall discuss any one or any combination thereof during my final martini." He bowed slightly and went to the bar. As he poured himself a drink, he inspected his teeth in the mirror. Impulsively, he folded a white bar napkin and arranged it in the empty pocket of his jacket. After a final approving glance, he returned to the couch. He touched the woman's glass gently with his own. "And now, my dear, to business. Or to pleasure. After office hours, I much prefer the latter I try to make pleasure my business, one might say." Smooth, he thought, smooth. Where the hell do you get this stuff, Maynard? You are a positive rake.

The woman's back arched slightly. It was a sudden erotic

gesture. "Yes," she said. It was not a sigh. It was an exhalation. Her hand rose slowly until her fingertips were resting under one side of his chin. She spoke softly. "Tell me what pleasure is, Maynard Drogin."

Drogin glanced quickly down at her hand. What a sensual thing to do, he thought. Yes, there was passion here. He felt his brow begin to perspire. He looked back into the woman's eyes. They were still bright blue, but deep within them he saw swirling purple billows, like mists that emanated from her mind. "Well, I . . ." he said. "Pleasure I . . ." he said. He could not think. It was the noise. Deep within some recess of his brain he began to hear his own heartbeat. Quietly at first, then gradually growing louder and louder. Above the rising noise, he spoke again. "Madam, I am in confusion. Your beauty makes the blood pound in my brain. I can hear it. I . . ." He stopped.

The woman's eyes flared excitedly. She pressed her fingers deeper into his neck.

"Your fingertips!" Drogin's voice was filled with wonder. "They touch my heart. I feel . . . I hear . . ."

The woman spoke. Her voice was low, each word a caress. "Shall I speak of pleasure, Agent Drogin? Shall I define joy?"

With a rapt, childlike expression on his face, Drogin stared into the eyes in front of him. They were purple no longer. Scarlet at the center now, they grew brighter as her words flowed toward him, engulfing the pupils like some minute but uncontrollable red raging fire. As he listened, the sound of his heartbeat grew steadily in volume until it mingled with her voice in a pounding, sensual rhythm. Enchantment filled him. A crimson aura permeated the room. It gleamed off the floor, the high wooden walls. He was immersed in the lush, sanguine air, a reflection of the eyes before him. The ancient melody of her words, soft notes of ecstasy, sang into his soul, until the room became a vibrant, red, pulsating world, sweet beyond imagining.

Drogin's eyelids fluttered. His head rolled back. A musky, primal scent filled his brain, arousing lusts he had never known, bringing perfumed, mystical visions. He was a snake curled tightly around a unicorn in an embrace of love; he swam with mermaids in a vermilion sea; lightning darted from his eyes; a flower called his name. He became the center of a universe of desire. The heartbeat sound became a thunder in his ears, unbearable, delicious, unbearable. A wild sexuality invaded his mind and body, so total, so powerful, that he emitted an unrestrained cry of joy.

Maynard Drogin did not see the face of the woman beside him change. He did not see the ruby eyes glow in their demonic passion, nor the hand rip away the silken blouse. He barely felt the grip of iron that forced his head inexorably down to the bared, heaving breasts.

Drogin grasped the nipple in front of him in his mouth. At the moment of contact, a sound tore through his consciousness, a feral scream of lust, pure and elemental. Soundless, it shook his being. Silent, it issued into his soul, destroying his sanity. Gone was his kingdom of exotic delights. He stood now in a new land, a secret forbidden realm. Maynard Drogin heard the life force of earth uttered in a single prolonged cry. It flooded his being like some terrific electricity. Horror ran through his veins. Fear that knew no limits constricted his heart.

Dying, still held in that immutable grasp, Drogin raised his tortured gaze to the face above him. The woman's head was thrown back, her eyes glowing redly in the darkened room. Her mouth was open in a snarl of joy, her lips raised above the long, white teeth.

Drogin's eyes rolled back until only the whites showed, as

the primeval shriek penetrated to the core of his mind. He was insane when his heart stopped. He was dead moments before he was dismembered.

The tall man let the night pour into him through the motel window. The woman sat behind him in the dark room, watching him. After a long silence the man spoke, his eyes half closed. "Do you hear it, sister? The black winds that sing in the firmament? Can you feel the stars burn? Oh, glorious night, night of fulfillment. A raging joy runs the earth. It ripples the meadows and shakes the tops of trees. Oh, ye mortals! Do not go down to the woods tonight!"

The woman spat her words out. "Fool!" she said. "Jotunn, our brother, is dead. Bestla, our precious mother, is dead. They are yet unavenged. Fool!"

The man continued to look at the star-filled sky. "Ah, the Marinos," he whispered. "The murderers. I have not forgotten them. No indeed, sister mine. They are on my mind. Nicholas. Christine. And their child. How I yearn for them! I am like a lover. How I want them!"

The woman's face became intensely alive. The total predator. "Well, Hyrmgar? Well?"

"Do you yearn for them too, my sister? Do you want them as I do? Then dream of them tonight. Tomorrow we shall be with them in Florida. Do you know about Florida, Thagnar? A true paradise, where all dreams come true."

The corners of the woman's mouth turned up in the semblance of a smile. It was not a smile. A long sigh of anticipation escaped her lips. The sibilance filled the room like the breath of a gold-green dragon lying in a cave of darkness.

6

NICK AND CHRISTINE lay in the huge bed listening to the rustling of the palms beneath their window. Nick's hard, tanned arm was around her shoulders; his hand rested lightly on her breast. Christine wriggled closer to him. "*Amore*," she said softly.

"Yes, my cabbage?"

"That was very nice. You were magnificent, as usual."

"I cannot accept that. Approval of sexual performance by women from Connecticut is meaningless. They have no experience to base it on."

Christine bit his hand gently. "My magnificent New York City beast." Her lips touched his chest.

Nick was staring at the ceiling, his face impassive. The lights from the pool below them cast white ripples about the room, bathing his features in glimmering waves. Christine regarded him for a long moment, the beginning smile slowly fading from her lips.

"Nick," she said, "what are you thinking about? Right now. This minute."

Nick did not look at her. "I was dreaming, my delicious. Merely dreaming."

"Of what? Tell me, Nick. Please."

"One does not divulge one's dreams. One's dreams are one's."

"That's terrible, Nick. That's a terrible sentence."

"Precisely selected, pal o' mine. My dreams. They are terrible dreams."

At his words, something suddenly raised its hideous head deep inside Christine's brain. Fearfully, secretly, her eyes searched her husband's face, remembering. She remembered the shadows of thrall that had transformed his features. She remembered the troll enchantment that had made him into an evil, unrecognizable beast. His face was calm now; his eyes were reflective. The shadows were not there.

"Sleep, my celery," he said softly. "That was a joke. I shall not joke again."

Christine reached up and held his hand, still remembering. A vague unease tensed her brow. She tried to frown it away, but it would not leave.

The jangling of the telephone in the sunlit room awakened them abruptly the next morning. One eye half closed, Nick searched for the telephone on the night table. "Now who the *hell* is that?" he muttered. He picked up the phone, dropped it, picked it up again. "Yeah," he said. "Who's this?"

The voice on the other end was subdued, tense. "Nick, it's Loreto."

"Pops!" Nick did not like the unfamiliar tone of his father's voice. He struggled to clear his mind. "What's up?"

"I don't know, Nick. I don't know. I don't like it."

"What? What is it, Pops?"

"I got a call this morning. My friend Captain Hinton from the Mill Harbor police. He was trying to reach you, didn't know where you were."

"Yeah? So?" Nick waited for his father to continue.

"I don't like it. I don't like it at all, Nicky." There was a long pause. "Nick, there were two murders in Mill Harbor last night."

"What!" Nick sat up, his eyes wide.

"Yeah. And there is another guy, went out jogging, they can't find him."

"No! Who were they?"

Christine sat up sleepily. "Nick?" she murmured. "What is it? Who is—" Nick stopped her with a raised hand, a glance.

"One of them was that detective, Lieutenant Broderick. The other guy was your friend Maynard Drogin."

"Oh my god," Nick said quietly.

Sudden fear etched itself on Christine's face. "Nick, what is it?"

Nick shook his head, asking for silence. "Do they know how it happened, Pops? Do they know who did it?"

It was several moments before his father spoke again. "Nicky, I think it's bad. Real bad."

"What are you saying, what are you saying?"

The other voice was low; the words were measured. "I think it's them, Nick. It's the Andersons. I know it."

Nick shook his head. "It can't be, Pops. The mother and son—they're dead, we killed them. I was there."

"Then they got relatives, Nick. They got a clan. Something."

Nick's eyes narrowed. His features hardened with the intensity of his thoughts. There was no fear there. "What makes you say that?"

"It's what the captain told me. The public won't get the details, but he thought you ought to know. Just in case. Broderick, Nick. Somebody picked him up in one hand. The fingers went into the back. They shook him, Nick. Broke almost every bone in his body."

Nick's voice was hard. "Drogin. What happened to Drogin?"

"Torn apart. Blood all over. Hinton said that mill looked like a house out of hell."

Nick nodded imperceptibly. He waited for his father to continue.

"There's more, Nick. God in heaven, there's more." He struggled to control his voice. "The woman who discovered Drogin. She works with him, was picking him up to take him to his office. She was hysterical, but the police managed to question her a little. She told them there was a big, blue-eyed bastard in the office yesterday. They were talking about the Anderson fire. And he was asking about *you*, Nick. Drogin told him the whole story. He told them where you are now. He even told him what hotel you're staying at."

Nick glanced at Christine. Her hand was at her mouth now; her eyes searched his face helplessly. He reached out and put his hand gently on her shoulder. Anger flickered in his eyes.

"It's them, Nick." Loreto's voice was steady now. "Trolls, bastards, whatever the hell that professor called them. Nobody else could kill like that. It's them. And they're coming after you, Nick. I can feel it." He paused, then continued. "Don't come home, Nick. Don't come back here. Get out, Nick. Get away."

Nick spoke quietly. "Hey, Lorry, we live there. That's our house. That's where we live."

Loreto's voice rose. "They'll kill you, Nick. They're after you because you killed the Andersons. They'll get you, Nick, they'll get you."

Nick's voice was like iron. "Fuck them. They'll get nobody. I'll get a gun. I'll shoot any bastard who comes near us. Fuck them." His words had a lethal ring. Flat, city-tough.

"No, Nicky, you can't handle it. You remember what that

professor said. You *know* them. They can change the way they look, change their shapes. You won't know who's coming at you. They'll get to you. They'll get to Chris. Nicky, they'll get to Joey."

At the mention of his son, Nick's expression changed. He shook his head in frustration. "But how can I—"

"Do it, son." Nick had never heard his father's voice like this. "Get out! Run! I'll take care of everything here. The house, everything. Don't come back until I find out what's going on, until they catch these sons of bitches. Go anyplace, Nick. Don't come back here, don't come back."

Nick stared into Christine's frightened eyes for a long time. Finally he spoke. "O.K., Pops. You got it. We'll leave this morning. I know where I'll go. I'll phone you when I get there."

"Don't phone me! Don't trust nobody! Nothing! Phone our attorney. Everything through him. They may be watching me. No mail, no phone. Through the attorney. You understand?"

Anger and sadness closed Nick's eyes. "I understand." He was whispering now. "I'll see you, Pops."

"Good-bye, sonny." Nick heard the unsteadiness in his father's voice. "Be safe. Be good. Take care of my grandson." A moment later: "Get out, Nick! Get out of there!" The phone went dead in Nick's hand.

Three hours later, the Marinos hurried silently through the Fort Lauderdale airport, white-faced, Aunt Henrietta trailing behind them like a tattered kite. They did not notice the tall man and woman eagerly stride past them. They were boarding the plane when the man gave a taxi driver the name of the hotel they had just left.

7

My sister,

The hunt continues. I search through Florida, an eager, ravening wolf. I snuffle here, I sniff there. Everywhere my rabid saliva blanches in the burning sun.

I have strange thoughts, sister. I do not want my search to end too soon. I love, I am possessed. An aching lust invades my veins. How I want them! My teeth grind with the exquisite longings of our race. Sweet hatred! Vengeance as desire! My loins tremble with the consummation yet to come. Never has life been so fulfilling. It is the hunt, it is the hunt. I am the cat who loves his mice, little playthings. Stealthily I shall stalk the states, my tail swishing back and forth, back and forth, until one day . . . Aha, aha.

Did you know, my sister, that our vengeance has already commenced? Oh, yes. We search for the murderers because they are gone. Logic dictates that they are gone because they know we search. Our imprudent ways in Mill Harbor saw to that. Further logic: if they know we search, fear is their constant companion. So you see, retribution has already begun. How the mice scurry to escape the taloned paw! And such a paw. Is that a Cheshire grin I see before me in the mirror?

When in the past have you seen me smile?

Stay in Mill Harbor, sister. Stay close to the father, the restaurateur. They will contact him sooner or later, I know it. Let us wait. Do nothing to disturb the tranquility there. Do nothing to arouse suspicions, impetuous sister, or they shall never return. Patience. Patience. The game has only begun.

HYRMGAR

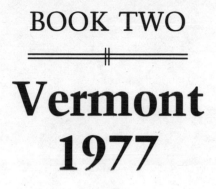

BOOK TWO

Vermont
1977

8

N ICK SAT STARING through the windshield of the
Volkswagen, a half smile on his lips. It had taken
him three years of work as a maître d' up here, saving
his money, learning the intricacies. It had taken the sale of his
house on Long Island for the down payment, but there it was.
His own restaurant. Everything about the chalet-style building in front of him pleased him. The gray wooden exterior,
the wide, tall windows, their window boxes filled with artificial red geraniums, and the view of the mountains from the
redwood cocktail deck. He raised his eyes to the sign above
the doorway. CHALET DU NORD. It's yours, pally, he
thought. Yours and Chris's and Joey's. His smile broadened.
Joey. The kid was a born restaurant man. He had watched his
son's eyes narrow as he explained how to select vegetables,
how to smell seafood. The kid knows meat as well as I do. He
must have been born with it. The Marino inheritance.

Nick had never realized how much he had learned from
Loreto throughout the years. He had worked for his father
since he was thirteen. Without his being aware of it, the
knowledge had flowed into him; he had absorbed the rules day
by day. They were simple. Rule one: everything the best.
From the rolls and coffee to the cigars and wine. Nothing but
the best. Attention to details, always. Rule two: a good bar-

tender and a good chef. Nick had gotten the best, and he paid them well. The long run, go for the long run. Rule three: never hire anyone when you or family can do it. Nick was everywhere, did everything. Christine as hostess was an enchantment, her quiet elegance was perfection. And Henrietta. He couldn't keep her away. She would not accept a salary. Not a penny. Nick knew what that meant. It was payment for her room and board. It meant that Henrietta was tired of wandering from relative to relative; it meant that Henrietta wanted to stay here with them. Nick shook his head slightly. She was a dear old girl, but . . . He'd see, he'd see.

The first snowflakes of winter thrust themselves against the windshield, driven by a cold October wind. Nick watched them happily as they clung to the glass for a moment and then melted their brief, crystal lives away. Come on, little pals, he said silently. Come on down and stick. Bring the skiers. Bring those hungry skiers. He had been lucky. The first month had been good, very good. But it was the winter season up here that made you. Made you or broke you. He beckoned the snowflakes down with a crooked finger, then got out of the car and entered the restaurant.

As Nick walked through the silent, dimly lit main dining room, he saw Henrietta at the bar. She held up a glass and polished it meticulously.

"You're late," she said, staring at her work.

"Henrietta, it is now two o'clock. We don't open until four. I am early, and those glasses have already been washed."

"Not by me they haven't. Dearie, where are my oranges, my lemons and my limes? I'll have to slice them myself. Eddie cuts them too thick. He's not a bartender, he's a dessert man. And raise the prices on the piña colada. Pineapples are up."

"I know I ask too much, auntie dear, but would it be possible for you to say 'our' instead of 'my' just once in a while? I have this inescapable feeling of being taken over by an irresistible maternal force."

"Get to work on time and I'll think about it. Don't walk on that! I just mopped over there."

Nick groaned loudly, retreated, and walked toward the kitchen. A voice trailed after him. "The lobsters are in the sink. I gave them their freedom for a couple of hours. It was the least I could do."

Christine and Joey arrived at the restaurant at ten minutes to four, each carrying a large bouquet of fresh flowers. Henrietta walked quickly toward them, took the flowers, and peered nearsightedly down into them.

"Ferns?" she asked. "Did you bring the ferns?"

Christine nodded her head patiently. "Yes, boss. If we had our spectacles on, we would be able to see them."

" 'Boss,' " Henrietta mused. "It has a nice ring to it. I should fire you for impertinence, but I don't have the time. Joey, help me with the flowers."

Nick and Christine slid their arms around each other as they watched Joey help place the flowers on each table, noticing the intent care he took, how he smoothed an occasional tablecloth or adjusted the silverware as he worked. "Marino genes," Nick whispered in her ear. Christine nodded.

The power that Henrietta had over their son was a constant source of wonderment to them. He did her bidding, especially around the restaurant, without a word, unquestioningly. They loved it, envied it.

As Joey passed close to them, he caught their rapt stares. "What's the matter?" he said, frowning

Nick pressed Christine's waist gently to keep her from laughing. "Nothing, pally," he said. "You do nice work. Maybe Henrietta will give this place to you when she retires."

"Ha!" The immediate answer came from behind the bar.

"Not if he dawdles like that with the nonpaying customers. Finish. And get me the maraschino cherries."

Christine glanced at her husband. His eyes had that special look, the soft glow that appeared whenever he watched his son. She looked back at Joey. At twelve, he was big for his age and handsome. He's not handsome, Christine thought, he's beautiful. Already he had the dark good looks of his father, that finely cut perfection of features that had so attracted her to Nick. Without taking her eyes off Joey, Christine spoke softly.

"I have good news for you, Daddy, and I have bad news."

"Tell me, my zucchini. I am all ears."

"How sexually unfortunate for me. However. First, the bad news. I can not get Henrietta to go home these afternoons to take care of Joey. We haven't got a sitter, we have a career woman."

"I know, I know. She fired me yesterday and I own the place. I cut the cheesecake too large. The woman is out of control."

"And now the good news, *amore*. The builder called. We can move into our condominium next week."

Nick looked down into Christine's smiling face. "Happy, honey?"

"Ecstatic." After a pause, Christine spoke again. Her eyes searched Nick's face. "Nick"—her voice was hesitant— "do you ever think about, you know, the house on Long Island? Do you regret that we, well, had to sell it, that we moved here?"

Nick's face hardened; his eyes grew cold. "Chris, listen. I love it here. I sort of always wanted to live up here." His eyes narrowed. "What I *don't* like is that some bastard out there *made* me do it. Some earthly or unearthly bastard pushed me. I don't like that, Chris. You know me by now. I don't push easily. I don't really push at all." He saw the troubled look on Christine's face. "You asked me, honey," he said gently. "I can't help how I feel." His face relaxed. "Let's forget it, Chris. I love it up here. This is my home." He held her closer. "And I love you. You are now and forever my antipasto delight of delights."

Christine raised her head and kissed his cheek. Her eyes flew open. "The butter!" she exclaimed. "Henrietta will kill me if I don't take out the butter to soften." She walked quickly toward the kitchen.

Without looking up, Henrietta called after her, "Take the butter out, dearie. I've only got two hands."

Christine had one hand on the huge refrigerator door when a strident screeching assailed her ears. She walked to the kitchen door and opened it. Standing between the large garbage bins were two cats. Unmoving, they glared at each other, their bodies tensed for combat. An eerie caterwauling came from their open mouths.

"Stop that!" Christine said severely. "Stop it! Get out of here! Go away! Go away!"

The cats did not move. The two tails continued to lash from side to side. They were both looking at Christine now, the feline brightness of their eyes tinted by the rays of the pale afternoon sun.

9

From the diary of Henrietta Knapp:

November 21

Fate has a funny way of never being right. Through the myriad decades of my life, from early transcendent beauty, to mature, fragile beauty, down to my present semi-Quasimodo state, never once has Fate said to me, Henrietta, how are you? You are where you ought to be, you are doing what you should be doing. As a matter of fact, Fate hardly ever talks to me. Until now. Lately, *some*body, *un petit voix*, has been whispering in my good ear, you're there, girl. Home. Career. *Vous avez arrivée*, girl.

Questions: Has Destiny finally stopped pummeling me? Is this Happiness I breathe through perpetually clogged sinuses? Dare I dream? How do I tell Chris and Nick I want to live with them forever? How can I tell Joey I love him as if he were my own? How can I explain *al dente* to that insane chef? Where is the silverware disappearing to?

Enough. *Ça suffit*. Put heavy socks on and to bed, to bed.

P.S. Too much bourbon in the Geritol tonight. Right eyelid fluttered for a full hour, kept me awake.

1:15 A.M. Footnote. My feet are killing me! Sneakers too tight?

November 22

Situation impossible *au* restaurant today. Simply cannot function in an atmosphere of idiocy. My crazed chef knows *rien* about sauces, but I mean *rien*. Tried to explain them to that Continental catastrophe in his native *français*, couched in the simplest terms, of course. His eyes glazed over, moustache twitched like the wings of a hummingbird. The man is *fou*, completely mad. Swung his hat at me. Threatened me with an Italian bread. An Italian bread!?!? Can't even do *that* right!

My bartender is sane. Too sane. Has a sly look about him. The customers love him. Seems charming enough on the surface. Cover-up? I know he's stealing from me, the only question is how. Watched him like an eagle for hours. Can't figure out how he does it yet. Caught him putting *two* olives in a martini. When I broached the subject to him, he referred me to Nick. Cool one, that one.

Nick and Christine insisted I take Joey home early tonight. God knows why, they can use all the help they can get. Can use the rest, however. The stress of the marketplace. Shall relax with a monumental gin and tonic and a hot tub laced with bubble bath that foams to the ceiling. To lose oneself in froth. How *jolie!*

November 23

Midnight. Snuggled cozily in my quilt, soaking my feet, hot buttered rum at my side. Should have taken my socks off. Demon rum, rum of my ruination. Ah, *la vie seul*.

Did not go *near* the kitchen today. Shall let the maniac slide to his own destruction on the grease of his incompetence.

Definite chill in the air. Is it Vermont or is it premonition? Can never forget why we are here, why we left Long Island. It's been three years, but some nights . . . some nights. My old bones can *feel* the things that roam in the dark. Tonight they positively ache.

Silly fool. Stop it. *Instanter*. You see a tree, black against the sky, and your bones ache. Your bones always ache, witch of the north. And if anything *is* out there, Nick has a gun. He will shoot it. And that's that.

Go to sleep, girl. Perhaps you'll dream. Dance with Fred Astaire in a marble nightclub in the sky. Champagne. Music. And there are no monsters in casinos high among the clouds.

10

Sister,

Too long the hunt, too long. The Marinos, whore father, slut mother, and their pig offspring, have vanished, they are not to be found. Vengeance, like a fever, still burns in my blood, but I have wearied of this hunt. I must have it now, my red consummation.

I have given it much thought, sister. The solution is simple. We must make them come to us. How can we make these very careful toads hop toward retribution? What will make these insects leave their hidden nest of dung, this close-knit family of worms who love each other so very much?

Have you guessed it, sister? Did you guess the beloved father, the restaurateur? He is our answer. Something shall have to happen to the worm father. Something sad, that will bring the loving whore son out of his secret whorehouse.

I return to Mill Harbor, sister. The night shall sing, and blood shall spatter the stars.

HYRMGAR

Loreto Marino opened the front door of his house and closed it quietly behind him. It was two o'clock in the morn-

57

ing, and he was tired. He was always tired lately. He turned on the hall light and looked at himself in the mirror. The tuxedo, the carnation, the neat gray hair. Too gray. Getting old, *amico*, he thought. No. Not old, Lonesome. Twelve years had gone by, and he still missed Louisa. The glass of anisette in the kitchen late at night, her quiet questions, the soft brown eyes, the gentle touch. He shrugged his shoulders. What do you do. You go on, that's what you do. You go on. He hung up his coat, turned off the light, and walked up the darkened stairs toward his bedroom. He did not go into the kitchen for his customary nightcap, so he could not notice that the lock on the rear door had been forcibly sprung.

It was an hour later that the noise began. Loreto awoke and sat rigidly upright, trying to clear the sleep from his brain. The sound, a loud, steady banging, reverberated through the house, shaking it. Loreto jumped from his bed, put his bathrobe on, and picked up a baseball bat that he kept in the closet. As he walked down the stairs, the noise grew in volume. He turned on the light. The noise was almost unbearable now. Within the thunderous bedlam, he heard a loud hissing. He whirled and faced the dining room. Only for an instant did he see a tall man with red eyes, sorcerer eyes that glittered into his own, bringing evil enchantment. Loreto blinked once. What he now saw in front of him almost stopped his heart. The head of a gigantic lizard filled the doorway, its yellow eyes gleaming in expectation. Suddenly, its huge, white, forked tongue slid out and flicked across his face. Loreto staggered back into the living room, automatically wiping at his mouth. The great reptile head turned to follow him, its tongue seeking him out in the shadowed room.

As Loreto retreated farther back in horror, something bit him sharply on the ankle. He looked down. Clinging to his flesh was a small black animal with the hair and body of a

Pekingese dog. Loreto's eyes widened in terror. The creature had a small, malignant, goblin face. The narrow, pupilless eyes glared up at him as the teeth ground into the bone. Acting out of fear, Loreto swung the bat down at his nightmarish tormentor, catching it flush on the side. A high, human scream rent the air as the thing lay writhing against the couch, where the force of the blow had sent it. It did not get up again, nor did it die. It lay there, screaming unceasingly. Loreto closed his eyes, raising one hand to his ear. The continuous thundering noise and the shrill cries tore through his brain unabated.

When he opened his eyes again, his hand tightened on the bat. Three more small monsters had appeared from behind the couch, their mouths moving in conversation; the slit, merciless eyes watching him slyly. Through the clamor that filled the room, Loreto caught snatches of a strange, unearthly language. Then, purposefully, one of them walked around behind him. They advanced on him with tiny, cautious steps, their voices never stopping. Loreto's grip tightened on the bat. His heart was pounding so heavily it shook his whole body. He coughed several times.

When the attack came, Loreto swung at them viciously, but they were too quick. As they darted in and out, he felt the painful piercing of their sharp teeth. Out of breath, he half fell, half stumbled onto the couch. They attacked him everywhere now. When he grasped them with his hands, they bit his fingers so painfully that he flung them across the room.

In the depths of his agony, a realization came to Loreto Marino. I'm dying, he thought. These bastards are killing me. Summoning all his strength, he stood up. He kicked, he cursed, he flung his arms wildly. There was a constricting pain in his chest, but he paid no attention to it. Coughing, he lunged for the stairs and began to run up. The horrific creatures followed him, shrieking in wild victory. Midway up, he fell. He could not catch his breath. Something ran up his back and sank its teeth into the back of his neck. Loreto rose, gasping for air, and staggered toward the top of the stairs. Suddenly, on the landing above him, a gigantic cobra reared up out of the darkness, its white underside gleaming in the light from below, its mouth agape, ready to strike. Loreto's eyes and mouth flew open, and his face turned white. It was a mask of pure terror. A moment later, his heart stopped beating. He fell sideways on the stairs, his head and one arm hanging down.

Immediately, the noises stopped: all creatures disappeared. Below, in the silent hallway, the tall man strode to the foot of the stairs and picked up the bat, which had rolled bumpily downward. He stared with bright anticipation at the unbitten, unmarked body.

"Good night, father of worms," he whispered. "Bring Nicholas. Yes. Bring the whore to me."

A biting wind whipped the coats of the people standing around the flower-strewn casket. At the outer edge of the crowd, it flapped the brim of the hat on the tall man's head and swirled the blond hair around the face of the woman beside him, but they did not blink. Their blue eyes glittering in the bright morning sun, they stared unwaveringly at the man, woman, and child who stood facing them on the other side of the empty grave. Deep within those arctic irises disturbances roiled, minute crimson volcanoes erupting, closing, then erupting again. The watchers concentrated totally on the three in front of them, their faces rigid in their eager attention. Not a movement, not a facial expression was missed. When the man bowed his head, overcome with grief, and the woman put her arm around him in compassion, the eyes of the tall man became even more intent, bright, in a strange amalgam of wonderment and hatred. When the man leaned over to talk to the young boy and the butt of a shoulder-holstered gun showed for a brief moment, the tall man's eyes flared open; he almost smiled. As the man continued to talk to his son, straightening his tie, then brushing the black hair away from his forehead, the tall man nodded his head several times, his eyes swirling red whirlpools now, the look on his face alien to this earth.

The tall man stood with his back against a pine tree. He looked down through the starlit Vermont night at the amber lights of the restaurant far below him. The woman stood at his side, her eyes as hungry as his; a wolf pair motionless in the night. Snowflakes swirled in front of them, drifting unnoticed onto their faces. It was a long time before the tall man finally spoke. "I had forgotten the sweetness of the pines, sister, the sweetness of the cold mountains."

The woman's eyes never moved. "Vengeance is sweet, Hyrmgar, vengeance."

The tall man raised his head. His gaze searched among the stars. He spoke quietly. "Vengeance is an art, precipitate sister. Wrought into a thing of beauty, it can be truly exquisite. Step on the insects and that is that?" He shook his head. "How beastly, the ways of an ogre. There is little enjoyment there, nothing to savor. Oh, the worms are dead. That is understood. But, ah, the manner of their death. It is open to question. The hunt has been a long one, sister. Should not the murderers suffer long, die slowly and deliciously before our eyes? Before our eyes! Ancestral magic shall afford us proximity, Thagnar. A small mouse in the cupboard, watching the gradual killing with bright and beady eyes? No, I think perhaps something larger, something more . . . participatory. There are many ways to kill. Artful vengeance dictates first the mutilation of the mind, the slaying of the soul. It dictates loss, it dictates devastation. I, artist, have meditated long on this, sister. It was at the funeral of the worm father that I finally realized what we must do." As he continued to speak, the woman's eyes slowly widened. Her head turned toward him with the stiff, quick movement of a striking snake.

When the tall man finished speaking, the woman nodded her head once. "Yes, brother," she whispered. "Oh, yes." A terrible smile raised the corners of her mouth. When she turned her head to look down at the lights below her, triumph and hatred contorted her features, flickering across her face like firelight. The smile disappeared as her mouth opened into a grimace of malevolence. The sound that issued forth violated the night. It was the rushing sound of vast, faraway waterfalls mingled with the screams of a hundred voices lost in the circles of hell. As the volume gradually increased, her voice coursed up the dark valley like some malefic wind from the ice rims of the world.

It was several minutes before the sounds of horror stopped. Silence once again enveloped the night. And then, suddenly, high above their heads, the top of the pine tree swayed and rustled in the still air. The smaller branches trembled and moved. The tall man glanced up quickly. In a moment he was standing at the woman's side, his body tensed in expectation. It was then, out of the distant reaches of the night, that another sound broke the stillness, as if in answer to the woman's hideous cry. It was a single note of ineffable beauty, neither male nor female, earthly nor unearthly. It streamed down the steep mountain valley, an ecstasy in the air, shimmering the trees in the starlight as it flowed above them. The eyes of the tall man and the woman shone as they stared out toward the mountains and beyond. Slowly, in rapture, in longing, they raised their arms to what was in the depths of the darkness.

11

THE MEETING IN the clubhouse had been called for eight o'clock. By seven-thirty, most of the condominium owners were there. The room quickly filled with smoke. The white wine in clear plastic glasses glimmered in the bright overhead lights like fireflies.

Nick sat staring out the window at the silent, icy ski runs, glinting blue in the moonlight. He recrossed his legs and lit another cigarette. Christine watched her impatient husband. She touched his hand. "*Amore,*" she said. "I know you want to get back. This won't take long. And they said it was important, Nick."

Nick grasped one of her fingers lightly. "Listen, my cabbage. Right now, at this very moment, my business, my dreams, my financial future are in dire jeopardy. Have you forgotten that we left Henrietta in charge of the restaurant? Did you forget that, my love?"

"Oh my god," Christine whispered. "Anyway, honey, we can always rebuild."

"That's amusing. That's very amusing, sweetheart. Hey, there's Amanda. Maybe she knows what the hell is going on." He waved at a tall black woman who had just entered the clubhouse.

Christine had met Amanda Birch once before at a social

function here in the clubhouse. As she watched the woman approach, she could not help but admire the easy grace with which she carried her slim figure.

"Hello, boys and girls," the woman said pleasantly. "I suppose you're wondering why I've gathered you all here tonight."

"Break it to us easy, Amanda," Nick said. "What are they springing on us now?"

"Beats me, baby." Amanda shook her head. "Even the Irishman doesn't know. And *mon* fiancé, Benjamin Kiley, he knows everything." She was looking at a sun-pinked, white-haired man standing several yards away, a cigar clamped in his mouth, his hands in his pockets. He was heavy around the middle with the slabby-stocky build of a man one should leave alone when the fighting begins.

Nick stood up suddenly and rubbed his hands together. "Anyone for liquor?" He looked down at Christine. "Sweetheart?" His direct stare and the subtle shading of his last word were not lost on Christine. There had been several arguments during the past few months about the amount Nick was drinking, creating a small, unaccustomed tension between them. Christine was annoyed, a little frightened. Nick was defiant, blaming it on the necessities of business. Christine shook her head, returning his gaze with temporary truce in her eyes.

As Nick sauntered away toward the wine table, Amanda sat down beside Christine, her eyes still on Ben Kiley.

"Isn't he something, that man," she said admiringly.

"He's cute," Christine agreed. "Does he always look that mad?"

"Always." Amanda sighed. "Being mad is a way of life to Kiley. He dislikes women, taxes, humidity, the Giants *and* the Jets, and all minorities."

"Is he really prejudiced?" Christine asked seriously.

"Benjy? No. Heart of gold. New York City detective for

twenty-five years. He just retired, but he still thinks he has to be tough on everybody. He even hates his own name. Thinks it sounds Jewish. Watch this." Amanda cupped her hands in front of her mouth and raised her voice. "Hallo, Benjamin dolling," she said in a terrible Jewish accent. "Finish your wine, dolling."

The white-haired man did not acknowledge her voice, did not even move his eyes, but clouds of smoke began to rise above his head in ever increasing amounts, and his face grew a deeper pink.

Amanda watched him and began to laugh quietly. "I get to him. I really get to him. The worst thing that ever happened to Lieutenant Ben Kiley was falling in sex with a black woman. The absolute worst."

"I'm sure he fell in love, Amanda," Christine said gently.

Her eyes suddenly serious, Amanda looked at Christine. "Yes. That happened, too. Later." She looked down at the floor. "We're engaged, you know. We've been engaged for five years." Once again her eyes met Christine's. She looked as if she were searching for something.

Christine touched her hand lightly. "Every morning I have coffee in number three oh seven, at ten o'clock. I wake up precisely at ten-fifteen."

The smile returned to the other woman's face. "I'll be there precisely. Maybe every morning." Her eyes widened. "Oh god, no!"

Christine looked up. Bearing down on them, cigarette held between thumb and forefinger, was a huge man in a baggy white turtleneck sweater. A mass of curly brown hair topped a pale face whose features were completely dominated by a large nose. He wore black horn-rim glasses and was as chinless as a shark. His heavy body was wide-hipped and joggled ponderously as he strode toward them.

"What's this, what's this? An employee of mine drinking?"

His voice was high but pleasant. "Squiffed on the eve of a workday? You know my rules, Amanda. I shall have to dock you. Vigorously."

Amanda sighed. "Malcolm, how can you speak to me of rules. You forget that I work with you, I keep your books. Rules! You have the morality of a snake and the libido of a mink, and your ethics would stun an anarchist."

"Nag. Amanda dear, don't you believe in introductions?"

"Ah, yes. I'm sorry about this, Christine. This is my employer, Erogenous Jones. Christine Marino. He's just bought the largest antique store in town. Some of his stuff is actually several years old. He is, for better or worse, one of our neighbors, Christine."

The large man took Christine's hand. His grip was soft and damp. "Malcolm Jones, Mrs. Marino. It's a pleasure to make your acquaintance. It's really so difficult to get loyal help these days. That vixen will be the death of me yet. May I say, Mrs. Marino, that it is a pleasure to see beauty once again in Torchester, Vermont."

Christine smiled patiently. "Thank you, Mr. Jones."

Something appeared and disappeared deep within the man's eyes. "Yes. Your husband has a truly extraordinary quality about him. Fantastic."

Christine was truly taken aback. "Oh," she managed. "Oh, well, thank you."

The man stared down at her. "My pleasure," he murmured.

Amanda Birch shook her head several times. "I done tol' you and I done tol' you. The man is awful. Go away, Erogenous. Go away."

Jones exhaled his newly lit cigarette. "Hag," he said.

"Hag? That's it. I quit. Hag?"

"My dear, you can't quit. It's quite impossible. Where am I going to hire another black woman as a token?"

"Malcolm, are you kidding? Token? I'm your only employee."

The large man leaned down and kissed her forehead lightly. "There. You see?" He smiled at both of them and walked away, his body bouncing up and down inside his sweater.

The two women stared after him. It was Christine who spoke first. "Amanda, you certainly can—"

"Don't talk about it. I don't want to talk about it. Yes I do. I know he's weird. I know he's neurotic. I've only worked for him for three weeks and I've never known anybody so wretched, so . . . interesting. He's like a snake. You can't stand him and he fascinates you."

"I'll buy the first part, anyway," Christine said with a half smile. She looked around the room. "Amanda, you've been here longer than I have. Who are all these people anyway?"

"Our friends and neighbors? Nice people. See that gentleman? The most important person here." Amanda nodded toward a large, bulky man sitting next to a larger woman in a corner of the room. He wore an ill-fitting black suit and tie, white shirt and socks, and a defiant expression.

"Who is he?" Christine asked.

"That's Truman Hooker and his wife, Gussie. He's the new maintenance man for Mountaincrest. Summer farmer, winter handyman. Without him I think all these nice, helpless people would eventually perish in their own plumbing. Be very, very nice to him. You may need him someday."

Christine looked into Amanda's eyes. "And the bronzed hero over by the sandwiches mentally undressing both of us. Who's that?"

Amanda glanced up and smiled briefly at the tall blond man, who waved his sandwich in salute. "That's Eric Teiler. He's gorgeous. Just ask him. He and his sister run the ski school for Mad Mountain. You and I are most probably the only two women he hasn't slept with at Mountaincrest. Unless there's something you want to tell me."

"Amanda!" Christine shook her head, smiling. "So that's the famous Mr. Teiler. I know about him already. My son just joined his ski school two weeks ago. He's been raving about him ever since. I've got to be nice to him, too." Christine looked up and smiled pleasantly into the blue eyes that were staring over at her. Teiler had the knowing, predatory look of a cheetah about to start a race that can have only one winner.

Their conversation was interrupted by the deep voice of a man who stood at a table in the front of the room. "Folks, if you'll take your seats." It was not a request. It was a command. The speaker was a heavyset man with a broad face and long blond-gray hair. "For the benefit of the newcomers," he continued as the voices gradually died away, "my name is Kyle Thorne. As chairman of the Mountaincrest board of directors, I've called all of us together tonight for a special meeting." A few catcalls, groans, and one cry of "Railroad!" floated through the smoke-fogged air. Thorne smiled briefly. "No, this is not a reassessment, my friends, this is good news for a change. Before I open the matter up for discussion, I would like to take this opportunity to welcome all you newcomers from the just-completed Northgate section. Welcome to the happy family of Mountaincrest owners. From my wife, Kirsten, myself, your board of directors, and all the old-timers from the first section. You're very lucky. This is the first good-news, noncatastrophic meeting we've ever held.

"Now, as many of you know, when Mountaincrest was first conceived and built, one hundred and ten acres were bought on the border of the Mad Mountain ski area. This was to house three separate sections plus our recreation area. With the completion of Northgate, our second section, plans for our third and final section got under way. But, as you may know, we've begun to have problems. Sewerage problems, water-supply problems, many of the general problems that come with overcrowding have begun to appear. Many of us thought that the last section—the largest, may I add—would only exacerbate these problems, and we told the builders exactly that. Their answers: reassessment, spend more money—our money, their money. We can hardly blame them. Their profits are tied up in the last section." This time the groans and expressions of anger were real. Thorne shook his head and smiled. "My friends, my friends, I told you that I have good news. This is a happy meeting. Practically jubilant. Because yesterday, my dear friends, your board of directors and the builders attended a meeting with representatives from Cabot Inns Limited. We all know that they are one of the biggest hotel chains in the country. And do you know what Mr. Baxter Cabot himself had to say to us?" Thorne looked around the room expectantly.

"He wants to buy my condominium." A voice from the back.

Thorne beamed. "Better than that, George. Mr. Baxter Cabot wants to put up a large hotel and resort at the base of Mad Mountain. Although the price has not been determined as yet, we are talking about bills of large denominations, my friends. Denominations that would dig more wells, correct our sewerage problems, widen our roads. Denominations that would pay for our swimming pool and our tennis courts, which, in turn, would make Mountaincrest a summer as well as a winter home. And let us not forget summer rentals, my friends, at very satisfying figures." Excited voices now filled the room. Thorne waited patiently for them to die down. "Of course, folks, everything is still up in the air. Much of this is still speculation at this point. Additional land for a nine-hole golf course would have to be purchased from some of the neighboring farms. First indications are, however, that our farmer neighbors would be more than willing. Mr. Cabot does not quibble over dollars, I am told. They *are* looking at several other sites, closer to the larger ski areas of Bromley and Stratton, but I am here to tell you that, as of this moment, Mad Mountain has the inside track. In any case, Mr. Cabot will make his decision within the next several months. Favorably, we hope.

"And now I am throwing this meeting open to questions or comments. We shall have another meeting here in two weeks to vote on this proposal. This should give us time to think, ask questions, and have our say. Please introduce yourselves so we can all get to know each other better."

As member after member rose and spoke in favor of the sale, Christine's brow began to furrow. Before she knew what was happening, she was on her feet. Kyle Thorne smiled at her and nodded expectantly.

"My name is Christine Marino. We have only recently moved into Northgate, and I'm sure I'm not aware of all the facts involved here." She drew in a deep breath. "However, I think we should look into this matter very carefully. We are having overcrowding problems already. I think a large resort might only make these problems worse." Christine looked at the faces around her. They were not pleased. She looked at Nick. He was staring at the floor. "At least," she continued lamely, "I think we should get legal and technical advice before making our decision." She sat down abruptly.

"That advice has, of course, already been solicited, Mrs. Marino." Kyle Thorne's smile was less benign now.

In the short silence that followed, a small bespectacled man rose stiffly to his feet. He was old and completely round: a round head, no apparent neck, round shoulders that sloped to a round body. He wore a black, vested suit with a gold watch chain draped across the front. He looked benevolent and irritable at the same time. "My name is Dr. Emile Landau." He spoke with a very slight accent. "When I was a little boy in Vienna, my mother used to ask me this question. 'Do you want your milk now, Emile, or later?' It always sounded to me like a fair question. It took me thirty years and three universities to realize that there was a third choice, which was, of course, no milk. No milk at all. With all due respect, my dear sir, I feel as if I am being presented with a similar question tonight. And I am thinking: perhaps no resort at all. I am retired. I have recently moved to Mountaincrest as a permanent resident because I have always dreamed of a quiet place in the country. I am not convinced that Mr. Baxter Cabot and his resort are the answer to my dreams. I agree with the young lady who just spoke. I think we should be careful. Very careful indeed."

Kyle Thorne was not smiling anymore. "Thank you, Dr. Landau. This is why we're here tonight. Anyone else?"

Several more people stood up and spoke in favor of the resort, and then Thorne adjourned the meeting.

Walking back through the cold, pine-scented air, Christine held on to one of Nick's fingers, looking at him thoughtfully. He had not spoken since they had left the clubhouse.

"Give me a hint, pal o' mine," she said finally. Nick glanced up at her and smiled briefly. "C'mon, Nick," she urged. "Get it off your chest. I did something. What is it? What did baby do?"

Nick stopped and lit a cigarette. He watched the wind whip the blond strands of hair across his wife's face. "You look beautiful when you're puzzled," he said.

"Give it to me, *amore*. In the *stòmaco*."

"Chris, I'm a businessman. I'm in the restaurant business. That's how I—we—make a living. This restaurant is located near the base of Mad Mountain, and, fortunately for both of us, very near the site of the proposed Cabot Inn. When we put these facts together, my love, do you know what they mean? Money. A great deal of nice, fresh money. For Joey, for us, for our boss, Henrietta. Therefore, wife of mine, let us become wealthy. Let us learn to love Mr. Baxter Cabot and his splendid ideas. Let us not, my sweetheart, speak of options, let us not louse it up. *Capice?*"

"Nick, all I said was that we should know all the facts. And I think we should. I think—"

Nick's gentle kiss interrupted her. "Don't think, Chris. Just be beautiful."

Christine's eyes became suddenly serious, almost sad. "In one sentence, Nick, you have just told the story of my life." She paused. "I'm not sure I like it." She turned and continued down the stone walk.

Nick looked at her through the smoke from his cigarette for several moments. "Does this mean," he called after her, "that I sleep in the den tonight, my broccoli?"

Christine stopped. She composed her features. When she turned around, she was smiling. "I never mix business with pleasure, pally," she said quietly.

Amanda Birch rang the bell at exactly ten minutes after ten the next morning. When Christine opened the door sleepily, the two women looked at each other and laughed. "If I had known you were going to look this bad, I never would have come," Amanda said.

"Coffee. Amanda, for God's sake, make some coffee. We didn't close until after three last night."

A half hour later, it seemed as if they had known each other for years. There was a dignity in movement and manner about Amanda that Christine admired. "All right, Amanda," she

said. "I'm tired of all this small talk. Let's get to the big talk.
What's this nonsense you told me about Detective Ben Kiley
and his five-year engagements?"

Amanda drew designs on the tablecloth with her forefinger.
"Christine, I've been through a lot in my life. I won't bore you
with details. But that man . . . that man. I've never been so
happy. And so sad. We love each other, Chris. We've loved
each other for five years. He's the marrying kind. His wife
passed away twelve years ago. He's got two beautiful teenage
kids. He's a family man, the Irishman is."

"Then what's he afraid of?"

"Ben Kiley? No man alive and Amanda Birch. She's black,
in case you haven't noticed. Get the picture?"

Christine looked down into her coffee cup. "I get the picture," she said.

"I have seen Ben Kiley handcuffed to a three-hundred-
pound homicidal maniac and eating a hamburger with his free
hand. That same man still bristles when we go into restau-
rants, that same man is afraid of what his children are going to
say."

"After five years?"

Amanda raised her empty cup to her lips and stared into it.
"Maybe forever." She sighed.

A soft knock on the door interrupted their thoughts. When
Christine opened it, a short, plump woman stood before her.
Her gray hair was tied in a bun, and a woollen shawl was
draped around her shoulders. Christine had seen her the night
before, sitting next to Dr. Landau. She looked just like him,
round and benign.

"Mrs. Marino. My name is Berta Landau. Excuse me, you
are in the middle of breakfast?" Her accent was stronger than
her husband's.

Christine smiled. "We're just having some coffee. Please

join us, Mrs. Landau." She introduced Amanda and set some hot coffee in front of her new guest.

Mrs. Landau shrugged apologetically. "I am so sorry. I feel like the intruder. You must only blame Emile. He sent me here, while he goes skiing."

"I liked what your husband said last night, Mrs. Landau."

"Yes, Mrs. Marino, that is why I am here. Emile feels that since you two were the only ones who did not jump with open arms at Mr. Thorne and Mr. Baxter, that maybe we should form some sort of a committee. To look into this resort idea, to find perhaps some facts about the advantages and disadvantages. These facts we could bring to the next meeting. For discussion. For evaluation."

"Say, this is great!" Amanda waved her hands expansively. "I feel like some sort of minor revolutionary. We could call ourselves the Terrible Trio."

Mrs. Landau's hands went to her face. "*Na! Himmel!*" She shook with quiet laughter.

"I have just decided," Christine stated. "You two and Ben and Emile are coming to dinner tomorrow night. It's the only night the restaurant is closed, and I never get a chance to cook anymore. You can't say no. My husband thinks I'm trying to put him in the poorhouse already. When he hears about our committee, I want you two standing in front of me. Cocktails at seven."

The following evening, Christine looked over her coffee cup at her family and guests. Although Nick had drunk far too much, and was still drinking, the dinner had been a definite success, she decided. Ben Kiley and Nick had grown up three blocks from each other in the East Village. They had even known an Angie Somebody together. Henrietta was talking to Mrs. Landau on a couch in the living room. The poor woman alternately nodded and shook her head as Henrietta spoke unabatingly, the noise from her braceleted, waving wrists jangling across the room.

Christine found Dr. Landau completely fascinating. The round little man had kept Amanda, Joey, and herself intrigued with stories about his newfound hobby, the study of the supernatural and the occult. She watched him now as he slowly swirled his brandy in his glass.

"I don't know which is more interesting, the natural world or the other. Sometimes I think they are the same."

"What do you mean, Doctor?" Amanda asked.

"When I gave up my psychiatric practice ten years ago, the Westchester police were kind enough to let me work with them on some of their weirder cases. The things I saw filled me with wonderment. Man—I shall phrase this mildly—is a complicated creature."

"Is that story true, the one you told us about the wolfgirl?" Joey's face was frightened yet animated.

"We must be very careful, my young friend. I mentioned that at one time there was a feral child who roamed the parks of the Bronx and Yonkers. I was, in fact, bitten by her. Although the poor child was incurable, we cannot label her a 'wolfgirl.' No full moons bringing hairy changes, none of that."

Amanda's voice was serious. "But, Doctor, what is the difference?" Nick and Ben Kiley had stopped talking now and were listening to the conversation.

Dr. Landau stared down with disdain at his ever present but unlit meerschaum pipe. He shook his head. "That is a deep question, young lady. A hard question. It is a question, I think, that may be impossible to answer. Hypothesis: Are there, my friends, more things on earth than we dream of? Is there a hidden, unknown realm where creatures silently glide? Is there an abyss from which creatures lunge and then quickly return, leaving us puzzled and multilated and dying? Are

there, truly, vampires, werewolves, elves, goblins, trolls"—
Christine glanced at Nick, who was staring down at the wineglass in front of him— "witches, fairies, horrors named and
unnamed?"

Amanda spoke quietly. "And what is your conclusion,
Doctor?"

"My conclusion, my dear woman, must be for the pres-
ent . . . no. A hesitant 'no,' a doubtful 'no,' but a 'no' neverthe-
less. My recent studies, my dusty books fill me with a secret
awe, they make my 'no' ever so feeble. Show me a true were-
wolf, a genuine vampire, show me one little elf dancing on a
mushroom, and I will change my tune, sing a different song.
But until then . . ." He shrugged his shoulders.

Ben Kiley stabbed the air with his cigar. "But, Doctor.
How did all these legends come into existence? Are they totally a product of someone's weird imagination?"

"I do not believe this, Mr. Kiley. I have been a psychiatrist
for fifty years, sir. I have worked with the police for ten years.
We do not need our imaginations to create these creatures,
these deeds, Mr. Kiley. We have a model to work from."

"I don't get you," Kiley said.

"You and I, sir. We are the models. Read your history. Pick
up your newspaper. There is nothing in the creature fables
that Man the Mad has not perpetrated. He is your model, Mr.
Kiley. Oh, an embellishment here, a little magic there. But
make no mistake. We are they. We are the stuff of legends. It
is we, my dear friend, who slouch toward Bethlehem."

Christine's voice was earnest, troubled. "Dr. Landau, you
speak of us as mad, as beasts. Man is also divine. He creates
beauty, he conceives the idea of God."

Landau's round head nodded vigorously. "Agreed. Agreed.
And that, Mrs. Marino, is precisely his predicament. He is
born into dilemma, he lives the cursed paradox. Divine. No-

ble. Trailing clouds of glory where he walks. And beast. In the dark forests of the mind, always there lurks . . . the beast."

Nick had been staring at the old man as he spoke. Abruptly, he stood up and walked across the living room toward the glass door that led to a small wooden deck. He stepped outside, closing the door quietly behind him.

As the conversation continued around him, Dr. Landau peered over his glasses at Nick's back, outlined against the star-filled sky. After several minutes, he excused himself and followed Nick into the chill night air. He stared at Nick for a long moment before he spoke. "Nicholas, I perhaps said something?"

Nick turned his head, a half smile on his lips. "No, Doctor. It wasn't you." He turned again toward the night. "It's not you." Somewhere in distant moonlight a train howled, a metal behemoth calling in darkness. Without turning around, Nick spoke again. "You are wrong, you know, Doctor. I have seen the beasts. They are out there, I assure you." He paused and then continued quietly. "You are a trained professional, Dr. Landau. When you look at me, what do you see?"

"I see an excellent host who knows his white wines." Dr. Landau tried a small smile.

Nick turned around, the look on his face enigmatic, strained. "What do you see, Doctor?"

Dr. Landau's eyes changed. "I see a man with scars, Nicholas. You hide them well."

Nick shook his head. "Not scars, Doctor. Not yet. It seems . . . that I am a slow healer." Landau said nothing. His eyes were locked on Nick's now. "I have not only seen the beast, good Doctor"—Nick's voice was low— "he has touched me. Oh, I have been touched. His mark is upon me. Faint but not forgotten. Echoes of evil melodies. Shadows of shadows. I am haunted, Doctor. Haunted at the core." Nick hesitated but could not stop. "I was one of them, Dr. Landau. They made me their own. That's why you see a man before you with . . . difficulties." He tried to smile. "I seem to be spoiling your retirement with my problems, Doctor. Please forgive me."

Landau waved one finger from side to side. "On the contrary, my dear, dear sir. Any mention of the supernatural whets the only appetite I have left. Please continue."

Nick watched the round little man sit down heavily, his unlit pipe held in his hand. "I'm going to tell you a story, Doctor. I'll put it in the form of a fable so you'll never guess the identity of the characters. Once upon a time"—Nick's voice was low, and his eyes were humorless— "in a land beside the sea—the North Shore of Long Island, to be precise— there dwelt a happy family in a happy castle. Everything was perfect. Until the beasts came. For, you see, dwelling next to the castle of Nicholas the Unlucky were two trolls, two of the bastard beasts you don't believe in. Make no mistake, Doctor. They were not madmen. They were your genuine supernatural article. They could change their faces and shapes. They could sing songs that enchanted the soul. Blood beasts. Decapitators with the strength of giants. My neighbors."

The little man's eyes grew wide. "What did you say? Decapitators?"

"Oh yes. They did that. It's sort of a trademark they have."

Dr. Landau stroked his nose. "My god, Nicholas. My god."

"And do you know what they did, these beasts, these hideous articles? Why, they fell in love." Nick tried to smile. It was a grimace. "Yes. The mother with Nicholas the Lovely, the son with his beautiful wife. And with their magic they enchanted him, they changed him. He was one of them, he was theirs. He ran the night. He sang their songs. Terror was in his heart, rapture ran through his veins. He was theirs. He gave his wife away with a smile, his soul away with a cry of joy." Nick stroked his forehead. His eyes were closed. "Tell me, Doctor," he said. "Why don't I forget? Why don't I heal? How long to endure a scarred psyche?"

Landau's gaze was steady. His eyes glinted with interest. "You say you were one of them, Nicholas. How did you break away?"

Nick's voice flowed like hot steel. "Simple. They made a mistake. They threatened my son. A big mistake, Doctor. It cost the unnatrual bastards their lives. My wife and I. We burned them, we smashed them, we killed them. Oh, yes. The bad guys lost. It was Hollywood. It was practically biblical. Love conquers sinister magic. Paradise is regained."

The other man removed the pipe from his mouth and gazed down at it thoughtfully. "Paradise, Nicholas? It is perhaps . . . less than beatific? There is, perhaps, a serpent?"

Nick shook his head slightly. "No, Doctor. The serpent is gone. His presence is not my problem."

Landau raised his eyes to Nick's. "Then what, my friend, what?"

Nick spoke, lost in private reverie. "My problem." He stared at the seated man but did not see him. "My problem. It would seem, Doctor, that there are wines we should not taste. Slumberers within us who should never be awakened." He ran his hand through his hair. "There are nights when I dream of the serpent. I can stand that. I've had nightmares before. My problem, what I cannot stand"—his voice lowered to a whisper— "are the nights . . . when I long for his return." He turned suddenly and faced the darkness.

Dr. Landau stared up at the dark outline of Nick's back, his face furrowed in thought. The two figures remained unmoving in the light of the stars that streamed down from the sky.

12

THE STEEL-AND-GLASS structure thrust itself into the dark Manhattan sunlight, gleaming dully. High in his penthouse office, Baxter Cabot sat staring out a large window, his fingertips pressed together in front of his face. Irritations, he thought. Always irritations. A forty-million-dollar investment that might be delayed by a committee of three bitches and an old bastard. Delay was out of the question. The interstate highway would be continued one mile from the Mad Mountain ski area. It had cost him a small fortune to find this out before anyone else, but he couldn't expect his edge to last forever. Kyle Thorne had assured him by telephone that he could handle everything before the condominium owners voted, but that was not the way Baxter Cabot played the game. He did everything himself. Properly and precisely. That way it was not a game at all.

Cabot swiveled his chair around toward his desk. He had the striking good looks of a male model, his gray eyes and dark hair in perfect unison with the gray pin-striped suit he wore. The suit seemed molded to his trim body. It was said about Baxter Cabot that when he was born he emerged fully and perfectly dressed, including a tiny vest and matching accessories.

Cabot pressed the intercom. "Eileen, would you please find

Turk Brandon and send him in to me, please." His voice was soft yet charged, the voice of a polite emperor. He released the button and began signing some papers that were lying on his desk.

Ten minutes later, a man opened the door to Cabot's office. He looked like a well-built fire hydrant. He had the thick shoulders, large hands, and slightly pigeon-toed stance of an athlete. His face would have been craggily handsome but it was simply too beaten up. The broken nose and multiple scars made it look like a battlefield where both armies had lost. Under the thickened brow, the eyes gave away nothing. "You summoned?" he said.

"My time is worth a lot of money, Turk." Cabot's voice was perfectly modulated. "Where the hell were you? Pinching asses again?"

"No, boss. Something far more important. Practically metaphysical. I was contemplating my navel through my shirt. I think I have a gift."

"What the hell are you talking about? Come in, Turk."

Brandon raised his hand. "Oh, no. Not me. If I do, you'll give me some work. I can feel it."

"I've got something very important I want you to do for me," Cabot said. He was forcing himself to be patient. "There's a small committee at the Mountaincrest condominiums that's causing me problems. I want you to go up there and set up a meeting with them. I want to talk to them within the next few days, straighten things out. You'll leave this afternoon."

Brandon nodded. "You have spoken," he said.

Cabot looked up quickly. "Dammit, Turk"—his voice was controlled— "you can really irritate the hell out of me. I don't understand you. When you were in pro ball you were a tiger, a killer. The best linebacker in the business. I was lucky to get your name for Cabot Inns. But this last year . . . How long have you been working for me, Turk?"

Brandon put a forefinger to his forehead. After a moment he stamped his foot two times.

Cabot shook his head, suppressing a slight smile. "Sometimes I think you're really crazy, you know that? You've been playing the clown around here for too long. And lately I think you're getting worse. You can do good work. I've seen you. Settle down, Turk. Be serious."

Beneath the scars, Brandon's eyes grew imperceptibly harder. "Why?" he said.

"Money," Cabot answered immediately. "Making money. It's a serious business." He stared at the other man. "Are you listening, Turk?"

Brandon was looking down at the floor, his hands clasped behind his back. "Yas'm, Mistuh Bax," he said.

Baxter's gaze rose to the ceiling in exasperation. "Here are some papers with my thoughts on this matter." He tried to keep his voice calm. "The background and details are being typed up right now. You can read them on the plane. Turk, I want you to make a serious effort here. Will you do that, Turk?"

The other man's head nodded vigorously. "Oh, yas'm," he said. He turned and began to shuffle out the door, one hand holding the back of his hip.

"And, Brandon. This is a business trip. No booze. No women. I want you back here tomorrow, not three weeks from now." Cabot's voice softened. "This is very important to me, Turk. Don't mess it up by screwing around." He stared in puzzlement at Brandon, who had turned around and was looking down at his shoes. "I want your assurance on this, O.K.?" The other man did not look up. "My god, Turk, answer me! Say something!"

Brandon sighed. He scratched his head. Finally, he spoke. "Feet, don't *fail* me now." He closed the door quietly behind him.

Cabot's gaze remained on the closed door. A spectrum of emotions flickered across his features. When his face finally settled, he had the look of a man who had seen something he could not understand.

It was ten o'clock when Turk Brandon rang the Marinos' doorbell the next morning. A woman's voice came out to him as he stood in the chill wind.

"Come in. Come in." Turk stepped inside and closed the door behind him. The woman's voice sounded soft and warm. "I'm just getting decent. Come in here, or take some coffee. It's good and hot."

Brandon tapped his fingers on the wall, then shrugged sadly and walked into the kitchen.

Again the lovely voice. "There's some cheesecake in the refrigerator that I stole from the restaurant. Take some."

Opening the refrigerator door, Brandon peered inside. "What kind?" he said loudly.

Within seconds, a woman flew out of the bedroom behind him, clutching a white bathrobe around her, her head turbaned in a towel, her mouth open.

"What kind, Mrs. Marino?" Turk repeated. "You were not specific."

Christine's mouth shut and then opened again. "My god," she said, "you scared me. I thought you were Amanda. Just who in the hell are you?"

Brandon shook his head. "Is it cherry? I hate cherry." He turned from the refrigerator and looked at Christine. He blinked once.

"Will you please get out of here." Christine was regaining

her composure. "I thought you were my friend. You'll really have to leave."

The man stood staring at her. With his green, piercing eyes, his bent nose and wind-ruffled hair, he looked to Christine like an eagle who had been soaring in the high winds too long. He raised one hand in appeasement. His other hand held his sports jacket open on one side. He peered down at it and pretended to read mechanically. "Mrs. Marino. My name is Turk Brandon. I am here representing Mr. Baxter Cabot of Cabot Inns. Mr. Cabot would like to talk to you and the committee you have formed. He understands that you are concerned about the various possible consequences to the residents of Mountaincrest should he decide to build a Cabot Inn at Mad Mountain. He feels that such a meeting would be valuable to all parties concerned and would like said meeting to occur at your earliest possible convenience." Brandon looked up at Christine, a smile of self-satisfaction on his face. He buttoned his jacket. "On a personal note, Mrs. Marino, if you refuse to see him, it will mean that I have failed in this most important mission. I may be fired. Do you want this on your conscience, Mrs. Marino?"

Christine's eyes were wide. The man was very weird. "No," she said. "I mean . . . no."

"I should think not. Mr. Baxter can be here Monday morning. Is that satisfactory?" Christine nodded, her lips parted in wonderment. "And now, Mrs. Marino, you mentioned hot coffee?"

Christine nodded again. Brandon poured himself some coffee and sipped it carefully. He looked at Christine pleasantly, as if she were a beautiful scenic view.

Christine found her voice. "Would you like to sit down, Mr. Brandon? Some cream or sugar? Some cheesecake?"

"No, no, no, and definitely no." His amused stare began to

unnerve her. After a short silence, he spoke again. "I am sorry, Mrs. Marino, that you feel you have to steal cheesecakes during the holiday season. Would you like to talk about it?"

"No," Christine blurted out. "I mean, it's all right. They're my husband's." Brandon's head shook sympathetically. "No, really. It's O.K. You see, he owns a restaurant." She was suddenly irritated. "It's really all right, Mr. Brandon." Christine decided suddenly that the man might indeed be crazy. He looked harmless enough. Or was he? I don't like the way he *stands*, she thought. He looks like he's about to pounce, or do *something* active. And his neck is much too thick for his body. And I don't like his hands. They're huge. And what really the hell is he doing standing in my kitchen anyway? She smiled artificially, glancing everywhere but at Brandon.

Turk gazed at her levelly. Something glided behind his eyes and was gone. He put his coffee cup down carefully. "I have to go now, Mrs. Marino. Thank you for the coffee. I shall return with my king on Monday. Until then, ta-ta." He waved two fingers and turned to leave.

Christine watched in annoyed awe as the man walked toward the front door. When he reached it he stopped, as if waiting for something. Christine spoke, not really knowing why. "You . . . you represent Cabot Inns, Mr. Brandon?"

Brandon smiled slightly but did not turn around. He thrust his shoulders back. "Somebody has to do it." He opened the door and stepped into the cold Vermont air.

During lunch, Christine told Nick and Joey about her visitor. Nick looked up in surprise. "Chris, you don't mean *the* Turk Brandon?"

"Why, I don't know, dear. How many are there?"

"Chris, the man was the greatest. What did he look like?"

"Good heavens, I don't know. He was incredibly . . . stocky. All beaten up. He couldn't have been more than thirty five, and yet he looked . . . gnarled."

"It's him, Pop!" Joey exclaimed. "The Turk was right here! Mom, you should have gotten his autograph!"

"I really doubt whether he can write, Joey, and besides, who—"

"Honey, you saw him on television a few years ago," Nick interrupted. "That's when he got hurt. The Super-bowl. Bad concussion. Put him out of business."

"Well, in my opinion, I don't think he's back in business yet. He is totally, totally strange."

"I can't believe you, Mom," Joey said through his sandwich. "You didn't get his autograph. I can't believe you!"

Christine looked at Nick and shrugged her shoulders, her eyes wide. She changed the subject. "If we may leave the topic of crazy football players for just a moment, I have something important I would like to discuss with you. I think I have a solution to the problem we've been having with Henrietta. We're all tired of the nightly battle that occurs in order to get her to stay home with Joey. Joey, what would you say if I found you another baby-sitter?"

"Baby-sitter!" Joey exploded.

"An unfortunate term. Another young-man-sitter."

"Who?" Nick asked.

"Berta Landau. I think Henrietta may have put her up to it, but she *did* volunteer, and it *would* mean solving a problem for us."

"Not to mention financial ruin for myself. This would put Henrietta in the restaurant every night."

Christine covered his hand with her own. "I've never seen her so happy, Nick. You've done that for her."

Nick looked at her in admiration. "I can never win with you, can I? I really ought to stop trying."

Christine smiled and nodded her head. "Well, what do you say, pal?"

"I'm twelve," Joey said incredulously. "I don't need anybody, Ma."

"We think you do, Joey. We don't want you here six hours by yourself. It will only be for a little while, until Daddy doesn't need me at the restaurant anymore. Right, Daddy?"

Nick shrugged. "Don't ask me. Go right to the top. Ask Henrietta."

"I don't care," Joey murmured. "She's O.K."

"Good," Christine said. "Then we'll try it. And because you're both so handsome and so nice, the dishes are on me."

Nick got out of his car. It was two o'clock in the morning and he was tired, right to the bone. He was also, he realized, quite drunk. Hosting these private parties did raise the nightly gross, but it was a little tough on the liver. Christine, mad at him for the second time this week, had gone home at midnight. He'd have to explain to her about the restaurant business. Maybe she was right. Driving home on the icy roads had been an experience. It was the brandy, he decided. No more brandy.

The night was windless and very cold. Huge banks of clouds swept up toward the moon, trying to darken the night. Nick put up his jacket collar and crunched through the snow toward his front door. As he put his key into the lock, he glanced down. Two tiny feet and a pink tail were sticking out from under the doorstep. Nick took off a glove and squatted down, plucking gingerly at the bare tail. He lifted the dead mouse up into the entrance light. The tiny animal was headless. Slowly, the expression on his face changed. It was as if his eyes and features were being gradually illumined by the rays of an inner, rising sun, until his entire countenance was bathed from within by the light of a fearsome and terrible dawn.

Holding the decapitated creature in front of him, he walked back onto the crusted snow. With angry eyes, he glared up at the unlit condominium windows that surrounded him. He stared into the dark, snow-laden pines that stood motionless in the night, and then out into the black valley beyond. Suddenly, with a furious gesture, he flung the mouse high into the night, almost falling down in the snow as he did so. He could not see where it landed, for the clouds, successful now, had covered the moon, giving the night back to the shadows.

13

THE MORNING WAS cold and cloudless. The bright sun glared off the ski slopes, making Christine's eyes squint. Lifting her face to the sun, she looked down along her nose at Joey. This was only his third ski lesson, but already he looked like an Olympic contender to her. He seemed to have a natural ability for the sport. Christine watched with pleasure as her son, his face tense with concentration, listened to the man standing in front of him. She looked at Eric Teiler. He was a perfect teacher. He spoke with an easy, knowing authority. It would seem absurd not to follow his instructions. He was even better-looking in the sunlight, Christine decided. Maybe I should take lessons. She didn't like Teiler's ski outfit, though. Knickers? Pom-poms? Emblems all over his jacket? Too ostentatiously European, too showy. Farther up the slope, with another group of beginners, she saw Teiler's sister. Same outfit, same aura of blond and bronze. Christine closed her eyes and gave her face to the sun.

The tanned image of Joey's face remained with Christine. Twelve years old and he looked like a man already. The hard, handsome planes of his father's face had just begun to form. Coupled with the total absorption, the innocence, of the eager learner, it made a beautiful mixture. A child-man. Little

Nick. Not so little. His body was getting tall and strong. He's going to be bigger than Nick, she mused. Two men in the world like that and I live with both of them. Lucky Christine. She wanted to cry. She smiled instead.

The ski lodge at lunch time was noisy and smoke-filled and smelled of fried food. Christine enjoyed it. She smiled as she watched Joey eat his lunch. There was no one in the world who enjoyed hamburgers as much as he did. She observed him in quiet amusement as he meticulously covered everything on his plate with ketchup, carefully applied proper amounts of salt and pepper, and adjusted the slice of raw onion to the exact width of the bun. It was a full two minutes before he was ready. As he hit the top of the hamburger with his fist to flatten it, he glanced up and caught Christine's rapt expression. They smiled. Christine reached over and pulled his ski hat down to the bridge of his nose.

Joey peered out from under the hat, his hamburger held in both hands. "Hey, Mom," he said. "You're really a pest, you know."

Christine nodded. Her smile deepened. She had never seen her son so happy.

Several minutes later Christine saw Eric Teiler weave his way through the chairs and admiring female glances toward their table. The cream-colored turtleneck sweater emphasized his deep tan; the blond hair fell across his forehead. The new Viking, Christine mused. Most probably wants to die with his ski pole in his hand. He was standing behind Joey now.

"Mrs. Marino, I must talk to you about your son." His European accent was noticeable and pleasant. German, Christine guessed. "May I sit down?"

"What's wrong, Mr. Teiler?" she asked.

"I tell you," he said, seating himself. "He is too good, your son. I think soon he takes my ski school away from me."

Christine turned to Joey. "Did you hear that, pal? Maybe you ought to fall down more, sweetheart."

Joey smiled and shook his head in refusal.

"I tried." As her head swung back to Teiler, she caught a look she had become familiar with. Oh boy, she thought. Too much fresh air for Thor. Oh boy.

Teiler shook his head. His eyes turned reluctantly to Joey. "I was afraid of this. Well, if the young man won't quit, I shall have to turn him into an expert. Do I have your permission to take him to the top tomorrow morning, Mrs. Marino? Just he and I. I think he is ready."

Joey's face filled with excitement. "Oh, yeah! Please, Mom. I want to go."

Christine had been taken by surprise. "Well, I don't know now. The top. That sounds dangerous. I don't know."

"Mom!" Joey's voice rose and fell, a hundred inflections in the one word.

Teiler smiled. "The air is different up there. Thin and rare. We can learn to yodel and watch all the novice ants scurrying toward the hot chocolate."

The look on Joey's face decided Christine. "I guess it's all right. But, Joey, stay next to Mr. Teiler."

"I shall be with him at every moment, Mrs. Marino. I shall take the best of care with him, the very best. I promise you." Teiler stared down at an ashtray in his hands. "I think, Mrs. Marino," he said quietly, "that you should take lessons along with Joey. I have watched you. You are a sun worshipper. You should be an athlete."

"Me?" Christine's eyes grew wide. "Oh, no. Thank you, but no. I shall never get on those things. Never. I would be sitting on the mountain more than I would be skiing on it."

Teiler put the ashtray down gently. "I think, Mrs. Marino, that the mountain would not mind this very much." He raised his eyes to hers.

Christine's expression did not change. Here we go, she thought. The chase is on. Innuendo and overtones. She raised her eyes to Teiler's in the bored, turned-off expression she had used so many times in her life. Teiler's reaction was to smile. Recognition of opposition. Equals in the game. He stood up, his eyes never leaving hers. He made a shooting gesture with his thumb and forefinger. "I bet you," he said softly.

Christine watched him walk away, trying to decide whether to be irritated or angry. She settled for both.

Joey's voice interrupted her thoughts. "He's a great guy, isn't he, Mom?"

Smiling down at her son, Christine nodded. "The best," she said.

Later that afternoon, the three women sat in the clubhouse awaiting the arrival of Baxter Cabot. Amanda was tapping a pencil, and Berta Landau was looking at the floor. No one spoke. Why are we nervous? Christine wondered. I feel like I'm waiting outside the principal's office. Her anxiety was not helped by Truman Hooker, who was adjusting a radiator in the back of the room. Over the dead cigar in his mouth, he shot covert, baleful glances at the three women, interspersed with long drinks from a small bottle he carried in his overalls. Christine looked at the heavyset man once in puzzlement and then decided to forget him.

At exactly three o'clock, the appointed time, Baxter Cabot's limousine pulled up in front of the clubhouse. Christine watched through the window as four men emerged from the car.

Christine and Amanda stared in unison at the first man to come through the door.

"It's Warren Beatty," Amanda murmured. Christine nodded.

As Cabot strode toward them, she recognized Turk Brandon at the rear of the group. As their eyes met, Brandon thrust his raincoat open and closed in flasher fashion and winked lewdly. Christine's mouth dropped open. That man is crazy, she decided. A true manaic. She found herself staring into the gray eyes of Cabot. Her hand was in his.

"Mrs. Marino," he said. "How nice of you and the committee to meet with us." When Christine tried to smile she realized that her mouth was still open. "This is Mr. Weil and Mr. Shannon," Cabot continued. "They are here, as I am, to answer any questions the committee has regarding the possible construction of a Cabot Inn adjacent to the Mountaincrest condominiums. I believe you have already met Mr. Brandon. Shall we begin?"

As the meeting progressed, Christine realized that the three women did all the listening and the men with Cabot did all the talking. Mr. Weil, a bald, irritable little man, spoke about water, sewerage, and the increase in land values. Mr. Shannon, large, immaculately dressed, discussed tax benefits and more jobs for the people of Torchester. This is getting complicated, Christine thought. I am getting in*volved*. Turk Brandon, sitting behind the other men, did not speak. The one time that Christine glanced at him, he was feigning sleep, a thumb stuck in his mouth. As she looked at him in disbelief, one eye flew open and stared at her wildly. She did not look at him again.

Suddenly, the meeting was over. As Baxter Cabot shook the hands of the other two women, Christine realized that she had barely said a word. It had not been an exchange of ideas.

It had been a lecture. Cabot pressed her hand cordially. Handsome, shining man, Christine mused. Used to success. In business, with women, in the stock market, she guessed. Cabot seemed oblivious to the impression he made, but Christine was sure that he was not.

"Mrs. Marino. So nice of you to meet with us." Cabot's voice had the tone of a bored king. "We shall be coming to Vermont for possible site determination in the near future. I look forward to meeting you again."

Christine glanced at him casually as he took her hand. No innuendo here, she decided. No secret hand pressure, no inflection of voice. Baxter Cabot was all business. Good. That's the way I like it. If you love it so much, why are you a little bit annoyed? Complex physician, heal thyself.

After the four men had left, Christine turned to Amanda. "Well," she asked, "what do you think?"

Amanda was still staring at the door. "Give him anything he wants," she whispered. "Anything."

"You're a big help, Amanda. Really great. Berta?"

The older woman was smiling. "I like him," she murmured. "He looks like a movie star."

Christine nodded her head in mock exasperation. "That's splendid," she said. "The three of us are really splendid. No one's going to push *us* around." The other women hardly heard her.

Amanda and Christine walked away from the clubhouse, a few drifting snowflakes touching their faces in cold caress. The clouds hung low and heavy. Thick mists raced across the dark green sides of the mountains.

Christine looked at the lowering sky. "This is ridiculous," she said. "It's only four o'clock and look how dark it is."

"It's the end of the world," Amanda agreed. "I'm sure of it. Thank goodness I've got clean underwear on."

"Don't talk like that." Christine shivered. "I have been known to frighten easily. Come and have coffee with me."

"Can't be done, baby. I'm late already. Bye. See you."

The moment Christine opened her door, she felt the cold air. Someone had left the glass door to the deck wide open. She walked through the living room and closed it quickly, shaking her head. It was when she turned around that she saw it. The head of a tall, slim china cat had been broken off and was lying on the table next to the delicate body. Christine frowned in anger. Joey, most probably. And then, slowly, her expression changed. She remembered. She shook her head in disbelief, but still her eyes grew wider, and the corners of her mouth turned down. She looked around with quick, sudden movements of her head. It was one of the few times in her life when her face was not beautiful.

The two figures stood on the snow-covered hillside, looking down at the bright Mountaincrest windows, their bodies as motionless as the pines above them. After a long silence, the man spoke.

"The murderers have received their second calling card by now. Holiday greetings from the North Wind. How I long to see that pale face at this moment! Ah, well. We must observe the holiday proprieties, my sister. After the card . . . comes the gift. It is time, Thagnar, for the gift."

The woman at his side did not speak. Her lips quivered back. Her teeth glinted dully in the gray light, transforming her face gradually into a mask of horror. The cold forest stilled to a deeper silence. And in the stillness, dark afternoon melted into darker night.

14

NIGHT.
Absence of moonlight.

Torchester, a modern Atlantis, lay under an ocean of black cold that pressed and cracked the houses, numbing the inhabitants into the icy sea dreams that rise from the waveless depths of the soul.

Christine dreamed. She was walking through deep snow toward a stand of dark pines in the center of a moonlit meadow. She was carrying a baby in her arms, protecting it from the cold. Suddenly, the baby bit her in the shoulder and leaped from her arms. It began to run away from her with the easy strides of a practiced runner, its movements strong and sure through the gleaming snow. In pain and shock, Christine struggled after it, calling its name. Once the infant turned and looked at her in a sly, unpitying manner, and then it raced onward, entering the snow-laden trees without another backward glance. As Christine approached, her footsteps slowed and stopped. Something emerged toward her from the shadowed pines, a malevolent force that filled her with dread. She began to circle the small woods, unable to leave, not daring to enter. She called the child's name again and again. There was only silence. And then she felt it. Something was there in the darkness, something was coming toward her, a thing of unutterable, immeasurable menace. She turned and fled, her body rising above the silvered snow, the wind carrying her wraith-like above the shimmering meadow, her legs swinging from side to side through the swirling, moonstruck drifts. Behind her, a faceless monster came lunging out of the dark trees in pursuit, howling in mindless wind-voice, rushing at a speed that was impossible to escape.

Joey dreamed. He was a black swan gliding on black water across a vast, misted lake. Astride his back was a beautiful, naked woman. Her thighs pressed closely about him; her long blond hair trailed after them in the ebon water. A swelling chorus of female voices perfumed the night air. The sweet music came from the water lilies along the shore, the gently swaying willows, the starlit ripples all about him, filling the night with rapture.

Deep in the mist before him, an island appeared. Crumbling marble columns rose at the shore, white steps led down into the lapping waves. A vague sense of foreboding made him stop, but the woman's voice urged him forward. As he neared the island, the music swelled to an unbearable exquisite intensity, mingling with the thunder of a distant waterfall. In a swoon of passion, he arched his long neck backward, placing his dark head between the breasts of the woman above him. She grasped his neck with one hand but did not look down at him. Her eyes were fixed in wild, expectant recognition on the thing that coiled on the steps in front of them.

Nick stood looking out the window as the first blue glimmerings of dawn silhouetted the mountains. The smoke from a cigarette half closed his eyes. He couldn't remember the last time he'd had a nightmare, but tonight had really made up for it. A real beauty. A corker. And he couldn't shake it. It was still vivid in his mind.

He had dreamed that he was locking up the restaurant. Inside, through the front window, he had seen the figure of a man walk past the night-light. The man was slim and wore an overcoat; his hat was pulled down, covering his face. Nick had opened the door and gone in, following the sound of the man's footsteps toward the unlit back dining room. At the center of the room, Nick had stopped, hardly able to see anything at all. He felt rather than heard that somewhere in the room the man had stopped and turned. Abruptly everything changed between the two shadowed figures. Fear flooded into Nick; the hunter became the hunted. In panic, he crawled under a table, his face pressed to his knees, his hands covering the back of his neck. And then unspeakable fear seized his heart. The man had sprung at him in the darkened room. As he did so, a primitive, bestial scream rent the silence, tearing at Nick's mind with claws of terror. Slowly, inexorably, the man glided toward him, arms outstretched, the ever increasing volume of his voice shattering the air between them. Then, suddenly, Nick was in his bed, trying to awaken. He huddled closer into himself, not daring to turn around to face his assailant. Half awake, half asleep, he knew that if the shrieking abomination behind him touched him, he would not be ripped and bitten, not killed. He would be lost. With a supreme effort, he climbed out of the fog and horror of his dream and awoke with a start. The voice was gone, but the memory of it still echoed in his mind. He reached for his cigarette pack, staring in wonder at his trembling hand.

Nick crushed his third cigarette out, his eyes on the distant mountains. He could not get that savage cry out of the recesses of his brain. He could not look behind him in the dawn-lit room. Fear that could not be suppressed darted in back of the anger in his eyes. He was remembering himself in bed. He was remembering how he could not turn around and look at who it was that came toward him out of the darkness.

Nick closed his eyes, fumbled for another cigarette. Somehow he knew that the last thing on earth he wanted to see was that face.

Night.
Absence of starlight.
The darkness lay like a terrific slumbering beast upon the land. Its gleaming, maniac eyes were closed; the great heaving black sides swayed the forests to the horizon. Fitfully the blackness slept, haunted by bellows of agony and ancient lusts, blending in the air with the piercing whine of police sirens, scurrying like shrill insects to some carnal feast of blood. Restlessly, it dreamed its unimaginable dreams, filling the night with a silent vibrancy that pulsed in unison with the giant heart of horror. Afraid to arouse that which pressed down upon the earth, the foxes of midnight did not hunt; the owls bowed their heads. Their animal efforts were in vain. Stirred by the sounds of primal crime in its depths, the slumberer arose. Terror awakened. Towering to the stars, the great beast lifted its head.

15

C HRISTINE STARED OUT the ice-flowered kitchen window at the gray morning sky. A sudden gust of bitter-
cold wind rattled the glass. Shimmering snowflakes
swirled against the pane in soft attack, bringing vague memories of nightmare. She shivered, drew her robe tightly about
her, and poured herself some steaming coffee.

The telephone rang.

Christine started, slightly spilling her coffee, and then
smiled. That must have been some dream, she thought. I wish
I could remember it. She picked up the receiver. "Hello?" she
said.

The voice on the other end was firm but pleasant. "Mrs.
Marino? This is Mrs. Dekalb, Joey's guidance counselor,
Torchester Junior High. Am I disturbing your breakfast?"

"No," Christine said quickly. "Is there anything wrong?"

"Well, frankly, Mrs. Marino, I was wondering why you
hadn't responded to my notes."

"Notes?"

"I have given Joey two notes requesting a conference and
I—"

"I haven't received any notes."

There was a pause. "I see. Perhaps you can talk that over
with Joey. At your convenience, Mrs. Marino, I would like

to discuss Joey's behavior with you. Before suspension, we should certainly—"

"Suspension!" Christine's eyes grew wide.

"I think we should sit down and discuss Joey's recent behavior at length, Mrs. Marino. The principal and I think that—"

"I'm ready to discuss it right now, Mrs. Dekalb." Christine had difficulty keeping the emotion out of her voice. "Will you please tell me what this is all about?"

"I would much prefer to discuss this with you in person, Mrs. Marino."

"Mrs. Dekalb, I have to go to work early today and simply will not have the time. I really shall have to insist that you tell me what is going on. Now."

There was a pause on the other end of the phone. "As you wish, Mrs. Marino. It has come to our attention that in the last few weeks Joey's behavior has changed considerably. I was wondering if there was anything that was bothering him, his home situation . . ."

"His home situation is fine, Mrs. Dekalb." There was a coldness in Christine's voice now. "Perhaps you could be more specific."

"All right." The other woman's tone matched Christine's. "Specifically, he is rude to his teachers, he is not doing his work, and his language has become offensive."

"Offensive?"

"Cursing, Mrs. Marino. I have been a recipient. 'Offensive' is an accurate word."

Christine's head was moving from side to side in surprise and dismay. "I don't understand. This doesn't sound like Joey. Not at all."

The voice on the other end grew perceptibly softer. "We're puzzled, too, Mrs. Marino. Although Joey has had his moments in the past, his attitude toward school has been excellent. It is only recently that his behavior has been . . . unacceptable. That's why I asked you if there was a home problem that might help explain—"

"But there's nothing! Nothing!"

"Mrs. Marino. Mr. Ettinger, the principal, and I both feel that perhaps there is something bothering Joey that you are unaware of. We would like to recommend that the school psychologist speak to him in order to—"

"I don't really feel, Mrs. Dekalb, that my son needs a psychologist. I think I know him better than you do. You can be assured, however, that both Mr. Marino and I will have a talk with Joey about his work and his behavior."

"Well, after what happened today I truly feel that professional counseling would be beneficial."

Christine's voice was level. "What happened today, Mrs. Dekalb?"

"Mrs. Marino, I've just spent thirty minutes in my office with Mrs. Ahlmeyer, Joey's social studies teacher. The woman was so distraught we had to send her home. She is a fine teacher, has been with us eleven years, and is not prone to hysteria, I can assure you."

"What has this got to do with my son?" Christine asked, not wanting to hear the answer.

"Joey apparently said something to her after class, as he was leaving the room."

"What is it he is supposed to have said to her?"

"Mrs. Ahlmeyer would not divulge this information to me. I suggest that you ask your son."

"I certainly shall. And thank you for your concern."

"Please think over what I said about counseling, Mrs. Marino. The next incident like this will almost certainly result in suspension."

"There will be no more incidents, I can assure you. Good-bye, Mrs. Dekalb."

Christine looked out the window once more, seeing nothing, disbelief and sadness drawing her attention inward. Impulsively she picked up the telephone and called Nick at the restaurant. His reaction was the same as hers. He simply did not believe it. He promised to discuss it with Joey later in the day.

Slightly reassured, Christine sipped her coffee, her eyes on the misted, silent mountains. Faint echoes, like sighing winds, drifted in the recesses of her mind, indistinguishable, fading quickly.

The telephone rang.

Christine stared at it as if it were a snake. She picked it up. "Yes?"

"How charming you are at eleven in the morning. Want me to call back after two, sweetheart?"

"Oh, Amanda, I'm sorry." Christine smiled slightly. "I'm not crazy about the phone this morning. Why haven't you come for coffee?"

"Couldn't be done, honey. Big doings last night. When the Irishman heard about it, his retired old eyes lit up like a Christmas tree. Don't tell me you haven't heard."

"Heard what?"

"Big excitement. Somebody had a bull killed last night. The last time something happened in Torchester, somebody took out a library book without a card. Ben and I are going down to the state police office for details. The captain's an old friend of his. I haven't been so excited since one of my fingernails broke."

"Will I see you tomorrow?"

"Absolutely. Bye, honey."

Christine hung up. Again the echoes called to each other in frail, sinister voices. Her mind still on Joey, Christine barely heard them.

Henrietta appeared in the doorway to her bedroom. Her

sparse hair was standing straight out, the sleeves of her cardigan sweater hung over her hands, and the previous night's eye makeup gave her a shadowed, ghostly appearance. A cigarette hung from her lips. She coughed. "What is this," she said in a harsh, croaking voice, "the stock exchange? How can I get my beauty sleep with that telephone ringing like that?"

As always, Henrietta could unknowingly lighten Christine's mood. "Your what?" she asked politely.

"You heard me, smart-ass. Why are you staring at me like that?"

"I was just thinking, auntie, how breathtaking you are in the morning."

Henrietta looked at her through the cigarette smoke, one eye half closed. "Which way?" she said.

"In the worst possible sense of the word, dearest."

Henrietta nodded. "You're fired. Give me some coffee."

Christine watched the older woman affectionately as she blew away the steam spirals. "Hen," she said finally, "that was the school on the phone before. It seems that Joey's been getting into trouble at school."

Henrietta's eyes flew open. "Joey? Nonsense. Forget it. All kids get into trouble at school at least once. He's a growing boy. Maybe the Marino juices are starting to flow. We Knapps have club soda in our veins, so it couldn't be our side of the family."

The frown melted slightly from Christine's forehead. "You think that's it, Hen? Growing pains?"

"Of course. Joey's my sweetheart. They're lucky to have him."

"I haven't noticed anything different about him. Have you, Hen?"

"Not a thing. The boy's a pearl." Henrietta paused.

"What is it?" Christine asked.

"It's nothing. I was just thinking. I haven't seen him at the restaurant lately. He used to stop by to help me out almost every afternoon. Girls, most probably. It's getting to be that time."

"I guess." Christine sighed.

Christine was still dressing for work when Joey came home. A moment later she heard him rattling around in the refrigerator.

Easy does it, she thought. Remember the growing pains. Still brushing her hair, she walked into the living room. "No basketball practice today?" she asked.

Bent over, Joey did not look up. "No," he said.

"Oh? Why not?"

Joey straightened and looked at her pleasantly. "Because I didn't go, Mom." He removed a plate of cold cuts and headed toward the kitchen table.

Christine took a deep breath. "Joey, I had a call from Mrs. Dekalb this morning. In regard to your work and behavior. I was very surprised to hear what she said."

Joey completed his sandwich and eyed it carefully.

"She called you disruptive, Joey, and said you were using foul language, and she said . . ."

Christine stopped. Joey had raised his head to her, his mouth wide in a smile she did not recognize.

"Mrs. Dekalb is a liar," he said matter-of-factly.

Christine stood still, unable to speak. She watched in a mixture of puzzlement and anger as Joey got up and began to put on his jacket, the sandwich held in one hand. Finally, she found her voice. "Joey! Where are you going? I want to talk to you. Your father's coming home from work to talk to you."

"Later, Mom. You can both nail me later. I've got to go to work."

"Work? What do you mean? At the restaurant?"

"No, Mom. I'm not working there anymore. I've been working for Mr. Hooker every afternoon after practice. He pays me two dollars an hour. You and Dad never paid me anything." Joey's voice was calm; the slight smile had stayed on his lips.

For a moment, Christine was too surprised to speak. She tried to make her voice sound firm. "Well, you be back here by five o'clock, young man. You can tell that to your father."

"All right," Joey said pleasantly.

Christine followed him toward the door, her hairbrush still held in her hand. "Before you go, Joey, I want to know right now what you could have possibly said to Mrs. Ahlmeyer that would upset her like that."

With one hand on the doorknob, Joey's head turned slowly toward his mother. For an instant his eyes, his face, came alive with his thoughts. Then his smile came back, and he opened the door and went out.

Christine watched uncomfortably as Nick paced back and forth across the living room. Every thirty seconds he looked at his wristwatch and took another sip from the glass in his hand. It was his third drink.

"Where is that kid?" he said impatiently. "It's almost six o'clock. It's the Friday before Christmas. Do you know what must be going on down there? Where the hell is he?"

The door opened and Joey walked in, his hat and jacket dusted with snowflakes.

Nick put his glass down. "Son, I thought your mother told you to be here at five," he said.

"I'm sorry, Dad." Joey began to take off his jacket. "I was helping Mr. Hooker with the generator. I guess I forgot about the time."

Nick waved him to the dining-room table. As Joey sat

down, Christine watched the snowflakes melt and disappear on her son's woollen cap. She was filled with a sudden protective tenderness toward him.

"Joey"—Nick's voice was calm— "your mother tells me you've been having problems at school. We'd like to talk to you about it. Maybe we can help."

"I'll handle it, Dad." Joey did not look at Nick.

Nick looked at his son speculatively. "We'd like to help you, son."

Joey shrugged impatiently. "I told you I would take care of it," he said.

Nick's eyes changed. "You just see that you do, Joey. See that you do. And, Joey, no more cursing. That's out. Get me?"

"Sure, Dad."

"And another thing. It's not a good idea to call Mrs. Dekalb a liar. She's only trying to help you."

"O.K., Dad. If you say so. She's not a liar."

Nick stood up. "All right, son," he said.

Slowly, Joey's gaze rose to his father. "She's a fucking bitch," he said evenly.

Sudden anger flared across Nick's face. His hand lashed out and slapped Joey's cheek. Hard. The sound stayed in the room, stunning the three of them.

"Get out," Nick said finally. "Go to your room. Get out."

Christine had always feared the sound of Nick's voice when it went flat and calm, the way he was speaking now. Sudden tears sprang into her eyes as she watched her two men stare at each other.

A slow smile spread across Joey's face. He rubbed the side of his face where Nick had slapped him, his eyes never leaving his father's. After several more seconds, he walked to his room.

It was only after Joey had left that Nick's expression changed. He walked to the bar and poured himself a drink, fumbling with the ice. He drank it quickly, staring at the wall in front of him. When he had finished, he walked to the hall closet. "Let's go," he said.

Christine watched as her husband carefully buttoned his coat. "Oh, Nick, I . . ." She stopped.

Nick turned to her. "Let's go," he repeated.

Christine nodded, biting her lip. She had never seen that look in her husband's eyes before.

When Christine answered the doorbell the next morning, she saw that Amanda had brought Ben Kiley with her. She smiled. "The police? What is this, a pinch?"

Kiley reluctantly threw his cigar away. "I might," he said, "if you give me some hot coffee."

Amanda looked at him sideways. "You always did like to live dangerously, didn't you. Wipe your feet and take off your hat."

Kiley scowled. He wiped his feet and took off his hat.

"You look disgustingly cheerful this morning," Amanda said, striding into the living room.

"I am, I am," Christine replied. "My husband and my son just hugged each other before they left."

"Is that extraordinary?" Amanda's eyebrows lifted.

"After last night? I'd say so, yes."

"Oh? Kiddie problems?"

"Growing pains. They talked, they hugged. It's all over, thank God."

"It happens," Amanda said, smiling. "Kids are kids."

"That's profound, dear. Deep," Kiley said, thrusting a box at Christine. "Here, Chris," he continued. "Doughnuts are doughnuts."

Amanda stared at the ceiling. "Boy, are you not going to get it when you get home. Ole Cap'n Ben's feeling good today, for a change. He's on a *case*. His state trooper friend has asked him to help investigate the killing of that bull that I told you about. What excitement." Amanda yawned.

Kiley stared into the jellied depths of his doughnut. "Could be interesting. Full-grown bull. Something mauled it all to hell. Broke its neck."

"Broke a bull's neck?" Christine's mouth was open.

"Yeah. They think they've got a big bear. A black bear couldn't do that. They think it might be a grizzly that wandered down from Canada. Nothing else could do a job like that. You had to see it." Kiley shook his head at his coffee cup, his eyes reflective. "That must have been quite an encounter. Sweet Jesus."

Christine shivered. This time she had heard the echo voices screaming terror from the depths of memory. It was only their message that still escaped her. "Could we change the subject?" she asked softly. "Please."

Amanda put a protective hand on her shoulder. She looked at Kiley through narrowed eyes. "Ben, you have a charm that won't quit. You're especially fun at breakfast."

Kiley shrugged and growled into his coffee.

"Change of subject." Amanda turned to Christine. "Guess who's coming to our Christmas Day gala?"

Christine shook her head, the fear slowly fading from her face.

"Baxter Cabot. *The* Baxter Cabot. That beautiful man." She glanced at Kiley. "Oh, the *charm* of the man. How can one man be so handsome? And so *charming!*"

Ben Kiley bit viciously into his doughnut. His eyes remained fixed on the table in front of him.

"What's the occasion?" Christine asked. "Why are we to be so blessed?"

"Kyle Thorne told me he was coming to announce his decision on the Cabot Inn. We're all supposed to be waiting breathlessly. With that kind of *charm*, he can have my condominium."

"Broke the damn bull's neck," Kiley said loudly. "Whacko!"

Amanda burst out in sudden laughter. Christine tried a tentative smile.

Exactly at five o'clock, as she did every weekday night, Berta Landau rang the bell. Although Nick was already waiting in the car, Christine stopped for a moment to talk to her.

"Berta, how has Joey been behaving with you? Have you been having any . . . problems with him recently?"

The older woman looked surprised. "Problems? But no. Nothing. He is a good boy, your son. Only . . ." She paused.

"What is it?" Christine asked worriedly.

"Only . . . sometimes I notice he does not like to do his homework."

Christine smiled in relief. "That's not a problem, Berta. That's a chronic condition. Good night, now."

A moment after Christine had left, Joey walked out of his bedroom and stood looking at Mrs. Landau.

"Good evening, Joey," She tilted her head to one side. "We play checkers tonight or must you do your schoolwork?"

Joey looked at her for a long moment, an unreadable look in his eyes. Abruptly, he walked back into his bedroom, slamming the door behind him. He stood there, looking around, his head moving from side to side. He sat down at his desk and picked up his science textbook. He read half a page, a slow frown gathering on his forehead. With no change of expression, he tore the page he was reading out of the book. Then, carefully, methodically, he started tearing the succeeding pages out, letting them fall silently to the floor.

16

THE CHRISTMAS PARTY was a definite success, the clubhouse filling before twelve o'clock. The room overflowed with red holiday decorations and Bloody Marys, the air filled with excitement, smoke, and the aroma of coffee.

The Marinos stood with Henrietta near the center of the floor, barely able to move. Christine smiled pleasantly at her aunt. "Another drink, auntie dear? How fortunate for you that the crowd will keep you from falling."

Henrietta's artificial smile was dazzling. "What are you, my accountant? Nicholas, both our glasses seem to be empty. Would you be a love?" She indicated the bar with a flourish of her hand. "I would go myself, but I think someone put my girdle on backward this morning. Dear boy." As Nick wove his way through the crowd, Henrietta's voice rose harshly. "And don't forget the lime this time!" Nick raised a glass in acknowledgment.

A moment after Nick had gone, Christine saw Eric Teiler shouldering his way toward her. He looked more tanned then ever.

"Mrs. Marino," he said, "I must ask you why you have never introduced me to your sister." Teiler smiled at Henrietta before his arrogant gaze turned back to Christine.

"Jealousy," Henrietta answered quickly. "Fear and jealousy." She played with her necklace. "Christine, who is this handsome, astigmatic man?"

After the introduction, Teiler spoke to Henrietta, but his eyes never left Christine's face. "You must convince your younger sister, dear lady, that she must take ski lessons. She does not seem to realize that there are things she can learn from me that she can learn nowhere else." Henrietta's eyes narrowed suspiciously.

"Mr. Teiler gives Joey his ski lessons," Christine explained patiently. "He seems to think that I should learn to ski also. I've told him that I much prefer to sit by the fire. The home fire." She returned Teiler's gaze pleasantly.

Teiler laughed. "This is such a shame. You are not . . . Vermont. You are missing, Mrs. Marino . . . so much."

Christine spoke with barely hidden annoyance. "I don't think so." She tried to maintain her smile.

"Oh, I am convinced." Teiler stared at her for a long moment before he walked away into the crowd.

Henrietta watched him leave. "Wow!" she said finally. "There's enough innuendo in here to fog up your glasses. Look out for that man, Christine. He's a tiger."

"He'd like to think so," Christine answered quietly.

"No, he's a tiger. A true predator. Stay away from him, dearie."

"Hold that thought," Nick said, coming up behind Henrietta and handing her a drink. His mouth was smiling, but his eyes, as they looked at Christine, were not. "Miss me, honey?" he said.

Christine's face flushed with anger. In all the years of their marriage, Nick had never been truly able to control his jealousy. In the early days it had given her a secure feeling, but now it merely seemed useless. Before she could answer Nick, the huge figure of Malcolm Jones appeared between them.

"Mrs. Marino," he said, his red lips wet with saliva. "What a beautiful outfit. You're gorgeous again. I have to admit it."

Beyond his shoulder, Christine saw Nick turn to Henrietta. "I guess I'd better get in line, right, Hen?" he said with the same nonsmile. He walked around Henrietta and stood behind Jones.

Suddenly I'm having a wonderful time, Christine thought desperately. I think I'll go home now.

"Mrs. Marino," Jones continued, "I want to talk to you about your son."

Christine's face showed nothing. "What seems to be the problem?"

"He is ruining my self-esteem. I started skiing at the same time he did, and already he's at the summit with Maestro Teiler, while I'm still floundering around the base. It's not right."

Relieved, Christine smiled. "He seems to be an excellent athlete, Mr. Jones."

"A dear boy. We've had many fine talks together. Oh my god, here comes Amanda. That woman. She's ruining me. She dusts, she rearranges, she insists that I pay taxes. Inconceivable! I think I'll fire her." As Jones turned to go, he came face to face with Nick. "Hi," he said, his eyes bright.

Nick's expression did not change. "Hi there," he said flatly.

As Jones walked away, Nick stepped up to Christine. "Next," he said.

Christine stared at him. "Nick, stop it. Please . . . just . . . stop it."

As they looked at each other, Nick's face gradually softened. He shook his head. "I'm sorry, honey. You know crazy old Nick. Besides, I think we can erase that last one, anyway."

"You can," Christine said, starting to smile, "but I won't." Their eyes met in silent mirth.

Amanda grabbed Christine's arm, nearly spilling her drink.

"My god, Chris, he's here. The great man is here. Now remember, we're the opposition. Be dignified. Be . . . opposing. Look at him. All my sexual fantasies. In ski clothes, yet." Behind her, the cigar in Ben Kiley's mouth shifted sides.

Christine watched as Baxter Cabot entered the clubhouse like a bright comet, trailing Turk Brandon and the two lawyers. A path opened before him in the crowded room as he headed for Kyle Thorne and shook his hand warmly. Thorne raised his arms, asking for silence.

"Folks," he said, speaking above the gradually quieting voices, "it gives me great pleasure to introduce you to Mr. Baxter Cabot. Mr. Cabot would like to say a few words to you, if we can get a little quiet in here."

Cabot waited patiently for silence. "Ladies and gentlemen," he said finally. "I would much rather join these festivities than interrupt them, so I shall be brief. I just want to tell you that my staff and I have recently decided that Mad Mountain would be an excellent place to establish a new Cabot Inn resort." There was scattered applause, which Kyle Thorne attempted to silence. "We think that Mad Mountain can be one of the biggest and best ski resorts in the East, and with your votes next week, I believe we can help you achieve this. As I've already explained to Mr. Thorne and to your committee, this will mean new jobs for the residents of Torchester, increased land values for them and for yourselves, new people, new excitement, new businesses. It is our estimation that a favorable vote on your part—and without your land it would be difficult for us to go forward—would prove to be beneficial for everyone concerned. And I can tell you this." He looked around at the now hushed audience. A sudden smile came to his lips. "I can't think of anyone else who I would rather have as some of my neighbors than the people of Mountaincrest."

Loud applause shook the room.

"He's good," Amanda said in Christine's ear. "Oh boy, listen to that."

Dr. Landau, standing on the other side of Christine, scratched his head. "I think 'oh boy' is a minimum," he said ruefully. "I think we are headed Forward into Progress."

Christine looked down at the round little man. She decided she liked him. "There's still the committee, Dr. Landau. We're still working."

Landau sighed. "Work harder, *Liebchen*. Or we are overcome with this Progress."

As Christine stood talking to Dr. Landau, she saw that Baxter Cabot was working his handshaking way toward Amanda and herself. In another few minutes he was standing in front of her, Turk Brandon at his side.

"Mrs. Marino. Ms. Birch." He took Christine's hand. "I've looked forward to seeing you again." Even though she knew it was his business smile, Christine was impressed. The moviestar face, the perfectly matched ski clothes, the gleam of the man. Those poor New York City women, she thought. "I've been giving you ladies some thought recently, and I think I've come up with a few ideas that may make you like me just a little bit better." Cabot had not released her hand. Christine glanced quickly at Nick. He was looking at their clasped hands. He finished his drink. "Before the voting I should very much like to meet with you, Mrs. Marino, and the rest of the committee, of course, to discuss this further."

"Sounds like a swell idea to me," Nick said, looking at Christine pleasantly.

In unconscious reaction, Christine withdrew her hand. She gave Nick one glance that translated into "Not now, not again." She introduced him to Cabot.

"So good to meet you," Cabot said. He shook Nick's hand briefly and swung his eyes back to Christine. Nick stood looking down at his hand.

"I shall be spending the coming week here, Mrs. Marino," Cabot continued. "Perhaps a dinner could be arranged."

"We'd love to," Nick said. His eyes appeared eager.

Cabot turned toward him slowly. His eyes measured Nick for an instant before he spoke. "You're on the committee, Mr. Marino?"

Nick nodded. "Oh yes. Yes. Recording secretary. The very heart of the committee."

Cabot's face remained impassive. "Then I'll look forward to meeting all of you very shortly."

Nick's eyes changed. "I'll bet," he said.

Cabot's gaze remained on Nick, beneath a slowly forming frown.

"Carmella!" Turk Brandon's loud greeting interrupted the two men. Brandon pushed past Cabot and threw his arms around a startled Henrietta. After a moment he held her at arm's length, his face alive with excitement. "To leave me in Rio de Janeiro with only a cryptic note? You ruined my life, left my American Express card a shambles. Now that I've found you, I shall never let you go again. Never!"

For the first time in her life, Christine saw Henrietta at a loss for words. In the confusion and explanations that followed, Baxter Cabot walked away, his departure hardly noticed. Brandon shrugged. "I don't understand it. There cannot be two such beautiful women in the world. Forgive me, dear lady." He embraced Henrietta again.

Behind her back, Brandon's eyes slowly rose to meet Nick's. The expression on his face was different now.

Gradually, the smile came back to Nick's face. The two men's eyes were locked in understanding, in the shared knowledge of men who were not strangers to violence.

17

CHRISTINE STOOD ON the small condominium deck staring at the bright, sunlit ski slopes in front of her. One hand was in her coat pocket; the other held her semiannual cigarette. She could hear the ski instructors yodeling their way down the summit stretches in their first morning runs, firming the powdery surface for the crowds of skiers soon to follow.

I need this cigarette, she thought. It is not nine o'clock yet and already it has been a bad day, a rotten day. She had been awakened early in the morning by the sound of the front door slamming loudly. As she was putting on her bathrobe to investigate, she could not help but notice that the bedroom smelled like a winery. Nick had begun drinking at the clubhouse yesterday and had continued steadily throughout the night. The scent of his alcoholic exhalations filled the room. Going into the dining room, she had found Henrietta in tears. It was something Joey had said to her before he had left for school. She would not tell Christine what it was. And at this very moment, Truman Hooker was hunched over her kitchen plumbing, alternately tinkering and glowering at her with small, steely eyes, driving her to deck and tobacco.

Enough bullshit for one morning, she decided, grinding her cigarette angrily into an ashtray on the railing. Time to take the bullshit by the horns. She strode into the living room and spoke in a firm voice.

"Mr. Hooker," she said. The man in front of her straightened up and turned around in one swift, fluid motion, startling Christine slightly. "Mr. Hooker," she repeated. "The few times we have met, it has been very obvious to me that, for some reason, you seem to dislike me." The man's bulk and unwavering gaze made her uneasy. She forced herself to continue. "Would you please tell me if my feelings are correct on this?"

After a moment, the huge man's head nodded, the corners of his mouth turning down.

Hooker's reaction disturbed Christine deeply. She collected her face. "May I ask why? I've done nothing to you, I . . ." She stopped. Hooker had turned his back to her and was once more adjusting her faucet. Christine's mouth twitched once. "I really don't understand, Mr. Hooker. As I say, we've never—"

Hooker spoke without turning around. "Mrs. Marino, you want your faucet fixed, you'll have to leave me alone. I don't work well, I don't work at all, with someone looking over my shoulder."

Christine's face hardened in anger. She turned and walked back out onto the deck. She glared at the distant, sparkling mountains, her face tense with emotion: rage and the first traces of an inexplicable fear.

It was late in the afternoon when the front door closed behind Joey. Nick and Christine sat at opposite ends of the couch, Nick sipping a martini, Christine reading and staring into the rose-glowing coals in the fireplace.

Nick's voice was firm. "Joey, may we see you for a moment?"

Joey came into the living room, his cheeks red from the frost air. "Yeah, Dad," he said. "What is it?"

"Joey, your mother found Henrietta crying this morning. I

believe it was because of you. I would like to know what happened."

His head shaking in impatience, Joey looked steadily at his father. "All I said to her, Dad, was to leave me alone. She tells me how to dress, what to eat, everything. She bothers me."

Nick looked at his son for a long moment. "She loves you, Joey," he said finally. "She's only trying to help you. Maybe you could let her bother you a little bit."

A half sigh, half laugh escaped from Joey. "I'd really rather not," he said. "And besides, she cries too easily, if you ask me."

Nick put his glass down. "Really?" he asked softly. Their eyes met.

"Yeah," Joey said. "Really."

"I'll tell you what you're going to do, young man." Nick's voice was deliberate, almost a whisper. "I'm going to call Henrietta in here right now. You're going to kiss her and tell her you're sorry. Do you understand?"

A slow smile spread across Joey's face. "Sure," he said.

Henrietta came in, smiling tentatively, her face heavily made up for work. Joey walked over and hugged her mechanically. Behind his back, Henrietta's face creased into a relieved smile, which she quickly controlled.

"Watch the powder, dearie," she said, trying to sound crisp. "I just put—" She was interrupted as Joey placed his lips on hers and kissed her firmly. When he let the astonished woman go, he turned to his father.

"O.K., Dad?" he said, his eyes bright. They remained looking at each other for what seemed to Christine an agonizing eternity. Then, suddenly, Joey released Henrietta and walked to his room. The three adults remained there, frozen as in a photograph, Henrietta with eyes closed, Christine looking at Nick, and Nick staring at the door that had just closed.

18

CHRISTINE SAT ON the large wooden deck of the Mad Mountain ski lodge, her legs wrapped in a car blanket, the blond hair cascading forward from her parka hood. What a sport, she mused. These people are all crazy. She shivered once and raised her eyes to the main ski trail, which ended twenty yards in front of her. Eric Teiler had taken Joey and several other students to the summit. Try as she might, she could not find her son among the tiny, weaving figures on the trail high above her.

Christine closed her eyes against the chill wind. She felt her hair blow across her face in light caress. Her features were serene, almost as if she were asleep, but her mind was not at ease. Why can't paradise ever be paradise? she wondered. Things are going wrong, and I can't stop them because I don't know where to begin. I don't really know what they are. Nick is drinking more and more. Something is eating him up inside, I can feel it. I can see it in his face. He won't tell me what it is, he just laughs and then pours himself another drink. Beloved, beloved Nick. I feel like crying. Wait, she told herself. Don't cry yet. There's more. Think about Joey. Think about your son. Then cry.

Joey's behavior in the past few weeks was a mystery to Christine. Oh, yes, she knew all about teenagers, she'd read the books. But she had seen something in Joey recently, something strange, something deliberate, something the books did not explain. And when he had kissed Henrietta on the mouth last night, there had been something very wrong, in his face, in his eyes.

The sun warmed her face for a brief, unclouded moment. Christine opened her eyes to see Dr. Landau slowly trudging up the stairs next to her.

"I am too old for this," he said, waving a greeting. "My wife is right. I am old and I am crazy." He was trying to catch his breath.

Christine managed a smile. "You are neither. You are a handsome man, that's what you are."

Landau shook his head. "*Na.* Cute, yes. Handsome, no. Why are you looking at me like that?"

Christine spoke with difficulty. "I was just wondering, Doctor, if it would be very rude of me to ask you . . . a professional question?"

"It is impossible for a woman with a face such as yours, Mrs. Marino, to be rude. Don't ask me to explain that, because I cannot." He walked up the rest of the steps and sat down wearily next to Christine. "Oh, that feels good. Now, what is it, my child? Your husband?"

"No, Doctor, it's my son. Lately, he's been behaving rather badly. He's defiant, he doesn't listen, I don't know, sort of . . . unloving."

Dr. Landau nodded knowingly. He placed his unlit pipe in his mouth. "Terrible, terrible symptoms." His face creased into a smile at Christine's wide-eyed look. "My dear Mrs. Marino. The disease is called growing up. It will last several more years and then fade away of its own accord."

Christine tried to smile. "I hope you're right, Doctor. But sometimes I'm not sure. Some of the things he does . . . some of the ways he acts . . ."

Dr. Landau spoke softly. "My dear, I have met your boy. He seems to me to be a fine young man. His only problem is that he is twelve."

This time Christine did not smile. She looked down at her hands.

Landau gazed at her intently before he continued. "I have, as usual, an excellent idea. *I* shall drive Joey home from the mountain today. We shall talk, he and I. Then I shall telephone you and tell you, I am sure, what I have already diagnosed. He is suffering from a chronological disorder called teens. It will go away, my dear. It will go away."

Christine raised her eyes to his. "Thank you, Dr. Landau. You are very kind." She touched his arm lightly.

"I am not kind. I am hungry." Landau rose stiffly. "And now I shall attack the food in the cafeteria, so that later on it may attack me. Everything balances. *Wiedersehen*, Mrs. Marino."

As the sun once more broke through the banked clouds, Christine leaned her head back. She felt as if a weight had been lifted from her. She didn't care whether she had imposed on the doctor, or whether she was being silly and overprotective. She was going to get a professional O.K. on Joey and that was going to be that. A tear trailed its icy way down her cheek. I'm the crazy one, she thought. I feel reassured, almost happy. So what do I do? She wiped at the tear, shaking her head.

A half hour later, Christine found herself looking at the figure of a man racing down the mountain, in what she assumed was perfect downhill form. His skis remained close together and his knees bent to the right and left in perfect unison with his body. It's got to be Teiler, she thought in grudging admiration. She was quite surprised, when the man took off his goggles at the end of the run, to see that it was Baxter Cabot. Why did I know he would ski well? she mused. The man looked even better than usual. His cheeks were ruddy, and his face had a liveliness to it she had not seen before. As he put his skis away in a rack in front of her, their eyes met. After a brief moment they both smiled cordially.

"Just the woman I want to see," he said, stopping on the stairs next to her. "But first, why aren't you skiing?"

"Never touch the stuff," Christine replied. "Snow causes wrinkles and cavities, and happens to be very cold."

"Not so loud." He put a finger to his lips. "Bad for the ski-lodge business." He studied her briefly. "Mrs. Marino, who does your hair?"

Christine could hardly hide her surprise. Mild humor from Baxter Cabot? Levity from the world of finance? She shrugged. "I am a mess and I know it. Ah, me."

Cabot continued to look at her. "Everything is relative, Mrs. Marino," he said quietly.

For the first time since Christine had met him, she liked the tone of his voice. "You said you wanted to see me, Mr. Cabot?"

"Yes. Yes, I do. Mrs. Marino, I feel that the entire Mountaincrest community seems to be with me with the exception of your committee. Before the vote next week, I would like a further opportunity to convince you that a Cabot Inn here would be beneficial for everyone concerned. It is one of the reasons I am staying up here. I am inviting the entire committee, and their spouses, of course, to dinner tomorrow night to accomplish this. The other two women have already agreed. If you will say yes, then we shall all meet tomorrow. I was hoping that you can recommend a good restaurant."

"Why, yes. The one I work in."

"An excellent idea. I've already made reservations there." Once again they smiled at each other.

As Cabot turned and looked back at the ski slope, Christine followed his gaze up the mountain. "Lose something?" she asked.

"Yes. Turk Brandon. We started out together, but I don't see . . . my god, look at that!"

Far up on the ski trail Christine saw a figure, arms and ski poles waving frantically, move diagonally across the white expanse and disappear into the forest at its edge.

"Is he a cross-country skier?" Christine asked politely.

"Not intentionally. It's his first time. I told him to take a lesson, but he . . . aha, the hero returns."

Christine watched, trying not to laugh out loud, as Brandon walked clumsily out of the trees, brushing snow off his arms. She watched as he laboriously pointed himself downhill and began a slow descent. Her eyes widened in awe as she saw him pick up speed, gyrating like a disco dancer, his arms and poles once again flailing in the air. The faster he went, the more antic his movements became.

"Great heavens!" Christine exclaimed. "The man will kill himself! Can't something be done?"

Cabot glanced at her. "What do you suggest? He'll be all right. He's too out of control to fall."

Christine bit her lip as the hurtling form sped downward, miraculously still upright. She smiled in relief as Brandon reached the bottom and began to slow down. At the end of the run, just before he would have stopped, he mounted a large pile of snow and, as if in slow motion, hung momentarily at its top, and then fell backward in a tangle of limbs and equipment.

Christine began to laugh and could not stop. As Brandon picked himself up after several unsuccessful attempts, stacked his skis, and walked toward them, she tried to contain herself, wheezing hopelessly. He approached them with dignity, the snow still falling from his ski clothes.

Her face red with her efforts, Christine spoke with difficulty. "How do you like skiing, Mr. Brandon?" she asked. "Do you find it interesting?"

"Love it," Brandon said, plucking snow from his collar and adjusting his hat. "Nothing to it. Piece of cake." As Christine covered her face with her hand, Brandon's eagle stare fixed on her. After a moment he spoke. "Do you know where the bar is? I really want the bar."

Christine shook her head helplessly. Brandon turned, took a step, slipped, caught himself on the railing, and continued up the stairs. He did not turn around when Christine shrieked.

Nick was already in the car and Christine was putting the final touches to her hair in the hall mirror when the telephone rang. Dr. Landau's voice was friendly yet professional.

"We spoke, your handsome son and I," he said. "He is quite a little man, your son."

Christine sighed inwardly with relief. "Then you think he's . . . all right? It's just a growing-up rebellious type thing?"

There was a pause at the other end. "It is, of course, so difficult, Mrs. Marino, to say anything after so short a talk."

Christine saw her expression change in the mirror. "But you think he's fine, Doctor?"

Another pause. "It is my opinion, Mrs. Marino, that a few talks with me might be beneficial. Nothing serious, please believe me. He is a wonderful boy. Only, I see . . ."

"Yes?" Christine's mouth tensed.

"Is it all right that he comes? I shall have to charge you, you know."

"Yes, yes, of course. And thank you, Dr. Landau."

"Good. Then it is settled. I will see you tomorrow night at the restaurant. We shall make arrangements. Good night, Mrs. Marino."

Christine hung up and looked once again into the mirror. She didn't like her face. A vague apprehension shadowed her features. The shadows had not been there a moment before.

19

THE RESTAURANT WAS crowded. The voices from the people waiting at the bar mingled with those of the diners in the dimly lit rooms. Sitting next to Nick, Christine caught his careful, calculating glance.

"Let's open up a chain," she murmured, placing her hand on his. Nick smiled slightly, his eyes on a green-jacketed young busboy leaning on the end of the bar talking to a waitress.

Christine looked around the large room. She decided it was perfect. The dark walls flickered with the light from electric candles. Fresh flowers, wine racks, gleaming silverware; everything combined into a magic amalgam of excellence. Nicholas knows his business, she decided. And she loved eating at this prominently placed table. It was like dining with the captain. Guests stopped constantly to whisper and joke with Nick, anxious to show they knew the boss. And she was Mrs. Boss. Not bad, Christine told herself. Not bad at all.

The dinner had gone well. She recognized the extra flourishes the maître d' always gave Nick's guests and smiled. Show biz. Baxter Cabot, seated next to her, had been charming and unbusinesslike. Henrietta's jewelry jangled like wind chimes in a hurricane, her occasionally twirled necklace flying perilously close to Turk Brandon's nose. Only two flies in the ointment, Christine thought, as the chocolate mousse was put in front of her. She wished Joey were here instead of at his basketball game. He liked eating at the restaurant as much as she did. And Nick had been drinking steadily. Too steadily. Three martinis and four glasses of wine. She had counted.

As Nick rose to attend to something for the fourth time that evening, Cabot turned to Christine and raised his wineglass.

"We of New York City salute you, Mrs. Marino. I have not tasted food like this beyond Fifty-sixth Street. Except at the Cabot Inns, of course." He smiled.

God, Christine thought. Even his teeth are beautiful.

"I accept for my husband," she said, raising her glass.

"Kiley, don't!" Amanda's raised voice was half serious. "Just don't."

"What is that man doing now?" Christine asked.

"That silly man wants to talk about his silly bull again. Ben, sweetheart, don't be a clod."

"I think it's interesting," Kiley said, holding his cigar out in front of him like a weapon. "You folks all hear about the bull that was killed?"

"Locusts?" Turk Brandon raised his eyebrows.

"No, my friend, a bear. And I mean a big bear. Broke its neck, whap."

Amanda held her forehead and shook her head from side to side slowly.

"To break a bull's neck, it is almost inconceivable." Dr. Landau hunched forward behind his pipe. "Have they found the creature? Have they shot him?"

"No. Not yet. Wind blew his tracks away. They don't know where to look."

"It seems a shame to kill a magnificent creature like that," Christine said.

"On the contrary, Chris," Kiley answered. "Bear like that could be dangerous. To humans. You never know."

Turk Brandon slapped the table with finality. "I know. Boss, *you* get the car in the parking lot tonight. Pick me up at the entrance."

"There's something else." Kiley stabbed at them with his cigar. "My man down at the station got the pathologist's report yesterday. He wouldn't let me see it. Known the man for twenty years. Now what do you make of that?"

"I like it. A beast who kills mysteriously," Dr. Landau said eagerly. "I used to help the police in cases like this. Maybe I can be of some use to you and your friend."

The quick, frightened look exchanged between Christine and Henrietta was lost on everybody but Berta Landau. "Now, Emile, you must stop this foolishness," she said with surprising firmness. "You will begin to scare us."

Landau turned to his wife. "But, Berta. It is true. We have ourselves a beast in Torchester. Even if it is only a bear."

"I would like to propose a toast," Henrietta broke in, looking at Christine's downcast eyes. "To New York City. And its environs."

Baxter Cabot raised his glass. "Hometown, U.S.A. Do you folks miss it at all, living up here?"

"Not really," Christine replied. Her expression had already relaxed. "Although sometimes I miss the excitement of it all, I'll have to admit."

"Yes." Cabot looked deep into his wineglass. "New York can be an exciting place, Mrs. Marino."

Christine glanced at him quickly. Had there been a hint, some subtle meaning behind his words? His face revealed nothing. She decided she had been mistaken.

"In what way, Bax?" Nick had come up behind them, brandy glass in hand. As Christine turned to greet him, her expression changed. She did not like his smile.

Cabot turned his head. "I beg your pardon?"

"I said, in what way? In what way is it exciting? I mean sightseeing exciting, gastronomically exciting, intellectually exciting, sexually exciting? You weren't clear about this, Bax."

The conversation around the table stopped, everyone staring at nothing.

"Nick," Christine said, placing her hand gently on his arm.

Nick shook it off and took another drink from the large glass held in both his hands. "No, Chris. This is interesting. I really want to know. In what way, Bax? If my wife were to go to New York, in what way would she find it exciting?"

Cabot's gray eyes gazed up at Nick steadily. "That would be up to Mrs. Marino, don't you think?"

"Oh-h-h, Bax." Nick's voice was low. His smile deepened. "Say . . . you live in the city, don't you? You know what interests me? What *really* interests me? I'd really be interested to know which one of those departments *you'd* take care of, pally." Nick stopped. The smile disappeared. Neither man moved. After a moment, Nick spoke again. "Say, I've got a great idea!" His voice became low, deadly. "Why don't you and I go somewhere and discuss this. What do you say, pally?"

At the other side of the table, Turk Brandon rose slowly to his feet. His downcast eyes watched as he carefully folded his napkin on the table in front of him.

Nick's eyes flashed at him, a strange recognition deep within them. The trace of a smile came back to his mouth. "Is that the way it is?"

Brandon did not look up. "That's the way it is, pally," he said quietly.

A polite mask covered Nick's face. "If you folks will excuse us, Mr. Brandon and I are going down to the cellar to discuss this further. I have some excellent wines down there, Brandon. Care to see them?"

"Why not." Turk's gaze slowly rose.

Christine looked at the two of them in disbelief. "Stop it," she said, more calmly than she felt. "Please just stop this."

Brandon's face softened slightly as he turned to her. "This isn't my idea, Mrs. Marino. I haven't even had my dessert yet."

"Oh, come on, Turk." Nick spoke too softly. "Talk first, eat later." He glanced down at Cabot. "You're a lucky man, Bax," he said. "It's so hard to get loyal help nowadays."

At Nick's words, Christine saw Brandon's face change. In a single instant he was no longer an unwilling participant, but something else, a sword drawn suddenly in sunlight: gleaming, dangerous.

As the two men walked away from the silent table, Christine rose and stood in Brandon's way. "Please, Turk," she said quietly. "Let it pass. My husband's had too much to drink. Let it go."

Brandon stopped. He did not look at her.

"Don't do this." Christine was almost whispering now.

In front of them, Nick turned around. "Chris, don't stand in the way of the hired help." His voice was like ice. "Coming, henchman?"

Again Christine saw the angry electricity pass through Brandon. He brushed past her and followed Nick through the open basement door. Quick tears coming to her eyes, Christine walked behind them down the dimly lit stairs.

There was a small cleared space at the bottom of the steps, lighted by a single bulb. Shelves of restaurant supplies enclosed the area. Bottles of wine shone dully in the racks beyond.

Christine was about to speak when she saw Nick turn suddenly and hit Brandon squarely in the face with tremendous force. The smacking sound of the blow almost made her faint. Brandon reeled back, clutching at the shelves, and then fell onto some large bags of flour. The moment he landed, he began struggling to get up, blood gushing into his eye from a cut on his brow where Nick's ring had struck him.

Nick watched him without emotion. "Stay there, hero," he said. "It's over."

Brandon rose unsteadily to his feet, blinking, looking around until he located Nick on the first step. "Hey," he said. "Hey. Where are you? Hey, cook, I want to talk to you."

Her hand at her mouth, Christine watched Nick walk toward the still-dazed Brandon. She had seen her city-street-bred husband fight before. They had not been fights. They had been mechanical executions. She saw Brandon shake his head and raise his fists as he squinted through the flowing blook at Nick. She closed her eyes as Nick hit the other man several times in the stomach and then sent him to the floor again with a blow to the nose. Almost immediately Brandon was on all fours, shaking his head, trying to get his legs under him.

Nick stared at the other man, his eyes unreadable. "I told you, pally," he said. "It's over." He turned and began to walk up the stairs.

Brandon scrabbled to his feet, his nose flowing red, a finger pointing at Nick's back. "Hey, wait, pally," he shouted hoarsely. "Where are you going? Come back here. Come back, cook."

Nick did not turn around. As Christine, horrified at what she had seen, began to follow him up the stairs, she looked back at the man below her. Standing straight up in the glaring light, his hands at his sides now, his face already swollen, Brandon looked like some defiant, tortured monster: bloodied, naked in defeat, yet so fierce. Totally fierce. Totally indestructible. The warrior.

20

CHRISTINE STARED AT the glowing coals in the fireplace. She watched as a log cracked loudly and broke in half, sending up a shower of sparks. The heat from the fire warmed her face, narrowed her eyes. She was thinking about Nick's face when she had told him that she wanted to stay home with Joey for a night or two. He had read more into her words than she had meant. Perhaps because it had been one of the few sentences she had spoken to him since the fight two days before. Christine had not been mad. She had simply found nothing to say.

Looking at her son sitting beside her, Christine forced a smile. It was not going too well. Joey seemed so impatient, so uncomfortable.

"Joey, isn't it good to be alone, just us two?" she tried. "We never get a chance to talk together anymore, just us two, like we used to. Remember?"

Joey glanced at her and then turned his gaze back to the fire.

"How's the basketball coming, Joey?" Christine's voice sounded bright. "I'm coming to the next game, whether Daddy fires me or not."

Joey smiled. "I'll go with you."

Christine looked at him quizzically. "What do you mean?"

"I mean I quit, Mom."

"You quit? When did this happen?"

"Yesterday." Joey was still smiling.

"But I don't understand. You didn't come home until after six. I was waiting for you. Where were you?"

"I was working, Mom. Mr. Hooker took me down to his farm. He just bought it a couple of months ago and he says there's too much for him and his wife to do. So I help him. He pays me for it, and I like working down there."

"But Joey, you should have checked with your father and me. You can't just . . . I don't think you should spend so much time with Mr. Hooker anyway. He's not exactly a favorite of mine."

Joey glanced at her quickly for a moment before his eyes returned to the fire. "He's already hired me, Ma," he said.

God, this is terrible! Christine thought. How many years of this? I want my son back.

Again she smiled. "How did your talk go with Dr. Landau today, Joey? Do you like him?"

A silent laugh. "He's my buddy." Joey turned toward his mother. "Why did you send me to see him, Mom? You think something's wrong with me?"

"Oh, no, Joey. It's not that at all. It's just that sometimes these teen years can be a little . . . confusing. He's just someone to talk to. That's all. Don't you want to go?"

"I don't mind," Joey answered, his eyes following the rising sparks that danced like tiny crimson fireflies toward the chimney.

Reluctant to try again, Christine stared at the crackling logs with her son. It was Joey who spoke first. "Mom, can I go now? I've got a lot of homework to do."

"Of course," Christine said, not looking up.

Several minutes later she rose tiredly and put on her coat. She knocked on Joey's door. "Honey, I'm going for a walk. Be back in a few minutes." When there was no answer, she opened the door and looked in. Joey was lying on his bed, a magazine open in front of him. Christine caught the flash of thighs and garters as Joey closed the pages quickly. "Excuse me," she said, ducking out and closing the door.

She walked into the cold, crisp night. She felt somehow relieved, almost elated. That was it. The answer to all this. She was convinced. Joey was growing into manhood. The hot blood of his father flowed in his veins. Sex had found her son, and he simply did not know how to handle it. She and Nick would try to help him, leave books around, anything. And he did have Dr. Landau. She wanted to smile and wound up almost crying.

The figure of a man approached her along the lamplit path. It was Turk Brandon. She had not seen him since the night of the fight. As they neared each other, Christine saw his still swollen, empurpled face. She looked everywhere but at Brandon.

"We've got to stop meeting like this." Brandon's voice was hushed. His one open eye stared at her penetratingly.

Christine's voice was tentative. "Oh, Mr. Brandon, I—"

"No more Mr. Brandon. Call me Turk. Turk the Vicious."

"Turk, I'm so sorry . . ." She did not continue.

Something moved deep behind Brandon's eyes. "Say, Mrs. Marino, I'm sorry too." He shook his head ruefully. "It's not easy being a henchman, you know."

"My husband didn't mean that, Mr. Brandon—Turk. I'm sure he wishes the whole thing had never happened."

"I'm with him," Brandon said, tenderly feeling the large bandage across his nose.

"And, Turk, thank you for—you know—not being mad."

Brandon's expression did not change. "Who says I'm not mad?" he said quietly. After a pause, he sighed and continued. "I see my face makes you uncomfortable. Well, that works both ways, so I shall say good-bye. I am going down to the local bar, where I intend to pick a fight with the first large man I see. It's my life." He lifted his ski cap and strode past her on the ice-covered path. Christine walked on, thinking about Joey, trying not to think of the bruised, one-eyed face she had just seen.

The engineering firm of Wendell and Winters called at nine o'clock the next morning. When Christine hung the receiver up fifteen minutes later, an uncertain look passed across her face. She picked up the telephone.

"I suppose you're wondering why I've gathered you all here," Christine said, looking at the morning faces around her dining-room table.

"Very funny," Ben Kiley grumbled. "This had better be good."

"Oh, it's good, all right. Maybe it's too good." She repeated what the engineers had found. "They're mailing me their report this afternoon. My question to this committee is, what do we do now?"

"Forget it," Kiley said quickly. "You ladies are going to be very unpopular if you bring this up before the vote tomorrow night."

"How can we forget it?" Christine asked. "This could be serious. I remember when we lived on Long Island. Everyone in Mill Harbor complained about things, but when we tried to get someone to *do* something, no one had the time, no one wanted to get *invol*ved. Well, this committee took the time. We are involved. I think it has to be brought up."

Dr. Landau put his coffee cup down firmly. "Christine is right. This should be public information. We have no choice."

Amanda shook her head. "They're not going to like this. Most of the people here are weekenders or skiers. They are not permanent residents like ourselves. They may not care, or may be more interested in the real-estate value of their condominiums once the inn goes up. Can you just see Kyle Thorne's face? Baxter Cabot's? Ouch!"

"I think it has to be done," Christine insisted. "Berta?"

Berta Landau looked at her husband. She nodded.

"Amanda?"

Amanda shrugged and looked at Kiley, who shook his head slightly. "O.K.," she said.

Several minutes later as Christine stood in the kitchen making more coffee and wondering how she was going to tell Nick, Ben Kiley came alongside her, unwrapping a cigar carefully. "Chris," he said, "you mentioned a place called Mill Harbor on Long Island back there. Why does that ring a bell in this old detective's brain?"

Christine's eyes closed for a moment. Oh hell, she thought. Dammit. What the hell is the matter with me. Stupid, stupid woman. She turned to Kiley, her face revealing nothing. "Just a place where we lived for a little while, Ben. Unimportant. If you come inside, I'll give you more coffee."

"Sure," he said. He watched her thoughtfully as she went into the dining room toward her guests.

"All right, people if you'll just settle down." Kyle Thorne, as usual, had his arms raised in an effort to quiet the crowded clubhouse. "This won't take long, folks. I know we'd all like to get this vote over with."

At his words, Christine shifted in her chair nervously. She exchanged glances with Amanda. The presence of Baxter Cabot at the back of the room did not make things any easier.

She was glad that Nick was at the restaurant. Because of Cabot and because of what she was about to do.

"All right." Thorne had finally gotten a semblance of quiet. "Now, is there any discussion before we vote?"

Christine took a deep breath. She stood up. "Yes. Before a vote is taken," she said, trying to keep her voice calm, "I think it would be advisable to discuss something that has come to this committee's attention." She held up her hand. "I have here a report we have received from the engineering firm of Wendell and Winters, here in Torchester. It is quite detailed, so I shall attempt to summarize it for you. It concerns water. Well water, to be precise. They are of the opinion that a large facility, such as the proposed Cabot Inn, and the septic and sewerage disposal it would entail, could, at some time in the future, conceivably contaminate the wells that service Mountaincrest. The underground rock structure is not good. I understand that there have been bacteria problems already. Seepage from a facility of this size, they believe, could give us very severe problems in the future.

"We feel quite strongly that this matter should be brought to everyone's attention, for discussion and perhaps further investigation. I shall, of course, leave this report here for your perusal." Christine sat down.

"Thank you, Mrs. Marino." Thorne's smile was forced. "I'm sure the efforts of you and your committee are appreciated. Anyone else? Annette?"

A young dark-haired woman with horn-rim glasses had stood up. "I think what Mrs. Marino said needs time to be properly evaluated," she stated seriously. "And I really would like to know why we had to find this out by ourselves, why we weren't informed about this right from the beginning."

Thorne's smile was barely visible now. "Thank you, Annette. Henry?"

The man who spoke now was dressed in a business suit. He was small and had excellent diction. "As a condominium owner and legal counsel for the Mountaincrest Corporation along with Kyle Thorne, you can be sure that I want what will prove to be the best for everyone concerned. It a Cabot Inn and all that it will bring to us is the best thing for us in the future, I'm all for it. What I don't like, however, is what I'm starting to see here tonight. We've always been a rather happy family here at Mountaincrest, I think you'll agree. But tonight, right now, we're not so happy. I see the beginnings of dissension, of friction. Before we become a house divided, as it were, I am hereby making a motion to postpone this vote for whatever amount of time it takes to properly explore the matter which Mrs. Marino and her committee have been good enough to bring to our attention." As he sat down there were several cries of "Second." As the discussion continued, it grew more quarrelsome, angrier. When the motion was finally voted upon, it was decided to postpone the decision for further investigation.

Christine did not feel victorious. Quite the opposite. The angry stares she was receiving, the muted conversations that were taking place as everyone filed out, puzzled and discomfited her. As she walked toward the exit, she caught the following glances of Baxter Cabot and Kyle Thorne standing together at the bar. Cabot smiled automatically, but Thorne did not. His eyes were calculating and unfriendly.

Cabot's smile disappeared as quickly as it had come. He turned to Thorne. "What happened, Kyle?" he asked.

Thorne was still looking at Christine. After a moment, he turned to Cabot. "She took me by surprise, Baxter. You saw it. What could I do?"

"That's not my problem. That's your problem." Cabot's voice hung in the air like the icicles on the windows behind them. "That highway information will be common knowledge in a month. I will then have possible bidding competition for this land. That could cost me money. A lot of money. The more it costs me, the more it costs you. You understand, don't you, Kyle?"

"Don't worry," Thorne stated flatly. "It will pass next time. You have my word. I'll handle it."

"Please do that, Kyle. Or I'll get someone who can."

Thorne was not intimidated. "I'll handle it, Baxter," he repeated.

Cabot nodded once, put his drink down, turned, and left the clubhouse.

21

From the diary of Henrietta Knapp:

January 8

La nuit sparkles as in a fairy tale. Moon-dusted snow-flakes swirl at my window, shrieking in tiny white laughter, beckoning. I have half a mind to go out into the night and romp with them, but the other half says, Henrietta, act your age. Stay in bed. Cling to your pillows. Be cozy. Your sheets are your friends. And they are right.

Vielle fou! Romp in the snow indeed. You can hardly warm this brandy with your hands. Discontinue.

Clouds covering the moon. Why does that always give me a sudden chill? Three quilts and I'm shaking like a willow leaf. The snow glitter has gone. It's dark out there now. Dark and so cold. If I were a *wolf*, I would stay home tonight.

Strangest feelings. Filled with premonitions. I can sense things I would not want to see, envision dreams I would not want to dream. Nice phrase, but I'm starting to scare myself. Time to stop. Sorceress, desist, cease, witch. Mystic, cure thyself.

The malamute puppy ran along the side of the huge barn, its tail wagging excitedly, its paws slipping on the ice-crusted snow. As it came to the corner of the barn, it stopped abruptly. Cautiously but unafraid, it sniffed at the shoe of the figure that stood, unmoving, in front of it. Before it had a chance to run, a hand fastened on its tail and lifted it high into the air. In the next instant, a whiplike snap of its body broke its neck. Below its lifeless form, a jaw distended in the manner of a snake. It bit the dog's head off and then clamped voraciously around its blood-spouting neck.

January 9

Foul night! Wind screeching through bare branches like lost souls. Windows rattling incessantly. Relieved. Thought it was my breathing.

Wonderful ride home with Nick tonight. Almost went off the road twice. Why is that man drinking so much? Been that way ever since "The Trouble." Getting worse and worse. Moody. Restless as a cat. I love him, but how can I admire a man who drinks almost as much as I do?

Saw Turk Brandon today. Face not so swollen now, but wish he would put the bandage back on his nose. How much can one appendage really take? Promised myself never to be a professional linebacker. Ha!

King Cabot returned to New York. Coming back on weekend. If it were thirty years ago, I would be with him right now. He wouldn't have stood a chance. Oh, the years are such thieves. Beauty flies. Henrietta, and all her parts, walk.

Simply cannot believe that wind!! What is this, the tundra? Heaven protect all little beasties on a night like this.

Horrible out there. A good night to scrunch down in bed, draw your quilts up under your neck, sip your medicinal tequila, and watch Clark Gable. You never answered one of my letters, Gable, baby. My god, look at that hair. The stuff of dreams.

The lamb stayed close to its mother as she circled the wooden enclosure with the other sheep. It called to her once, but its voice was drowned in the frightened bleatings of the milling herd.

Two hands, like great talons, gripped it suddenly, one at the base of the spine and the other on its neck. Struggling helplessly, it was lifted upward. Its struggles ceased as it was mercilessly bent in two, the snapping of its backbone unheard amidst the howling of the icy wind.

January 10

The clouds have gone, *enfin, enfin*. A return to starlight.

Stayed home with my sinuses tonight. Poor company. Tried to talk to Joey. Grunts and closed doors my reward. How I love Old Grumpy! Tried to recall if my teens were this bad. All I could remember were the Charleston, that I would have died for Valentino, and my recurring dream of Teddy Roosevelt attacking me as if I were a hill.

Cold unbelievable tonight. Finished the entire thermos of anisette and espresso and my toes still feel like they belong to someone else. *Je ne voulez know* what the temperature is out there. Coldest night of the year. The century, most probably. A night not fit for man nor beast.

Predicament: how to turn on the television without freezing to death.

Solution: hurry. And take quilts with you.

The black-helmeted driver raced through the night, the noise from the snowmobile rending the silence. Like an alien beast, man and machine streaked out of the forest trail and entered a great, moon-gleaming meadow. As it progressed across the white expanse, a figure emerged from the trees behind it and began to run in pursuit, his powerful strides tearing through the crusted snow as if it were not there. Unaware of the figure that was gaining on him with every stride, the driver gunned his machine to its limit. And still the distance between the two dark figures closed relentlessly beneath the moon.

Suddenly, two other snowmobiles droned into view. The three drivers waved to one another and roared in unison along the blue surface.

The running figure stopped, hands thrust forward, head lowered. The baleful hunter's eyes glowed red watching the departing racers disappear in silver snow mist.

22

I S THERE ANY vodka in here, or what?" Henrietta held the large goblet up to the fire for inspection, her brow furrowed suspiciously. The eyes of everyone in the Marino living room turned toward the shining red liquid held high in her hand.

"A Virgin Mary, auntie," Nick said, patting her wig. "Sweets to the sweet. Albeit unwilling."

"Albeit? That means no vodka, right?"

"Section forty, rule six, of Marino's Law. No employee shall drink before going on duty. Witness your employer. A Virgin Mary. You and I, auntie, are going to drink less from now on. Your employer has spoken."

"No vodka." Henrietta shook her head. "My body is not going to like this."

"I will have to ask you to keep your body out of the conversation, old dear. Let us remember, we have guests."

Ben Kiley looked into Amanda's eyes. He clasped her hand. "I hope we never get like those two," he said.

Amanda nodded. "Familiarity breeds familiarity. Isn't it awful?"

Henrietta fixed her one-eyed stare on them. "Very funny. Just for that, I'm preparing my specialty for you tonight."

Nick groaned. "Let me see what's holding up the hostess. Be right back."

Henrietta's head turned toward Nick's retreating figure. "Employee?" she shouted. Nick winced but did not turn around.

Her mascara brush poised in her hand, Christine glanced up in the mirror to see Nick standing in the doorway. Handsome man, she thought. What a handsome man. "I'm ready, I'm ready," she said.

Nick contemplated his wife's face. "Sounds good to me," he said wistfully. "However, we have to go to work."

Christine turned to him. "My, Nicholas, we are in a good mood tonight. A long time coming, my love."

Nick held up his glass. "New leaf, Chris. Less booze, more love. I shall deal with my heebie-jeebies now, and I shall deal with you later."

Christine's feelings showed in her face. "I'm with you, Nick," she whispered. "Darling, do you know why I love you so much?"

Nick leered. "Yes," he said. He stepped back quickly and closed the door behind him.

Turning back to the mirror, Christine saw that she was smiling. Things have a way of getting better, she decided. For a long time now she had watched Nick struggling with something that she could not understand. It was not alcohol. It was something deep within him that he would not share. But these last few days he had seemed more at ease, less restless. The old Nick. Tough Nick. Nick could handle anything.

But best of all was Joey. In the last week, while the three of them had spent that long weekend in Montreal, and in the few days since they had been back, Joey had changed. He was almost Joey again. Whether it was his visits with Dr. Landau or merely getting away from Mountaincrest for a while, Christine did not care. He had laughed. He had even kissed her. All in all, she mused, a good week for my men.

As she completed her makeup and stared at the finished

product, her eyes changed. Not, however, a perfect week, she thought. In the five days since the meeting she had noticed things. Little things, disturbing things. The hard stares of people she didn't even know. Kyle Thorne and his wife looking at her coldly and whispering to each other. And Truman Hooker's glare had gotten meaner, more intense. She could swear that Gussie Hooker had slammed her shopping cart into her own at the supermarket two days ago. The two women had exchanged long looks, and that had been that. Christine shrugged slightly. So be it. Such is the life of a revolutionary. She would gladly exchange a few stares for the happiness of Nick and Joey. Any day. She picked up her purse and left the room.

Christine entered the living room holding her hands out. "Here I am," she said. "Wasn't it worth the wait?"

Henrietta affixed her eye on Christine. "Very dramatic. Welcome, Bette Davis."

"Hey, Ma," Joey said. "You look beautiful."

Christine walked over and hugged her son. She remained that way a long time, her eyes meeting Nick's in happiness. When she finally released him, Joey looked at Nick.

"O.K., Dad, can I have a quarter now?"

Nick beamed. "Look! Look! My son made a joke. Sunlight! Sunlight!"

As Christine was putting on her coat, Joey walked up to her, his eyes on the floor. "Hey, Mom." His voice was low. "Can I go with you tonight?"

Christine adjusted his hair. "But, honey, you told me you had two tests on Monday. Don't you think you ought to study?"

Joey looked up at her. There was something in his face, his eyes. "Please, Mom, can I go? Can I please go? Dr. Landau said we should spend more time as a family. Take me with you."

Nick tried to look upset. "'Dr. Landau says.' I used to be the boss around here, and now it's 'Dr. Landau says.'"

Joey looked past his father at the door. "Take me with you, Dad," he repeated.

Nick walked over and kissed the top of his son's head. "Tell you what, pally. You study tonight and tomorrow we'll take you out, the works. Is that a deal?"

Joey shook his head once, biting his lip.

Nick's eyes softened. "Hey, old sport," he said. "Who's your best friend in the whole world?"

Joey looked at the floor. "Dr. Landau," he said quietly.

The startled look on Nick's face melted into laughter. He tousled Joey's hair. "O.K., comedian," he said. "Hit those books. Surprise your teachers."

The door closed behind the two couples. Joey did not look up. The grandfather clock beside him struck six o'clock. Joey raised his eyes to it, not seeing it. A log dropped in the fireplace. Joey wheeled and stared at it as if it were a small, menacing animal. After a moment he raised his eyes to Mrs. Landau. She smiled at him, the firelight flickering in her glasses.

At the sound of the car starting in the driveway, Joey turned to face the door. A look of panic came into his eyes. He walked to the door, flung it open, and stepped out into the cold night. The chill, damp air bit into him. He began to flail his arms in an effort to stay warm. Below him he could see the taillights of his parents' car as it headed down the hill toward the main road. He began to walk, his eyes still on the tiny, receding red lights. After several moments, he started to run, trying not to fall on the slippery road, his breath steaming before him in white billows. When he could no longer see the car, a sound escaped his lips into the night. He increased his speed.

As he started down a long, straight stretch in the narrow road, bordered closely by crowded pines, he heard a low rumbling. The darkness above him gradually filled with a dull thunder that poured down on him from the shifting, wind-driven clouds.

Joey stopped. The fogbound road, the black trees, the thunder that now shook the air filled him with a strange dread, fearsome, yet somehow sweet, expectant. He stood there, looking about him, unable to continue.

Suddenly, the dark night was rent by a flash of gold-red lightning that illuminated the scene before him, flaming the earth, turning the ice-covered road into a burnished, glittering pathway. High in the sky above him, illuminated in the glare of the sudden light, a terrific figure soared, its encrimsoned wings framing a woman's face and breasts of scarlet. Joey stood there transfixed. He heard it utter a piercing cry and then watched it dive down toward the treetops, disappearing into the gray mists above them. Trying to follow its downward path, Joey found himself gazing into the pines that surrounded him. An exhalation of fear and ecstasy issued from his open mouth. In one golden moment, he saw the gilded world behind the world. Exquisite visions of erotic enchantment gleamed at him from a forest of bronze light. People and creatures of rapture beckoned him toward jeweled flowers, toward trees of copper and silver and gold. Sounds and fragrances filled his senses, swelling his veins with unbearable passions, unquenchable desires.

And then, as quickly as it had come, it was gone. Misted night settled in again, silent and white.

Joey stood staring into the woods. The fear on his face was slowly replaced by an intent, eager look. His eyes never leaving the trees, he walked with quick strides off the road, plunging his way through the deep snow toward the dark and waiting forest.

23

TORCHESTER CLARION
February 25

LARGE TURNOUT FOR SPRING
SKI CARNIVAL EXPECTED

Plans for the annual Mad Mountain Ski Carnival, two weeks from today, are in the final stages. Mayor Rutledge said today that this year's carnival should be the biggest in the resort's ten-year history, with racing participants and onlookers coming from many adjacent states and Canada. Men and women entrants for all events have already been selected. Carnival committee chairman Kyle Thorne has stated that an ice sculpture competition and the selection of a Snow Queen will be added to this year's festivities.

MOUNTAINCREST VOTE DELAYS
PROPOSED CABOT INN

In a close vote last night, the residents of Mountaincrest condominiums postponed their decision to sell their third section of land to

Cabot Inn Enterprises, pending further investigation.

There will be a meeting concerning this matter at the Town Hall tomorrow night at eight o'clock. The mayor has stated that a large turnout is expected.

MYSTERY ANIMAL SLAYINGS PUZZLE POLICE

Two more animals were mysteriously slain recently, making a total of three killings during the past few weeks. On Thursday, Calvin Turner's three-month-old puppy was found near his barn. Friday morning, Sy Kenmore reported the killing of one of his lambs. The two carcasses were found by their owners, uneaten, apparently the victims of a ruthless night marauder. As in the case of the Kilgore Farms' bull, neither the owners nor the police would comment on any further details. The presence of a large grizzly bear in our area has been suggested, but no proof of this has, as yet, been ascertained.

Chief Knowlton has urged that all animals be locked up at night until his investigation into this matter has been completed.

Christine put down the newspaper and looked out the window. She closed her eyes at the snow glare and at something else. She had heard a scream, solitary, terrified, in the recesses of her being. She remembered Mill Harbor. She remembered how her dogs had been killed. Suddenly her eyes flew open. She remembered the head of her china cat on the table in front of her. She stared at the table, her face drained.

Christine shivered. She pulled her sweater around her. Stop it, she shouted to herself. Just . . . stop it. You are being ridiculous and you know it. Do you like to scare yourself? Is that it? Shaking her head, she flung her hair back and squinted out at the bright, sunlit hills. The color had not come back to her face.

Nick crumpled the newspaper page in his hand, kneading it into a small ball in his fist. His eyes were grim, his face was set in anger. Don't be a fool, he told himself. It's a coincidence. Just like that mouse. A coincidence. It's not them. It's not those fucking beasts.

He threw the wad of paper with all his might against the wall of his restaurant office. He reached inside his jacket and felt the hard metal butt of his revolver. As he touched it, his eyes became veiled and cold. And in the one chance in a million, he thought, that it *is* some of those unnatural bastards, why they're dead. I'll shoot anything that comes near me or mine. The fuckers are dead. I'll kill them. I'm not moving again. I'll kill them.

He frowned. What the hell are you doing? This is stupid. You're going crazy, that's what you're doing. You've got more diners than chairs tonight and you're raving like a maniac. He took out a bottle of Scotch and a glass from a lower desk drawer and poured himself a drink. He sat staring at it as his hand slowly went back inside his jacket.

Ben Kiley sat looking at the newspaper, his face crinkled in thought, the end of his cigar pointing up toward the ceiling. After several long moments, his eyebrows slowly went up. He snapped his fingers once. He rose, walked into the kitchen, and picked up the telephone.

24

So it's decided then. Mountaincrest's contribution to the spring carnival will be an ice sculpture. Is there any further discussion?" Kirsten Thorne looked around the clubhouse. "All right. Refreshments are in the back, courtesy of the carnival committee."

Amanda leaned toward Christine. "Did you ever get the feeling," she whispered, "that the whole world is run by the Thorne family?"

"Amanda!" Christine flared her eyes.

"And look at La Hooker with her. They look like the forward wall of the Pittsburgh Tigers or whatever."

Christine looked at Gussie Hooker. The woman was not fat, just large. Short hair, no makeup, small eyes. Bad eyes, Christine decided. A mirror of her soul? Her glance encompassed Kirsten Thorne. Almost as big, but totally different. Artful makeup, excellent clothes. She exuded . . . what? Confidence? Power? A chairperson in her nursery and from then on ever upward.

Her musings were interrupted by Henrietta's querulous question to no one. "What am I doing here? My chef is blow-drying his hair over the soups, my bartender is leaning on his elbows eating my olives, and I'm here talking about some silly carnival to which I'm not going because I have nothing to wear."

"Try it, dear." Amanda smiled. "You might get elected Snow Queen."

"Don't count on it," Christine said. She closed her eyes and shook her head.

"Fresh kid." Henrietta pouted. "Sometimes I'm sorry I keep refusing your husband's advances."

"Committee work is good for you," Amanda pontificated. "It is the essence of the community of man, the lifeblood of society. Why, Christine and I thrive on it, don't we, darling."

"I'm not so sure." Christine remembered her speech in front of the Mountaincrest residents.

"You're not? But you're on so many of them."

Christine turned toward the speaker. Kirsten Thorne stood above her, trying, unsuccessfully, to look pleasant. "I beg your pardon?" Christine said, looking at the firm mouth, the unsmiling eyes.

"I just assumed you loved them, Mrs. Marino. You appear to be so . . . involved. In this. In that."

The conversation around them grew subdued and then stopped. Several women gazed with unfriendly interest at Christine.

"I do what I can, Mrs. Thorne." Something had appeared in Christine's eyes that did not match her smile.

The other woman appraised her once from head to toe before she spoke again. "Very worthwhile, I'm sure. I've always approved of noble effort. In the right direction, of course."

Christine's voice did not change. "I really wasn't concerned with your approval, Mrs. Thorne. One way or another."

Kirsten Thorne's face hardened slightly. "Charming," she said. She held Christine's gaze a moment longer before turning and striding out the clubhouse door.

Watching her walk away, Christine tried not to let her consternation show. She could not help but notice that most of the women had begun to leave within a few moments of Mrs. Thorne's departure.

Amanda looked around the nearly empty clubhouse, then at Christine. "And what the hell was *that* all about?"

Her eyes still on the door, Christine spoke quietly. "It would seem, Amanda, that Queen Thorne does not like unruly subjects. It's the Cabot Inn thing. Apparently we are cast in the role of bothersome, revolting serfs."

Henrietta arose and adjusted her girdle. "You two may be revolting, but I'm cute." She walked over to Christine and kissed the top of her head. "You did good, dearie. Real good. A true Knapp. I'm proud of you."

One eyebrow went up as Christine nodded slowly. "I did do well, didn't I." She suddenly realized how angry she was. And charming to you, Madame Thorne, she thought. And your glowering friend, Gussie Hooker. You want to battle, so be it. And your husbands, too. And throw in Baxter Cabot. Nick and Christine will take you all on. Nick and Christine and Joey. Little tough Joey could do it all alone. My Joey. She was surprised to find herself smiling.

Walking home from the Hooker farmhouse, Joey sensed the evening darkening swiftly around him. When he came to the long stretch of road that led toward Mountaincrest, he hastened his steps, not daring to look at the snow-laden trees, remembering. A sudden gust of wind brought a heavy scent of pine to him. He inhaled it deeply, took another few strides, and stopped. He stood there, the aroma flooding the air, filling his senses. And then the breeze brought a new fragrance: something that emanated from the wilderness beyond the trees, beyond, beyond. A primal perfume from the deepest core of Nature entered him and possessed him. He felt his feet drawn toward the bowels of earth, his head toward the twilight clouds. He became a giant of longing, of desire. As he stood there unable to move, a female voice floated to him out of the forest—calling, unutterably sweet, wanton in its need.

Joey could not look up. He hung his head shyly. A sly smile gradually creased his mouth. He remained that way until, at last, the voice faded away into stillness. Only then did he continue on his way, the smile still on his lips.

25

N ICK PRESSED THE lever and watched the espresso coffee trickle down into the cup. He enjoyed these Monday evenings. At the restaurant he was always too busy to help with the cooking, but on the one night that it was closed he let himself go here at home. He dabbled, he experimented. Tonight he had outdone himself. The veal had been magnificent, the linguine, the sauce, the salad. Everything magnificent. He carried two filled cups into the living room.

"Ah, the chef returns," Amanda said. "We didn't think you'd have enough nerve to show up again."

"Actually, the veal wasn't that bad," Christine joined in, taking a coffee cup from Nick. "I think it was the salad that is making me feel so nauseous."

"Do you think it's *easy* to get leeches at this time of year?" Nick answered, his eyes widening madly.

Amanda shrieked, almost spilling her coffee.

"And besides," Nick continued, "my cooking is superb and you all know it. Anyone for Strega, Galliano, Sambuca, Amaretto?"

"Yes," Henrietta said.

Christine laughed. She looked around happily at her guests.

Amanda, Ben, the Landaus. These Monday nights had become almost a ritual now. She loved it. Especially when Nick insisted on doing the cooking. Nice people, a fire, a husband who cooks, she mused. My cup runneth over.

Nick sat down on the fireplace hearth next to Dr. Landau.

The little man raised his cup. "I have said it before, my friend, but it bears repeating. You are an excellent host. To the manner born, as they say."

Nick nodded acknowledgment. He stared into the fire. When he spoke, his voice was low. "I just want you to know, Dr. Landau, what it means to my wife and me. Your helping Joey. It means so much to us." Dr. Landau waved his hand from side to side. "He's the light, you know," Nick went on. "He's the boy."

Dr. Landau smiled. "Of that I am aware, Nicholas." They both looked toward the other end of the room, where Joey was watching with rapt attention as Amanda animatedly described her recent first attempt at skiing.

As the eyes of both men returned to the fire, it was Dr. Landau who spoke first. "And you, Nicholas, my host. I remember our last private conversation. How is it with Nicholas?"

Nick did not look up. "I'm coping, Doctor," he said. "My family, my business, alcohol, time. They all help."

"And I, Nicholas. May I help, too?"

Nick shrugged. "I wish I could tell you how." It was a long time before he spoke again. "I can tell you this, Doctor. I hate it all. The memories, the foul residue within me. But most of all I hate the beasts. Dwelling in the evil, sweet darknesses of the earth. Singing their shadow songs. Bastard inhabitants. Sons of bitches. How I . . ." Nick stopped. He kicked the fire angrily with his foot.

Dr. Landau leaned over and spoke to him gently. The two men continued to talk, their low tones drifting up the chimney with the smoke from the fire.

Joey watched Amanda's hands as they moved descriptively in front of her. When she spread them apart, his eyes remained on her breasts, covertly following the curved lines that disappeared into her blouse toward the faint outline of her nipples. He looked away, only to return his gaze. He watched as her breasts shook slightly as she lifted her arms. His gaze grew more intense each time the soft flesh trembled with her movements. Slowly, his eyes went to her narrow waist, her flared hips, to her swelling buttocks and thighs, and then back up to her breasts. His eyes closed, his body arched slightly. Abruptly, he stood up and walked into his room. He locked his door quietly behind him, his eyes closing once again. When he opened them, there was a wildness there that gradually transformed the rest of his features. He threw himself facedown on his bed, his arms outstretched, his body grinding rhythmically into the mattress beneath him.

26

ALICE DWORSKI CROSSED in front of the school bus and began to trudge up the snow-covered dirt road toward her house. Holding her books in front of her, she picked her way carefully on the icy surface, once nearly slipping and falling. The thickly falling snow made it difficult for her even to see the trees along the side of the road. She thought about the two things she hated most in the world: her biology teacher and the way her gum hardened in this cold weather so that she could hardly chew it. Then she thought about her three favorite things in the world: cheerleading, a really good movie, and Joey Marino. When he had gotten off at her bus stop today, she had almost fainted. He's going to walk me home, she had thought, maybe carry these stupid books. But he had just smiled at her and walked off in the other direction. Boy, that guy was shy!

Alice stopped. She turned around and looked at the snow-clouded road behind her. She thought she had heard a footstep, like something breaking through snow crust. The kids in school were all talking about that grizzly bear. It gave her the willies. She looked at the white-mantled trees a moment longer before she turned and continued on through the deepening snow.

As she neared her house, she stopped again. She had heard nothing, it was only a feeling she had. As if something was out there, following her in the darkening afternoon. She stopped chewing and listened.

Joey stood motionless, one raised foot resting lightly on the surface of the deep snow. He knew he could not be seen through the trees, through the blanket of snowflakes between them. He watched as the girl began to walk quickly. He smiled as she broke into a run, dashed hurriedly up the front stairs, and slammed the door behind her.

What a game, he thought. It had been more fun than he had expected. Beats basketball. Beats everything. He had been so close to her at one time, he could have jumped out on her, scared her, done anything. Anything.

He remained standing there, the snow falling on his unblinking eyelashes, covering his head and shoulders with the crystals of winter.

27

Nick sat at the bar, the telephone hunched between his ear and shoulder.

"And, Maury." He took a sip of Scotch. "Only the best. Send the mediocre steaks to my competition up on the hill. And you *know* I weigh. Send me a pound over instead of a pound under. You'll go to heaven." He smiled at the loud reply he received. "Yeah," he continued. "Just about as far as I can throw you, fatso. And I need it tomorrow, *capice?*" Nick nodded as he took another drink. "And I love you, too, *paisan.*" He hung up and gazed at the rose-lighted rows of bottles in front of him. He was lost in thought as Ben Kiley sat down on the seat next to him.

"Doesn't the house ever buy a drink around here?" Kiley asked no one in particular.

Nick turned to him. "Benjamin! What brings you out of bed before cocktail hour?" Nick nodded to the bartender, who walked quickly over to them.

Kiley took the plastic stirrer out of his drink and swirled the ice with his finger. After a moment, he spoke. "I have a problem, Nicholas, that I need help with."

"Name it," Nick said.

"Ah, ah." Kiley raised his hand. "Don't be so quick to help. Because it is you, Nicholas, who are my problem."

Nick looked up, puzzled. "What's the matter, pally?" he

said. His voice had a barely perceptible edge to it that was not lost on Kiley.

The detective sighed. He relighted his cigar. "Nick, a policeman is a policeman is a policeman. He never stops. When that bull was killed out there, my retired salivary glands started flowing like one of Pavlov's dogs. Then, when those other animals were killed, it started to ring bells. Police alarms. And I started to remember. Four years ago. A case out on the Island. Horses and dogs killed. And I remembered murders. Cold, terrible murders." Kiley took a long drink. His eyes narrowed. "But nothing meshed. Dead animals, Torchester, Long Island. Nothing meshed," he repeated, exhaling his cigar smoke slowly. "That is, until I found my tie-in. My hook."

"And what's your tie-in, Ben?" Nick's eyes had narrowed slightly.

Kiley glanced at the bartender's back. "Let's go into the office, where you keep the good Scotch, O.K.?" he said.

Nick followed his glance, rose from the bar chair, and walked toward his office. Once they were seated, his eyes leveled into the other man's. "What's your connection, Ben?" he said quietly.

Kiley put his glass down carefully. "Why, it's you, Nick," he said. "The Marinos. Residents of Mill Harbor, Long Island, four years ago. Left right after the Big Trouble. Didn't even go back for your furniture. Currently residing in Torchester, Vermont."

Nick was taken by surprise. His eyes showed only rising anger. "Where'd you find all this out, old sport?"

Kiley looked down at his cigar. "I told you, I'm a detective. Once a detective, et cetera. I made a lot of telephone calls. It all checks, my friend. You're the hook. You're the boy."

Softly, Nick placed his thumb and forefinger on the bridge

of his nose. He closed his eyes. "You're a busy man, Kiley," he said, his voice low.

Kiley's attention was still on his cigar. "I like to keep my hand in. As a matter of fact, I used to be pretty good. Intuitive, you might say. I used to be able to recognize patterns. Like to think that I still can. Pattern: Mill Harbor, four years ago. Animals killed, torn apart. After that, five people were . . . slaughtered, one of them a police lieutenant. Now, in Torchester, animals broken, mutilated. It bothers me. Makes me ask myself questions. Like, do we have ourselves the same pattern here? And if we do, why? And another question. Why does my friend Nicholas carry a gun?" He sighed. "You know what I think? I think that last question is really an answer." Kiley turned and faced Nick. The two men's eyes locked together. "You are my friend, Nick, so fuck the denials. You didn't kill them all, is that it? Is that it? There are more trolls, or whatever the hell you call those bastards, out there. Maybe they've found you, maybe they're playing with you, maybe they're planning . . . who knows?"

With an effort, Nick controlled his voice. "That possibility has recently crossed my mind, yes."

Crushing his cigar out angrily, Kiley drained his glass. "This could be a coincidence, Nick," he said. "You've got to think of that. Just a damned coincidence. There could be a bear out there, a big grizzly. Wolves, anything."

A soft, mirthless laugh escaped Nick. "That would be nice," he said, almost in a whisper.

It was a long time before Kiley spoke. "Maybe you should leave, Nick. Just in case. Get the hell out. Disappear again."

Nick's face hardened. He shook his head. "No, Ben. I'm not fucking leaving." His voice was resolute, flat. "I've done it once, I'm not pushing again. My family is happy here, I've got a business here, my son's in therapy here. I'll shoot the heart out of anyone who comes near us, I swear it. I'm not fucking moving."

Kiley nodded. He fumbled for another cigar. "O.K. How can I help you, Nicky?"

"Don't mention any of this to anyone. Not the police, no one. Especially Chris. I don't know what the hell is going on, but I want her left out of it. Understood?"

Kiley gave him a long look, his face serious. "Say something clever. I said, what can I do?"

"It's simple. If it is them, find them and shoot them."

"Easy. What do the bastards look like?"

Nick grunted. "Find them in a minute. Eight feet tall, tusks, red eyes, arms that reach the floor. Only one small hitch. They can change their shapes, their faces. They can look like whoever the hell they want to."

Kiley released a large cloud of smoke. "What! What the hell are you saying!"

Nick looked at him tiredly. "You can believe it or not, Ben. It's true."

"Well . . . shit." Kiley's white head shook unbelievingly. "That's going to make them a little hard to find, isn't it."

Nick stared at him, his face grim.

Kiley rose heavily. Neither man heard the footsteps of the retreating bartender, who had been standing by the partially open door.

Kiley's brow furrowed as he looked at Nick's face. "We'll find them," he said quietly. "If they're here, we'll find them, Nick. Thanks for the Scotch." He turned and left.

The bartender watched the heavyset man leave and then glanced at Nick's closed office door. He picked up the telephone under the bar and dialed Kyle Thorne's number. He spoke in low tones to his father-in-law for several minutes. When he finished, he picked a glass up and began to polish it carefully.

28

As his limousine wound at a steady pace along the curves of the Taconic Parkway, Baxter Cabot watched the headlights in the opposing lane swerve toward him and disappear. He spoke to the small dapper man seated beside him.

"I still don't believe it, Harold," he said. "An operation like this held up by a committee of three women who have nothing better to do than screw things up."

The man next to Cabot brushed back some imaginary hairs on his freckled pate. "You've just stated Weil's Law, my friend. If a committee of three women can screw things up, they will."

Cabot's face remained grim. "I spoke to Turk this morning. He thinks the consensus right now is about fifty-fifty. How do you like that? From close to one hundred percent to fifty-fifty. Unbelievable."

"Ah. A consensus from Turk. That certainly ought to be accurate. Money in the bank."

Turning, Cabot's gray eyes regarded the other man coldly. "You don't seem to be too crazy about Turk, Harold. What seems to be the problem?"

"You used the word 'crazy,' not me. I think I would have selected something more like, oh, 'maniacal.'" He looked down at his manicured nails. "The legal mind, by necessity, is an orderly thing, Baxter. Neat, methodical, precise. It has a natural abhorrence for the antic, the chaotic. It's none of my business, of course, but I never really understood why you hired him in the first place."

Cabot was gazing out into the deepening twilight once again. "You're right, Harold," he said. "It's none of your business."

Weil shrugged his shoulders. "So be it," he murmured.

It was several moments before Cabot spoke again. "Tell me, Harold. Has your precise legal mind come up with anything new? The time is getting short."

"A few things here and there. We'll see. I'll tell you this—it wouldn't hurt to work on that Marino woman, throw her off the track for a week or two. Charm her, maybe throw her a fuck."

Cabot squinted into the juggernaut lights of a speeding van. "You're not serious, are you?"

"Why not? Mix business with pleasure. You've done it before—with excellent results, I might add."

Lost in thought, Cabot said nothing.

The thin lips of the attorney broke into a smile. "And don't worry about that jealous husband of hers. Turk'll set *him* straight."

Cabot reacted immediately. "I told you to leave Turk alone, Harold. I won't say it again."

Weil pretended to cower, throwing his hands up in front of him. The smile was still on his face.

Irritably, Cabot reached for the car telephone and dialed a number. "Hello, Kyle?" he said. "I've got to make a few stops. I'll arrive around Saturday. How does it look up there?" Cabot listened, nodding his head several times. "All right, you can explain the rest to me when I get there. Meanwhile . . . do whatever has to be done. We want that vote, don't we." He hung up, his thoughtful gaze returning to the passing head-lights that veered past him like countless twin comets swirling in darkness.

Christine watched Nick chain-smoke another cigarette as he stared into the ash-filled fireplace.

"More coffee, honey?" she asked. When Nick shook his head, she filled her own cup and walked over to where he was sitting. She kissed the top of his head. Nick put his arm around her waist, his eyes still on the fireplace.

"Anything wrong, pally? You look a little pensive this afternoon. Tell mama."

Nick managed a smile. His hand squeezed her hip. "Big mama," he said. "Just business—the price of shrimp, the price of laundry, Henrietta wrestling with the chef. The usual."

"Are you sure?"

"Would pally lie? Sit down next to me and drink your coffee."

The doorbell rang. When Christine opened it, she saw Kyle Thorne standing in front of her.

"Mrs. Marino. If you're not too busy, I wonder if I could have a few moments of your time?" Thorne's voice was smooth, neither friendly nor unfriendly. He did not talk to people; he addressed them. When Christine nodded, he entered, removing his hat. "Ah, Mr. Marino," he continued. "I'm glad you're here. I really wanted to talk to both of you. May I sit down?"

The attitude of Kirsten Thorne to his wife, as Christine had told him, was still fresh in Nick's mind. Without warmth he indicated a chair with his hand. "Talk?" Nick said. "About what?"

Thorne adjusted himself comfortably and folded his hands. "I'll get right to the point, Mr. Marino. My wife and I have lived in Torchester for a good share of our lives. We have raised children here, I have established my legal practice here, and we are both quite active in civic affairs. As a permanent resident of Mountaincrest, and as chairman of its board of directors, I think you can see that I have a vested concern in our community here."

Nick looked at Thorne blankly. He waited for him to continue.

"To be frank, Mr. Marino, I'm rather disturbed." Thorne dusted something off his hat. "My son-in-law, Edward Hobbs, telephoned me yesterday and gave me some information that has puzzled me and caused me a great deal of concern. Because this information was relevant to the welfare of the community he and I both cherish, he decided it was essential that he share it with me, and I fully agree with him on this."

Nick regarded him levelly. "You said you would get to the point, Mr. Thorne."

The other man's face hardened imperceptibly. "Certainly. It's in regard to a conversation Edward overheard between you and Mr. Kiley yesterday afternoon."

Nick's eyes widened. He glanced at Christine. Before Nick could stop him, Thorne continued.

"It would seem that Mr. Kiley has . . . suspicions about certain problems we've been having around Torchester recently. The killing of animals, to be specific. Apparently, he seems to feel that they might be connected with certain . . . difficulties you may have had before you came to live with us up here. When you lived on Long Island, I believe."

Nick saw Christine's quick look of fear as she glanced at Thorne. He swung his head toward the other man. "Get out of here, Thorne," he said, his voice a menacing whisper.

Christine put her hand on her husband's shoulder. "No,

wait a minute, Nick," she said. "I want to hear this. I want to know what's going on."

His large hands unclenching, Thorne regarded Christine and Nick closely. "I'm truly sorry if I've said anything to upset you, Mrs. Marino. That was not my purpose. It would seem that your past problems are much more serious than I was aware of. My only concern is for the welfare, shall I say, the safety of the residents of Torchester and Mountaincrest. I think you will agree that we would not want your problems, past or present, to become our problems."

Nick stood up. "I told you to leave, Thorne. That's good advice. Take it."

Rising to his feet, Thorne looked at Nick coolly. "In a moment. It was not my intention to stay. I understand you like to solve things with your fists, Mr. Marino. I prefer other methods. But you will find that I am not an easy person to intimidate. Not at all."

"Nick, stop it!" Christine said, her voice rising. "Don't you see what's going on? It's the committee. First his wife and now it's him. They're trying to threaten me in some way, turn people against me. It's the committee! It's all for their precious Cabot Inn. My god, Thorne, is that it?"

Thorne was almost smiling. "I have rarely been the cause of so much emotion outside the courtroom. Mrs. Marino, I cannot deny that I think your committee has done a disservice to my community by trying to block the proposed inn. A true disservice. If you believe that I am threatening you in any way because of this, I shall not try to dissuade you. You seem so convinced, I feel I would be wasting my time."

"Just tell me, I want you to tell me." Christine was almost breathless. "If I had quit, disbanded the committee yesterday, you wouldn't be standing here now. Am I right? Am I the hell right?"

Thorne looked at her for a long moment, his face devoid now of any pretense of civility. "But you haven't, have you, Mrs. Marino," he said softly. He walked to the door, opened it, and turned around. "I am sure," he said, "that we all hope there will be no further . . . untoward incidents in this area in the near future. I think that you will agree that in the interest of public safety, the local residents and the police would have to be informed in order to take the proper precautionary steps." He looked at Nick. "And, Mr. Marino—don't bother to fire Edward. I've already assisted him in finding employment elsewhere." He closed the door behind him.

Nick took out a cigarette and sat down. He glanced at Christine's face. He did not like what he saw there. He waited for her question.

"Nick, what's going on? Tell me, Nick."

"Nothing's going on, Chris. Ben Kiley was playing detective, that's all. He found out about what happened to us on Long Island. He thinks there could be a tie-in to the animal killings that have been going on around here. He's wrong and I told him so," Nick lied.

Christine's hand rose to her mouth. "Oh god, Nick, it was me! It's my fault. I mentioned Mill Harbor to him by accident. It's my fault. What a fool I am! What a fool!"

Without looking up, Nick shook his head. "I wish you hadn't done that, Chris. Now, thanks to my son-of-a-bitch bartender, every time someone loses an animal around here we're going to get blamed. Oh, well, what the hell. What really the hell." He looked up into Christine's face. He saw the hand still covering her mouth, the fear in her eyes. "Honey, what is it? What's the matter?" He reached for her arm.

"Oh, Nick, is it them?" Christine's voice wavered. "Is it them? Have they found us?"

Nick controlled his face. His voice was firm. "No, Chris. It's nothing. It's nobody. A policeman's pipe dream. It's so silly, I didn't even want to mention it to you. Damn Thorne. Damn him anyway." He stroked his wife's arm. "Forget it, honey. Come on. We've got to go to work."

Christine's eyes remained troubled. "Nick," she said. "Nick, I never told you."

"What is it, baby?" he asked.

"The cat. The china cat. One day I walked in here and . . . and . . . the head of the cat. It was broken off, Nick. It was lying on the table. I thought it was them, Nick. A warning. I thought they had found us. That they had been here, that they . . . they . . ."

Nick stood up and wrapped his arms around his wife. "Baby, baby," he said quietly. "Forget it. It must have been Joey, maybe even me. Forget it. It's nothing and there's no one. Now, come on. Go get dressed. We've got a restaurant to run. Come on, babe."

Christine's eyes searched his face. The love in his eyes, his tough smile, reassured her. "O.K.," she said, brushing her cheek, "O.K."

As he watched his wife walk toward the bedroom, the smile slowly left Nick's face. He was remembering the mouse. A headless cat and a headless mouse. Cat-and-mouse. His eyes glinted. He looked out the window. If someone is playing games, he thought, why, let's play. If you're out there, troll bastard, you're on. Hey, sport. You know how to play death? I'll teach you, sport. It's easy. You get shot. You lie down. And you die.

29

T HE TWO CAMPERS sat on a fallen pine, their arms
around each other, staring into the burning coals of
the fire. The evening was fading quickly into night,
the lake in the distance and the few patches of spring snow
already glimmering in the early moonlight. The young man's
red hair and beard, the girl's long auburn hair, lake-fresh, still
wet, blended with the flame-hued trees around them. Drawing the girl to him, the young man kissed her, his hand going
under her sweat shirt. The girl pressed herself to him, her
eyes closed, the firelight ruddying her hard thighs.

High above them, silhouetted against the blue-and-orange
sky like dark stones, the two figures sat, their knees drawn up,
their eyes riveted on the people below. As the lovers embraced, the figures glided down, between the trees, moving in
silence like encroaching shadows. When lips parted and talk
resumed, the figures became still once again, immobile statues
of menace.

The bearded man rose, put several large branches on the
fire, and removed his clothing as the girl watched him. Yelp-
ing with the cold, he ran to a nearby sleeping bag and jumped
in, beckoning to his companion to follow. As she hopped
around, trying to remove her shoes, laughter floated under the
hovering branches. Finally, nude except for her heavy shirt,

she squeezed into the bag next to him, their arms and legs instantly intertwining in an effort to get warm. Again their laughter startled the forest.

As the sound drifted up to the silent watchers, their mouths opened slowly in terrible anticipation. Awakening lusts burned crimson in their eyes. They did not acknowledge the great white wolf that loomed out of the trees behind them and seated himself at their side, his jaws opened, too, in predatorial hunger. Stealthily, wrapped in desire, the three figures inched forward in slow and soundless pursuit.

Seated astride her companion now, her hands locked in his in mock combat, the girl was gradually drawn down toward another fervent kiss. When at last she was released, she straightened and removed her shirt, her eyes on those of the man below her. Tenderly, his hands began to stroke her flame-bronzed nudity. They remained that way, locked in quiet caress, flickering in silence, children of the fire.

It was only the wolf who heard it at first. Gradually, he lowered his head, his ears flattened in abject fear. As the sound shivered the blue twilight air once again, his body began to tremble slightly. He turned his head toward the still pines behind him, the humans forgotten. When it became audible to the figures beside him, they twisted their heads in the same direction, their necks drawn back like snakes about to strike.

Something, a presence of light, was coming toward them through the darkening forest. Shimmering whitely against the tree trunks, a silver earth lightning approached, each brief flash followed by soft and delicate thunder. The being that stepped out of the woods a few moments later caused the wolf to cower still lower, the hands of the other two hunters to grasp and tear the tree roots out of the forest floor beneath them. Inhuman, he had the head and body of a man. He walked on large, splayed hoofs with sly, tentative steps. A small pair of silver elk antlers rose from his head. His sexual organ probed in front of him like a hungry, questing reptile. The creature was encased entirely in a skin of bright silver that glinted when the moonlight struck it, sending off pale shafts that emblazoned the surrounding trees, that filled the air with murmurs of dread.

Sensing the eyes that were upon him, the apparition halted and turned his head slowly. The silvered face, with its perfect features, should have been beautiful. It was the square cast of the open mouth and what lay behind the eyes that made it hideous, a visage barely possible to behold. Moon-gleaming, his body tensed, he regarded the three figures in front of him.

Violence coursed through the still air. It was the red eyes of rage that broke the confrontation, returning once again to the firelit humans—not in defeat, but in recognition of rivals too deadly for combat. Following their gaze, the silver figure's mouth compressed into a manic, licentious smile. He thrust his hands down and to the side, fingers slowly spreading in desire, while his organ pulsed and squirmed in a frenzy of lust. In an instant, he, too, became a stalker, his silent hoofs landing on the soft earth in poised, measured steps.

Their lips still touching, the man put his hands on the girl's shoulders and pushed her down along his body. As he entered her, the girl sat up, her back arched, her hands on his chest. She smiled and closed her eyes, throwing her fire-tinted hair back with a shake of her head.

Down and downward, gliding in silence. Soft paws, eyes of madness, hands with the strength of giants. Close and closer, out of the night, at firelight's edge. So close. To smell the flesh, to hear the pounding blood. Oh, so close. Red, riven ecstasy. So . . . close.

The girl's first moan was joined by a wild cry of joy. Running in an alien, stilted gait of horror, a silver form raced toward her through the glittering light. He was followed quickly by other figures, whose screams of longing rose high above the forest, an abomination on the soft winds of night.

30

CHRISTINE LOOKED AROUND at the dim interior of the tavern. What am I doing here? she thought. She had spent an hour cajoling Nick into this night off, and she had wound up in a place where the smell of smoke and stale beer filled the air like a miasma. The pool table behind her clacked incessantly; hunched figures sat at the bar, dark and silent.

She glanced up at Malcolm Jones, the red neon Piels sign in the window reflecting off his glasses. "It's charming, Malcolm. So . . . out of the way."

"I don't believe you took us here," Amanda chimed in. "Business just can't be this bad."

"You ladies will regret your sarcasm," Jones answered, "when you taste the chili. It's not only good, it's quick. Your meeting starts in twenty minutes."

Christine shrugged her shoulders. She had found out only this morning that the major portion of the meeting at Town Hall tonight was going to be devoted to the proposed Cabot Inn and its benefits to Torchester. Kyle Thorne, she had read, was going to be the principal speaker. At the last minute, she and Amanda had decided to go—to listen, maybe to ask a few questions. When she had picked Amanda up at the antique

176

shop, Malcolm had dragged them in here to eat God knows what, and do it in darkness.

Jones looked at his watch and then peered around in the gloom. "Where is that girl?" he said. "Isn't this ridiculous? Bartender!"

At the far end of the bar, the bartender was drawing some tap beer. He did not look up.

Jones's voice rose. "Bartender!" He snapped his fingers.

At the sound the bartender gave him a hard stare. "I heard you the first time, mister," he said evenly. "Why don't you just hold your horses."

Taken aback, Jones glanced at the two women. As the three of them sat in uncomfortable silence, a figure at the bar turned around slowly, a beer glass in one hand, a glass of whiskey in the other. His thin, handsome face had the look of a man who spent his life in the outdoors.

"Well, bless my finger-snappin' soul," he said after a long moment. "What do we have here?"

Christine and Amanda exchanged glances. They did not look at the speaker.

Another man turned around. He was short and stocky, his full red beard giving him a leonine look. He took a long drink of beer. "Looks to me, Gillespie, like a little bit of everything."

At his words, Amanda stiffened. Malcolm Jones turned around and squinted through the smoke at the speakers.

"Yep," the stocky man continued. "I believe we got us our own New York City melting pot right here at the Red Rooster."

"The Red Cock Lounge," the other man corrected. "Let's show these folks we got some class, too." His eyes returned to Jones. "What are you starin' at so hard, sugar?"

Christine put her hand on Jones's arm. "Let's get the hell out of here. Now?" She stood up.

As they walked past the two men, Jones stopped. "Say," he said, "is your name Gillespie?"

The slim man nodded, smiling.

"Well, Gillespie," Jones said pleasantly, "why don't you just go and fuck yourself."

The man put his drink down carefully. "Why don't you do it for me, sweetheart." His voice was barely audible.

Again Christine put her hand on Jones's arm. "Malcolm? Please?"

"Malcolm!" the bearded man exploded. "Listen to blondie, Malcolm. She knows. Listen to the pretty lady."

A hulking figure on the bar chair beside him spoke without turning around. "You got one of the best bird dogs in the county, Moon. You mess with Mrs. Marino there, why, you're just liable to lose him."

At the sound of Truman Hooker's voice, Christine stopped. She whirled around, her heart suddenly racing with quick anger, quick fear. "What did you say, Mr. Hooker?" She tried to keep her voice steady. "What did you say?"

Hooker swung his head toward Christine, his heavy-lidded eyes boring into her. "I was only saying, Mrs. Marino. My friend, Mr. Turner here, is a nice, simple country boy. I wouldn't want to see him get mixed up in no big-city problems, that's all."

His words drilled into Christine's brain. Thorne! she thought. Damn Kyle Thorne.

Hooker directed his sodden eyes at the thin-faced man next to him. "Lot of funny things been happening around here lately, Alex. Animals killed. Killed a goddamn bull. Ain't no bear. Shit. How long's your brother and Lucy been missing in the woods now? Two, three days?"

The other man's eyes widened. "Jeffrey? What the hell has blondie over there got to do with Jeffrey? You ain't makin' any sense, Truman."

"Oh, I'm makin' sense all right. You ask Mrs. Marino, Alex, if I'm makin' any sense. You ask her."

The implications in his words stirred unforgotten horrors in Christine. She closed her eyes. This is a bad dream, she thought. This place is hell, but I am not really here. When she opened her eyes, Hooker's slouched back was again turned toward her. Christine half ran to the door, opened it, and hurried out into the cool evening air.

The incident with Truman Hooker had so shaken her that when the meeting was over Christine realized she had heard very little of what had been said. The theme of Kyle Thorne's speech and that of everyone who had spoken after him was identical. The Cabot Inn meant jobs; anyone against the inn was against the people of Torchester. Neither she nor Amanda had spoken, not even to ask a question.

Glancing around the room, Amanda spoke to Christine without looking at her. "We seem to be minor celebrities. There are people here who are looking at us as if we wanted to take the bread out of their kiddies' mouths." She gazed down at her hands. After a pause she spoke again. "Is that what we're trying to do, Chris? Are we turning into the bad guys?"

"Amanda, I . . ." Christine stopped. She was staring at the two men who had spoken to them in the tavern. Gillespie was talking intently with Kyle Thorne. At the tall man's side, the other man was looking at Christine as he listened to the conversation, his bearded face set in harsh lines.

Sudden fury mounted in Christine. That bastard, she thought. He's talking about me and my family. First to Hooker and now to those two mean bastards. She looked around for a telephone to call Nick. Nick would shut Mr.

Kyle Thorne up. Very quickly. She shook her head. No, she decided. This is one time when Christine will handle things. Christine, not Nick. She rose, picked up her purse, and walked over to the three men.

"Mr. Thorne," she said. Her emotion made it difficult to keep her voice firm. "I understand that you have been discussing my family and its private affairs with Mr. Hooker. Is that true, Mr. Thorne?"

The lean man turned around and glared at Christine. She kept her eyes on Thorne.

"Mrs. Marino. I really don't believe this is the proper place to discuss our . . . differences, but since you have chosen to do so, by all means, let us discuss them." Thorne's voice flowed smoothly over his steaming coffee cup. "The only *affairs* I discuss with Truman Hooker," he continued, "are the ones that concern the safety of the residents of Mountaincrest. You will agree, Mrs. Marino, that a rising amount of incidents—crimes, if you will—have been occurring in this vicinity recently. Crimes that have yet to be accounted for. Mr. Turner's father lost a fine dog. Mr. Gillespie has just been speaking to me about his brother Jeffrey and his fiancée. Their disappearance is already in the hands of the police. I feel I would be remiss in my duties if I did *not* tell Mr. Hooker to take all available precautions to protect the people of Mountaincrest. Yourself included, Mrs. Marino." There was a glint of victory in the blue eyes, in the faint smile.

Unnerved by the number of people who were now listening to them, Christine tried to keep her voice low and in control. "I shall protect myself without Mr. Hooker's assistance. And in the future, Mr. Thorne, my husband and I would appreciate it if you kept us out of your discussions with anyone. I don't know what you're saying, but I assume you are aware of the libel laws in this country."

Thorne's eyes glittered now. "My profession keeps me abreast of the various laws in this country, Mrs. Marino." He paused. His features seemed to soften, except deep within the eyes. "Mrs. Marino, I consider myself a fair and ethical person. If you can assure me without any reservations whatsoever that there is absolutely no possibility that the recent ills that have beset Torchester have any connection with any problems that you and your family have had in the past, I will do two things. I will publicly apologize to you, right here, right now, for anything I may have said or implied, and I will give you the name of an excellent libel attorney, so that you may institute proceedings against me." His eyes narrowed. "Can you give me this assurance, Mrs. Marino?"

Looking into the face of Kyle Thorne, at the hostile faces of the two men next to him, and then at the circle of curious faces around her, Christine felt her rage leave, her anguish begin. No matter how angry the smug man made her, somewhere in the recesses of her mind she knew that Thorne could be right. That the possibility did exist that, at long last, the bastard beasts had found them, bringing revenge, bringing murder, bringing havoc. She fought the quick tears that welled in her eyes. She did not answer.

Christine turned and walked through the huge room toward the front doors. The stares of everyone around Thorne swelled at her back like an angry wave.

Hurrying along beside her, Amanda asked, "Honey, what is that man talking about? What problems? What is going *on* around here?"

Christine stopped. She looked into the face of her friend, eyes wide with the beginnings of terror. Then, moving as if in nightmare, she ran through the opened doors, down the steps, and into the star-lit streets.

31

THE DEEP BARKING of a dog awoke Nick. He peered through sleep-misted eyes at the clock beside him. Five A.M. As he turned around, he saw Christine sitting up in bed, staring at the wind-blown curtains, listening to the sound that invaded the room.

"Chris?" he whispered. "What is it, honey?" Christine bit her lip and turned her head away from him. Nick was wide awake now. "Baby, what is it?" A single sob escaped Christine's lips. Nick stretched out his arm. "Baby, baby, come over here. What's going on?" Christine flung herself on his chest, crying softly. Nick stroked her hair and kissed the top of her head. "It's O.K., baby," he murmured. "It's O.K. Tell Nicky what's wrong."

"Nick," Christine said into his chest. "Nick, I'm so afraid. Nick, tell me, have they found us? Are they going to kill us? Tell me."

In the dawn-tinted room Nick's face grew rigid. The tender kiss he placed on his wife's hair did not match the look in his eyes. "No, baby. Nobody's going to touch us. No one."

"But Kyle Thorne said—"

"Thorne again?"

"At the meeting last night. He said that everything that has been happening around here could be our fault. From, you know, before. And he's telling people, Nick. You should see the way they looked at me, Nick. It was terrible."

"Kyle Thorne," Nick said grimly. "Maybe if I bust his damned jaw he won't talk so much."

Christine looked up quickly. Her face was wet with tears. "No, Nick! No! Maybe he's right. Animals killed, Nick. Just like on Long Island. And now there are two people missing. Two campers. You know those beasts, Nick. You know what they do. Are they warning us, Nick, torturing us? God, Nick! Oh god!" Again her head went on his chest. It was a long time before she spoke again. "Nick, let's get out of here. I want to move. I want to get out of here."

Nick's eyes narrowed. "No, Chris. Thorne is wrong. You are wrong. There's nobody out there. And if there was, what good would it do to move? If they can find us once, they'll do it again. We're not running again, Chris."

"But, Nick. Joey. Joey."

"All right, let's talk about Joey. Joey's in school, he has friends, he has a life here. He's been uprooted once before. They're not going to push him away again. Chris, our son has had problems which he is working out. Do you want him to leave Dr. Landau now?" Christine shook her head sadly. "The best thing for our son, Chris, is to stay right here. You know what Dr. Landau said last Monday night? He said that Joey is making splendid progress. That's the word he used. 'Splendid.' I don't want him to give that up, Chris. We're staying. We're not giving everything up to run from shadows that may not exist. We're going to stay. For us. And for Joey."

Joey sat at his school desk staring down at the blue test booklet in front of him. Methodically, he wrote his name and the date, April first. He laid his pen down and raised his eyes to Mrs. Ahlmeyer. With a dull intensity, his gaze took in the glasses with the silver chain, the sweater thrown over her shoulders, the heavily powdered face. His eyes narrowed.

Old slut, he thought. Fucker of pigs. How I would like to ram this test down your scrawny throat, or up your spider-webbed crotch.

Educator who tests me, what do you know? What does the snake think in the recesses of the night, mindless whore? Who sings in the darkness, causing the flowers to uproot themselves in yearning? What does the thunder say, the lightning reveal? What whispers the wind to the pine trees in the amber twilight? Foul slut, you know nothing.

His mouth twisting in disdain, Joey's attention turned to Alice Dworski, sitting directly in front of him. His glance roamed down her long blond hair to the outline of her blue-jeaned buttocks. He nodded his head slightly.

Your turn is coming, temptress. It is the time of delights, the time of your flesh. I am tired of following you, glaring through tree branches. I am tired of hiding and not touching. I am tired of being harmless.

Joey leaned forward and whispered something in the girl's ear. She turned to him, her eyes and mouth crinkled in shock. Angrily, she stood up, dropped her purse, picked it up, and walked out of the room.

A silent laugh shook Joey. He knew where she was going. The principal's office. He'd hear all about it from Nick tonight. The long lecture. The threatening lecture. A dog barking at an intruder. Did you know, Nicholas, that intruders can threaten, too? A game of threats. Bark and counterbark. Until, in time to come, a howl signifies a winner. And then the game is over.

Restless, unable to sit still any longer, Joey rose and walked to the pencil sharpener. As he watched his pencil slowly disappear into the machine, a sound, a melodic sigh, pressed against the windowpane next to him. Startled, he looked out at the meadow that bordered the school and to the forest beyond. For an instant, he caught a glimpse of a white-clad female figure walking among the trees. Again he heard the sound, a plaintive call, as if the wind were singing to him across the flowing meadow grass.

Struggling with the unused window, Joey finally wrenched it open. He stood there straining toward the voice, the wraith-like singer, his eyes bright.

"Joey!" At the sound of Mrs. Ahlmeyer's voice, Joey's mouth twitched. He did not move. "Joey! What are you doing? Close that window immediately!"

The sweet, sighing melody stopped. Uttering a gasping cry of loss, Joey turned and looked wildly at Mrs. Ahlmeyer, at the uplifted faces of the students around him. Another desperate cry escaped his lips. He threw his pencil down and ran from the room.

As he raced down the stairwell, his progress was blocked by the outstretched arm of Mr. Ettinger.

"Marino, I was just coming to get you. Come to my office. Now."

Joey stepped back, his body tensed, his eyes on the doors in front of him. "No," he said.

The principal's voice rose. "I said *now*, Marino. What do you think—" The look on the face of the boy in front of him stopped him in midsentence. In another moment, Joey had sprung past him and run down the school corridor, bursting through the heavy doors into the afternoon sunlight.

Halfway across the meadow, Joey halted. Again, stronger than before, the haunting siren song came to him in tones of rapture too sweet to bear. His eyes, mad now in their intensity, caught a female form among the trees in front of him. He began to run once more, the music pulling him toward the figure that glided deeper and deeper into the gleaming birches. As he ran, his hands tore at his clothing. When he entered the edge of the forest he was naked, the sunlight through the trees speckling his body in shifting patterns of light and shadow.

Directly in front of him he saw a fawn looking back over its shoulder at him with a knowing, human smile. It bounded into the surrounding wood, the laughter of a young girl trailing in the air behind it.

Walking quickly after it through the impeding branches, Joey stepped into a small clearing. A swiftly flowing stream glittered among the tree roots, gurgling in liquid, crystalline melody. A large, deep pool, rippled by the small waterfall at its source, blended its exquisite murmurings with the music that now began to fill the air from everywhere. Enchanted, Joey looked up, the fawn forgotten. The tops of the trees were swaying now, as if in a storm, against the afternoon sky. Music from the budded limbs, the sun-glistening pine needles, poured down on him in a swelling chorus of delight. In pure, driven longing he raised his face toward the thrashing tree-tops. He stood immobile, his mind and body ravished by the sounds that poured down on him.

It was a long time before he opened his eyes. When he did, the look in them was unrecognizable. His features were contorted by the passions that raged through him, his body twisted as if in pain. He looked around with quick, manic motions of his head. Moving as if in a trance, he mounted a large rock by the side of the pool and pressed his body against it, his bent knees clasping it on either side. He placed his lips on the wet, cold surface. In an agony of lust, he turned on his back and arched his body toward the frantic branches above him, his moans blending with the primordial chorus around him. Close to death, he became a part of the most powerful force of earth.

Suddenly, a delicate hand reached out of the blue depths of the pool and fastened around his ankle. With unexpected strength, it pulled him into the icy waters. Dazed, his head resting beneath the softly flowing waterfall, Joey saw the small head of a woman rise in the center of the pool. Pupilless, deeply slanted eyes gazed at him curiously above a smiling, blue-lipped mouth. He heard tinkling laughter come from behind him. A tiny pair of legs emerged from the waterfall and encircled his neck; a cold pair of hands covered his eyes. In the water all about him now, he felt the movement of minikin bodies as they slid over his chilled flesh, biting him gently, touching him, disappearing. Joey threw his head back against the small body behind him. He inhaled the vernal perfume of the forest floor, the strange, watery musk of the elfin mistresses that surrounded him.

Then, as quickly as they had come, the small figures vanished. Joey sensed rather than heard the approach of something coming toward him, a presence of terror and joy. Above him now, the trees bowed almost to breaking in a single direction. The sweet, inhuman singing that issued from every living thing about him rose to an ecstatic crescendo. Transfixed, Joey watched as great golden shafts of light pierced the forest in front of him, burnishing the trees and rocks, turning the water that poured down on him to amber and then to bright, sparkling scarlet.

Radiating light, the figure of a woman emerged from among the trees. Long gold-silver hair blew about a face of unutterable beauty. Her body was clad in a flowing white gown that revealed the shape of love beneath. Two monstrous beasts shuffled on either side of her, their long arms reaching to the ground, their great muscles gliding under the mottled blue-and-gray skin. Long tusks grew upward on their huge faces, almost reaching their eyes of fire. Not daring to look at the woman's face, they slouched, apelike, beside her, their side-long glances at her feet and legs betraying their adoration. As she entered the glade, one of the shuffling monsters touched her with the side of his head. Like lightning in a silent sky, her features flickered and changed, arcane desires dissolving her face into insatiate wantonness, into a visage of horror. When she placed her hand lightly on the shoulder of the beast for a moment, he bent his neck around and bit where she had touched, drawing his blood in a paroxysm of love.

Standing at the far edge of the pool, the woman looked down at Joey, her face a mirror of carnal realms beyond imagining. He lay there, trembling in fear and an unbearable expectancy as flowers from her windblown hair fell about him in the crimson water like scented, purple raindrops. Slowly, she raised her arms until both hands extended toward him, in demand, in yearning.

Joey's whole body shook as if jolted by electricity. He gasped, he writhed in wild abandon, twisting and rutting, his mouth gaping, only the whites of his eyes showing in his transfigured face. Abruptly, his body bent rigidly upward, racked by a sexuality that knew no boundaries. Then he slumped back, unconscious, the water cascading down on his shoulders in a gentle, red caress.

32

"Joey!" Christine called. "Joey, your eggs are getting cold. Don't make me call you again."

Nick looked up from his paper, a coffee cup held in front of him. "Joey!" he shouted. There was no answer.

"He's going to be late for his skiing," Christine fretted. "Nick, can't you come with us today? They're practicing the torchlight ceremony for the carnival next week. After last night, I thought it might be a good idea." She could still remember the scene, the raised voices caused by the telephone call from the school principal.

"Can't, honey," Nick said, behind his paper again. "I've got over two hundred lunches booked and a load of seafood coming in for tonight's crowd. Don't knock it."

"I know, Nick, I know. It just seems that you don't spend much time with him anymore."

"I will, baby. I will. The season's almost over." Nick raised his voice again. "Joey!"

Joey came out of his bedroom dressed for skiing. He sat down at the table without a word and began to eat.

After a few moments, Nick put his paper down and looked at his son, his eyes troubled. "Joey," he said, "are we straight now? I don't want any more telephone calls from your school. You'll remember that, won't you, son?"

Joey raised his eyes to his father. They looked at each other for several long seconds.

"Well?" Nick said.

"Well." Joey's voice was almost a whisper.

Nick's mouth tightened. "Don't start that smart-ass stuff with me, pal. Not again." He looked at his son intently. "What the hell is the matter with you?"

Only Joey's mouth smiled. "Yes. What the hell is the matter with me." He looked down at his plate.

Christine and Nick exchanged a perplexed glance. The rest of the meal was eaten in silence.

Christine watched as her son finished his milk. "Get your boots on, Joey. We're going to be late."

After Joey had left the room, Christine looked worriedly at her husband. Nick shook his head slowly. "I don't know him anymore, Chris. He's so damn . . . cold."

"That didn't sound like 'splendid progress' to me, Nick. Isn't that what Dr. Landau said?"

"Yeah. Maybe we'd better give the good doctor a call and see what the hell is going on. I don't like it, Chris. I . . ." He stopped.

Christine nodded. "I'll do it. Right now."

After an exchange of pleasantries, Christine got right to the point. "Dr. Landau, I called you to ask . . . Well, how is Joey doing?"

"Joey is doing very well. Why do you ask?"

"We're worried about him, Doctor. We thought he was doing so much better, but recently he's been so moody and quiet, and this morning . . . it wasn't good, Dr. Landau. We thought he'd be, you know, improving."

The doctor's voice was soothing. "Patience, my dear. We must learn patience. These things do not develop in a day, and they do not disappear in a day. We are probing, he and I.

Very deeply. You must expect some reaction on his part. There will be anger. You must expect this. These things often appear worse before they get better. I cannot discuss it further, but you must remember, Christine. If I may say so, I am very good at what I do."

Reassured, Christine repeated to Nick what Dr. Landau had said. "It's going to be all right," she added hopefully. "The way I understand it, this attitude, this anger, means that progress is being made."

Nick stared at the smoke from his cigarette. "I hope he's right, Chris. He's the only game in town. He damn well better be right," he said after a moment.

"He is." Christine rose and kissed him on the forehead. "We've got to go, dear. I'll call you later." She followed her boot-clumping son out the door.

When Christine found out that the ski practice would take at least two hours, she walked over to the small pond at the base of the mountain and rented a pair of ice skates. As she carefully tied her laces, she thought about what Dr. Landau had said. Things always got worse before they got better. Landau's Law. She thought of the events of the past few weeks. Joey. The committee. Lawyer and Mrs. Lawyer Thorne. Truman the Bastard Hooker and friends. The stares of the townspeople and Amanda's question. This must be the worse, Christine decided. The better *must* be coming. Meanwhile, I'll handle it. I'm getting better at coping, just like the grown-ups do. And I'm only thirty-five.

As she stepped out onto the ice, she caught a glimpse of Turk Brandon through the other skaters. She smiled. She didn't think it could be possible, but it was true: his ice skating was worse than his skiing. Brandon did not skate. He walked, tentatively, with little steps, his arms held straight out to the sides. Her hands on her hips, Christine watched in amusement as he slowly approached. When at last he was in front of her, he did not stop but smiled modestly. Christine shook her head and glided up to him.

"My compliments, Mr. Brandon," she said. "You are a total winter sportsman."

Brandon's eyes remained on his feet. "Don't touch me," he said firmly. "I'm in training."

Christine's smile broke into a laugh. "My god, for what?" she murmured. She grasped one of his outstretched arms gently. "Turk, I can't stand it. Let me help you."

Skating slowly around the outskirts of the pond, Christine could feel the physical presence of the man beside her. The compact body seemed to be made out of metal, his arm a bar of steel under her hand. She remembered him scrambling to his feet in the glaring basement light, refusing to stay down. Hard man, this, she mused. Just like Nick.

She did not know precisely why they fell, but they did; gradually, grandly, landing on the ice in a tangled heap.

"That's it," Turk said, lying flat on his back. "I don't want to overtrain. Mrs. Marino, if you will sort out what belongs to you and arise, I will buy you a cup of cocoa. That's my final offer."

Slightly embarrassed, Christine got quickly to her feet. She looked down at him. "I'll take it," she said.

Seated in the bright sunshine on the large wooden deck that stretched out in front of the base lodge, Christine warmed her hands on her cup and looked at Turk. "You know, Mr. Brandon," she said, "my son worships you. Apparently you were a better football player than you are a skater."

Brandon shrugged.

"My son says you were something called a linebacker. Doesn't that involve a lot of tackling?"

Amusement lit up Brandon's eyes. "When it's done right, yes."

"Don't you have to be mean and rotten to do that job?"

"Ever so." Brandon was smiling now.

"And you *liked* making a living doing something like that?"

"It was a good living, Mrs. Marino." A pause. "I loved it."

"Well then, why did you quit? You look healthy enough to me."

Brandon stared down at his cup. "It's very simple, Mrs. M. Someone hit me. Rather hard. Hoist by my own petard, you might say."

"Why did you go to work for Mr. Cabot? If I may say so, you don't seem to enjoy it very much."

"Several reasons. First, although I did make a good deal of money, I spent it. All. We shall not discuss how. Second, I needed a job. Cabot's was the best offer I had. And, lest we forget, Turk Brandon was a household word. I was an athletic feather in the Cabot cap. And now, if this interview is over, I would like to stop. My cocoa is getting cold."

"No," Christine persisted, "it's not over. I have two more questions." Turk sighed. "Why does Turk Brandon, tough guy, all-American, always clown around, play the fool, if I may say so."

Brandon answered promptly. "Because I'm a fool."

"I don't believe it for a minute. I get the impression that there's more. Much more."

"There is. I'm also crazy."

"You're not crazy, Turk. You have a gift. You can laugh at life, at people, particularly at yourself. You're a lucky man."

Glancing up, Christine caught Brandon gazing at her speculatively, his smile almost gone. He said nothing.

"Last question. I have reached a moment in my life when it

would help me to know. I need to know the secret."

"The secret?"

"Yes. Tell me. What the hell is so funny, Turk?"

Brandon looked at her unwaveringly. "I'll tell you, dear lady. Why, it's us. You and me. The human race. We are *funny!*"

"But we're not!"

"Oh, yes. Yes. We are. Listen, Christine. Did you ever watch people chew? I mean really watch them. Did you ever see someone cough? Or take a good look at a human ear? How can you take someone seriously who's got two of those?"

"But that's not really funny."

"O.K., O.K. How about mating? That's funny. Or someone with a bad cold? It's all hysterical, I tell you. We're a comical bunch."

Christine shook her head. "That's not fair, Turk. That's all physical. Look at what the mind of man has accomplished. It's magnificent, but it's not funny."

"Ah, yes. Symphonies. Bridges. Satellites and calculus. Laser surgery and computers. But you forget, Christine, trapped in the body of the beast as we are, we are all of us ridiculous. Charles Darwin put bloomers over his head, I'm sure of it; Copernicus would rather look down between two mammary glands than up at the stars; Henry Ford invented the rumble seat in order to make out; and Alexander Graham Bell, I'm convinced, made the world's first obscene phone call. Ridiculous creatures. We can only be objects of thunderous, divine laughter."

Christine stared at him in mock amazement. "Thunderous? Divine? Is that linebacker talk?"

"No. I speak in the language of a world-class skater. Finish your cocoa."

Over the steaming liquid, Christine glanced at the ugly-handsome face. Hard to know, hard to reach, this henchman. Is there such a thing as a profound clown? she mused. She raised the cup to her lips.

As they sat in silence, she saw Baxter Cabot approaching them across the deck. As always, he was dressed perfectly, his handsome face tanner than ever.

"Mrs. Marino," he said, holding the back of Turk's chaise. "I must ask you not to interfere with Mr. Brandon's work. His time is extremely valuable." It was meant to be a joke, but Christine noticed a slight edge in the tone of his voice.

Brandon closed his eyes. "Ssh, boss," he said. "I'm forming a conglomerate. I think you're going to like it." Beneath the humor, Christine again felt something hidden, a fencing.

"Mrs. Marino," Cabot continued, "is your husband here?"

"No, he's at work. Why do you ask?"

"Self-preservation. I would like you to join me for lunch. I think my staff and I have come up with a plan that would resolve the problems that exist between us."

"Does it include the building of a Cabot Inn at Mad Mountain?"

"Of course." His smile was friendly. "You're going to lose the vote next week, Mrs. Marino. That is the consensus at this time. In the interests of future peace, however, I hope your committee will be pleased by what we propose to do. Please come to lunch and I'll explain everything to you."

Christine looked up toward the ski trails. "I'm waiting for my son. I'm not sure exactly when he'll be finished."

"Perhaps Turk here can keep an eye out for the boy. Will you recognize him, Turk?"

Brandon nodded his head vigorously. "I can do it, boss. You just . . . leave it to me."

Cabot extended his hand toward Christine. As she rose, she glanced at Turk. He was staring straight ahead, his scarred face an enigma.

As the two figures walked away, Brandon swung his head to watch them. He reached down alongside the chaise and picked up a large handful of snow. After packing it methodically, he drew his arm back suddenly and threw it as hard as he could, his eyes never leaving Cabot's back.

The snowball flew past Cabot's head, missing it by inches. He whirled around, staring at Brandon.

"Damn kids, boss," Turk shouted. The two men's eyes locked for a long moment. Then Cabot swung around and continued walking toward the lodge.

Seated at a table near the bar, Cabot ordered two drinks, sat back, and regarded Christine, his eyes narrowed.

"Yes?" she said, returning his gaze.

Cabot smiled. "Sorry. I was just thinking about some legal advice my attorney gave me recently."

"About Mountaincrest?"

"Indirectly, yes. However. Christine, here is the plan we have come up with. I hope it meets the approval of you and your committee. When we build here at Mad Mountain, we would like to—"

"When? Not if?"

"I've told you, Mrs. Marino. The result of the vote next week has already been ascertained."

As Cabot continued, he stopped several times in midsentence, appearing increasingly distracted as he spoke. Finally, he slammed his empty glass down on the wooden table. "That son of a bitch," he said, almost in wonder.

"What?" Christine stared at him.

"My apologies, Christine." Cabot's eyebrows furrowed in

anger. "That . . . idiot! He was aiming at my head just now. Damn him!"

Embarrassed, Christine looked down into her drink.

"Damn him!" Cabot repeated. "Now why the *hell* would he do a thing like that? Was it about you, Christine?" He regarded her closely.

Christine shrugged her shoulders. She did not look up.

"The man's insane." Cabot's voice was lower now.

"No, he's not insane, Mr. Cabot. I think he's very . . . complicated."

Cabot almost laughed. "No. He's insane. You don't know him. The things he does. Did you ever see him play football? Only an insane man plays with broken ribs, a broken nose, a broken hand."

Feeling somehow defensive for Turk, Christine looked at Cabot. "I have to ask it," she said. "If you knew all this about him, if you thought he was crazy . . . why did you hire him?"

Cabot took a drink from his refilled glass. It was a long time before he spoke. "I don't know, Christine. I've thought about it a hundred times. I don't know." Suddenly, his eyes changed. Following his glance, Christine saw Turk Brandon approaching the bar. His face filled with cold anger now, Cabot waved Turk toward them.

Standing next to the table, Turk looked down at Baxter Cabot. Above his slight smile, his eyes had the look of patient expectancy. "Joey's taking off his skis, Mrs. Marino," he said. His eyes never left Cabot's face.

Cabot's voice was almost a whisper. "I've had it, Turk. That was a stupid, infantile thing to do. I want an apology. Right here. Right now." Brandon's deepening smile brought Cabot's voice up in volume. "I'm not kidding, Turk. I want to hear it."

"O.K., boss." Brandon's voice was calm. "I was sorry a moment after I threw it. How could I miss an easy shot like that?"

Cabot's features contorted. "Damn you, Turk. Damn you. I don't need this nonsense. I don't . . . need you, Turk."

Looking down at Cabot, Brandon's eyes held a strange, reflective look. "Don't you?" he said softly.

"Now what the hell is *that* supposed to mean?" Cabot's voice rose again.

Brandon adjusted his face. The smile returned. "Beats me." His eyes swung to Christine. After another moment he spoke. "Ask Mrs. Marino. Beautiful women know everything." He turned and ambled out of the bar, raising his hand in salute as he left.

Cabot watched him go, his eyes wide in disbelief. "Oh my god," he said. "I don't believe it."

"What? What is it, Baxter?"

Cabot's head was shaking now. Wonder had replaced the anger in his face. He turned to Christine. "Did you see the way he looked at you? Did you see it? Turk Brandon is in love! He's in love, I tell you. The old, crooked horse. I can't believe it. I know that crazy bastard. It's you, Christine. I tell you, it's you. He's . . ." Cabot stopped. His eyes followed Christine as she stood up and walked between the tables toward the door. The look on his face changed. It was not pleasant.

Christine caught up with Turk on the sunlit deck. She touched his shoulder. The moment he turned around, his eyes were naked in the scarred face. In another instant, the mask had fallen on it once again. "First you land on me while skating, then you touch me. Mrs. Marino, I cannot take this sexual pressure anymore. I am not a toy."

Christine did not smile. "Turk, why did you throw that

snowball? Why do you talk to him like that? He's going to fire you, I know it."

"You have just answered your own question, Christine."

"I don't understand." Christine shook her head.

Brandon sighed. "It's . . . involved."

"Tell me," Christine insisted.

"Let's just say I'm tired, Christine. I'm tired of being a pet. I'm tired of being a high-priced flunky. I'm tired of giving manhood lessons to ol' Bax. I am living out of my style, Christine. Getting fired would solve all this."

"Why don't you just quit, Turk? Solve it yourself?"

Brandon scratched his head. "The thought has occurred to me. It is immediately followed by contemplations of poverty. There is not much call for linebackers on the marketplace. Put me down for a gutless procrastinator. Interview over? Or is there something else? You're staring at me."

Christine looked away quickly. "Interview over," she said softly.

Brandon cocked his head to one side, his eyes leveled on Christine. "No, it's not. You had a very funny look on your pretty face just then. Be a good interviewer. Ask it."

"It's nothing. It's silly, Turk."

"Ask it," Brandon said firmly.

Christine raised her gaze to the fierce eyes in front of her. "It's just that back there at the bar, Baxter said that . . . he thinks that . . . you're in love with me. I told you it was silly."

The bird-of-prey eyes in front of her softened for a moment. Finally, Brandon spoke. " 'Silly' is not the word for it," he said. "Good afternoon, Mrs. Marino."

Christine watched the stocky man walk across the deck. Something within her wanted to see the look on his face at that moment, but Brandon did not turn around.

33

NICK SHUFFLED THROUGH the papers on his desk, trying to concentrate. Although the restaurant, as usual, was closed on Monday, he liked to spend the morning hours there, tending to his paperwork. This morning it was difficult. The scene with Joey at breakfast had been bad, the worst ever. Christine crying, Henrietta staying in her room. The works. Torn between anger and love, Nick stared at the papers in front of him, reading nothing. He raised his fist slowly and slammed it down on the desk top. "Dammit," he muttered.

There was a knock on his office door. Startled, Nick glanced up. "Yeah?" he said.

The door opened and Ben Kiley walked through it. "Hello, Nick," he said. He walked over and sat down in front of the desk. As he thoughtfully plucked the cellophane off a fresh cigar, he spoke quietly. "Buy us a drink, Nicky."

"At ten o'clock in the morning? What's up, my friend?"

"Get the bottle out and then we'll talk. You're going to need it."

As Nick withdrew a bottle of Scotch and some glasses from a desk drawer, his eyes remained on Kiley. "What is it, Ben?" His voice was low.

"*It* is not good, Nick. My friend in the state police just let me look at the pathologist's report on that bull that was killed. The broken neck we knew about, but there's something new. It's bad, Nick. That bull had most of its blood sucked out of its body. Teeth marks on the neck, everything. Just like that poor horse back on Long Island."

Nick stared at him in disbelief. "Damn!" he exploded. "Dammit! Dammit!"

Kiley's face was grim. "That's not all, Nick. Want to hear the rest of it?"

Nick nodded, his eyes wild with anger.

"Those two campers that disappeared a few days ago. Well . . . they found them, Nick." His voice grew husky. "What the hell kind of fucking beast are we dealing with?"

"Tell me, Ben. Tell me!"

"They were raped, Nick. I will not describe it to you. They were decapitated and drained of blood. One of them was hung up on a branch and the other was stuffed up a hollow tree. The *strength* of the bastards. I can't imagine. I've been a policeman a long time, but this . . ." Seeing Nick's face, he stopped.

Nick sat unmoving, his forehead cupped in his hands. When Kiley spoke again, his voice was gentle. "It's them, Nick. The bastards have found you. Are you going to leave?"

"I can't," Nick said without looking up. "They'll find us again. I can't."

"Well, I'd say we have problems."

"We!"

"You don't listen. I said I wanted to help you. Do you think I could let something like that run around, knowing what they do? I intend to find the supernatural bastards. I hope I have to shoot them."

Nick's voice sounded tired. "Shoot who, Ben? I told you. They can change their shapes, look like anybody they want to. They could kill someone tomorrow and take his place. Who do we shoot?"

Kiley smoked his cigar reflectively. "O.K.," he said. "Let's see what we've got here. These . . . things. They've found you. They want revenge because of what happened back on Long Island. They're toying with you, Nick. Playing their bastard games. Repeating the pattern of what happened before. First the animals, then those two poor people. It's all for you, Nick. And, soon now, they'll want *you*. End of game."

Nick's eyes were cold, but his mouth was drawn in pain. "I'm not afraid for myself, Ben. I'll shoot anyone who comes near me. It's Chris, Ben. And Joey. They'll go after them. You don't know them."

"I know what they're capable of," Kiley answered, without removing his cigar. "I read the report." After a pause, he continued. "There's one thing for sure. They wouldn't come out in the open to terrorize you like this unless they had you pegged. It took them a long time to find you; they don't want to lose you again. They're watching you, Nick. Hiding in the forest, or it's like you said." Nick looked up. "Yeah. They're even closer. Maybe right here in Mountaincrest. Some of our friends and neighbors."

"Ben, who knows about all this?"

"Just the police. And yours truly. They're notifying the next of kin today. They're going to try to keep . . . the details out of the papers, but I don't know how long they can do it."

"Ask them to keep a lid on it as long as possible, Ben. If Chris finds out, it will kill her."

"I'll try, but you can't hold something like this down for long." He exhaled a large cloud of smoke. His eyes drilled into the other man. "You know, Nick, you're getting out of shape. What you need is some exercise. What do you say we take a little walk in the woods tonight? You and me."

Nick shook his head. "Thanks, Ben, but you stay home. Maybe I'll take a look around later on. It's me they want."

"But—"

"Shut up," Nick said softly, his eyes returning Kiley's gaze. He leaned forward and poured another drink. "For the road, pally," he said.

Arriving home in the early afternoon, Nick was startled to see a state police car parked in front of his condominium entrance. As he got out of the car, a small group of neighbors walked by, looking at the police car and then at him quizzically. Hurrying through the front door, he saw Christine, white-faced, pulling on both ends of a handkerchief, seated on the living-room couch. A police lieutenant was standing by the fireplace. As Nick strode into the room, Christine looked up at him in fear.

"Chris," Nick said. "What is it? What's going on?"

"Oh, Nick, it's terrible. Two people have been killed in the woods around here. The lieutenant just told me."

Nick sat down by his wife and put his arm around her shoulder. He looked up fiercely at the officer. "Can I help you?" he said.

The lieutenant's voice was practiced. "Just a routine investigation, Mr. Marino. We've had a double homicide. We're asking the residents of Mountaincrest if they might have any information."

"We have no information, Lieutenant. We know nothing about it. My wife seems quite upset. If you have any further questions, perhaps I can discuss it with you at another time."

The lieutenant studied Nick for a moment. He put on his hat, adjusting it carefully. "All right, Mr. Marino. I'll check with you in a day or two. Good-bye, Mrs. Marino."

Nick followed the officer out the door. "Lieutenant," he

said, closing the door behind him. "Lieutenant, how many residents of Mountaincrest have you seen already?"

"You're the first, Mr. Marino."

Nick nodded once. "And the last?" he asked.

The man's face grew hard. "What seems to be the problem, Mr. Marino?"

"My problem, Lieutenant, seems to be that someone told you to come here. To see my wife and me. Someone out there seems to be my problem. Some legal person, perhaps," he added evenly.

The man's eyes were as steely as Nick's. "I'll check with you very soon, Mr. Marino. Good-bye."

Nick watched the car drive away, anger once again welling inside him. He took a deep breath, relaxed his features, turned, and went inside to Christine.

The midnight moon shining down on the misted trees gave them a haunted, spectral look. As Nick walked down the fog-shadowed road, he felt no fear. He had checked his revolver twice. He was ready. He would shoot. His anger made him deadly calm, a hunter. He wanted an attack, that was what he was there for. Kill the beast or be killed, but end it, end it.

Silence flowed around him. The air was heavy with the scent of pine. Inhaling the spring darkness, Nick gradually felt the forest fill his being. Soft, delicate voices, exquisite and wild, sang in his memory, remembered echoes.

Nick stopped. He shuddered once and raised his eyes to the clouds that flowed like a gray river in front of the hidden moon. The anger was gone now, replaced by many things. And then he heard it. He closed his eyes, waiting. The sound came again. It was a small voice, the voice of a child. Mischievous. Evil.

"Nicholas," it whispered. "Nicholas and Nicholas."

Without hesitation, Nick stepped off the road toward the dark trees. Again he heard the voice, this time in tinkling, silvery laughter, still childlike, yet ancient, knowing.

It was the laughter that stopped him. Immobile, he realized that his hands had begun to tremble. You foolish bastard, he shouted to himself. Where the hell are you going? Are you that easy? One whisper after all these years and you're theirs again, foolish bastard? You weren't going to hunt them just now. You were going to join them. They want to slaughter you and your wife. They want to kill your son.

With the return of rage, the trembling stopped. Walking back to the road, he stood with his back in the direction from which the voice had come. Nick waited, staring at the stop sign directly in front of him on the other side of the road. After several minutes, he released his grip on his gun and walked across the road. Drawing back his fist, he struck the side of the sign with all his might. His fury mounting with each blow, he struck it several more times, until it was almost bent in half. Exhausted, he thrust his bloodied hand back into his jacket pocket and began the long walk up the hill toward his home.

Nick did not go inside. Instead, he entered his car, wrapped his fist hurriedly in a handkerchief, and took out a bottle of Scotch from the glove compartment. He took a long drink and stared through the windshield at nothing.

Son of a bitch, he thought. Son of a bitch. When does it end? He took another drink. You go to shoot them and what do you do? It's not their bastard magic, Nicholas, it's you. What the hell's the matter with you, pal? Nick shook his head slowly and lifted the bottle once again to his mouth.

Turk Brandon shivered against the night chill. Two o'clock in the morning is one hell of a terrific time to be taking a walk, he mused. He felt exhilarated, free for the first time in years. No wonder he hadn't been able to sleep. Baxter Cabot's furious face had kept looming up before him. He could still hear the breaks in Cabot's controlled, angry voice when he had asked him why he was quitting. Poor old Bax. And poor old Turk. Maybe very poor from now on.

As Brandon turned his collar up, he noticed a figure slumped over the steering wheel of a car he was passing. He stopped, peered into the window, and then opened the door. The car reeked of Scotch. An empty bottle rolled out between his feet. Why, it's old Nick, he thought. Drunk as a skunk. Passed out.

As Brandon put one of Nick's arms around his shoulder and started to lift him out, Nick's eyes rolled open momentarily.

"Whozat?" he said. "Whozat?"

"It's me, pally." Brandon's voice was patient. "Your buddy. Shut up."

The moment Christine opened the door, Turk raised his hand. "He's O.K.," he said. "Too much to drink. Where do you want the body?"

Christine was still too frightened and surprised to talk. She pointed to the bedroom. As they removed Nick's shoes together, his unseeing eyes opened again.

"Whozat?" he repeated.

Turk dropped a shoe. "Your husband has a very inquiring mind," he said.

Christine shook her head. "It's not funny, Turk. This isn't the first time this has happened."

"Sorry," Brandon said. "Bad joke."

As he walked into the living room, Brandon turned and watched Christine close the bedroom door quietly. When she looked up, there was a moment of awkward silence.

"Well," Brandon said.

"Well. I want to thank you, Turk. This was very kind of you."

Brandon gazed at her troubled face. "Don't worry about it, Chris. Man's got to tie one on once in a while."

Christine bit her lip and nodded. "Yes," she said.

"Well," Turk said, rubbing his hands together. "Lovely slippers. I have some just like them."

Christine tried to smile.

"Yes. Oh, I meant to tell you. I gave Cabot my notice this morning. At the end of the week, I shall be free. Very free and very poor."

This time Christine did smile. "Oh, Turk, I think that's great. The price you were paying wasn't worth the money you were getting. You were losing on the deal, Turk."

"Tell that to my landlord. I'm going to tell him you made me do it."

"You'll be all right, Turk. You'll be fine. You're a tough cookie."

The expression on Brandon's face changed. He looked almost shy. "Well, if I ever can't afford doughnuts and coffee, remember, I'm your responsibility."

Christine's voice was tender now. "Anytime," she said.

A smile flitted across Brandon's rough face. "Yeah," he said. "Good night, Chris."

After Brandon had gone, Christine sat down on the couch, unmoving. She felt her eyes glisten with unexpected tears. She had seen the same look in Brandon's eyes that Baxter Cabot had seen. Fleeting, quickly hidden, but unmistakable. Turk Brandon, the old crooked horse, was in love with her.

34

From the diary of Henrietta Knapp:

May 6

Quel temps! Une semaine mystérieuse. Police in the living room? Very neat and good shoulders, but what was he doing here? Shall *never* venture out of the bedroom again without full makeup. The man looked at me as if I was a *suspect*.

Terrible scene in the clubhouse this A.M. Nick accused that man Thorne of something or other. Couldn't make out what they were saying between the threats and Anglo-Saxon dialogue. Chris and I *so* embarrassed. Everyone listening. Ugh!

May 7

In town with Christine today. People so unfriendly. Rudeness *incroyable!* What did we ever do to them? My sweetheart near tears several times.

Mountaincrest neighbors no bargain either. Got very quiet when we walked into the clubhouse for coffee this afternoon. Like we were *lepers* or something. So what else is new. Nobody's touched me in ten years anyway. What's going *on* around here?!?!

May 8

Trouble with the menfolk. Joey's behavior I shall not discuss here. It would break my heart. And my poor Nick. I've never seen him this way. Probably worried about Joey. A week one would not want to *répéter*.

Why do I get this feeling, vibrations of catastrophe? Like the sky is falling down on us. Slowly, but very hard.

35

C HRISTINE DROVE THE car carefully around the winding curves that led to the Mad Mountain Lodge. The melting snow made rivulets that streamed down on either side of the road. The traffic was heavy. Busloads of skiers and tourists headed toward the carnival site struggled up the slippery road ahead of her, filling the sunlit air with the smell of gasoline.

She glanced in the rearview mirror at the silent passengers in the back. Joey was staring straight ahead, Henrietta adjusting her wig in a hand-held mirror. Beside Christine, on the front seat, Amanda shook her head impatiently at the line of cars ahead of them. Although their relationship was as friendly as ever on the surface, something had come between the two women since the night of the Town Hall meeting. Christine knew what it was but could do nothing about it. She could not explain to Amanda, to anyone.

"Baxter Cabot says we're going to lose the vote this week," she attempted.

"*That* we knew," Amanda replied. "Well, the good fight. All of that."

"I think we accomplished a lot, Amanda. He told me he was going to spend a good deal of money, take every precaution available to ensure the safety of the Mountaincrest water.

Without our committee, I'm positive this would not have been done."

"Well, we did that, anyway." Amanda was looking out the side window at the small river of melting snow.

Christine glanced at her. "Amanda," she said softly, "what is it? Something's wrong between us, I can feel it."

Amanda did not turn her head. "It's nothing, baby," She sighed. "It's just that I hear things," she continued reluctantly. "People are talking about you, your family, the police, the things that have been happening around here. When I ask Ben about anything, he shuts up like a clam." She looked at Christine now. "Chris, I don't give a damn about people and their gossip. I *do* care about you. I feel as if you've shut me out. Hell, honey, if you've got problems, tell me about them. Maybe I can help." Seeing the expression on Christine's face change, Amanda's voice grew urgent. "Let me help you, Chris." The pleading look in Christine's eyes was her answer. She returned her gaze to the glistening snowbanks, the car creeping slowly upward in silence.

It was a long time before Amanda spoke again. "Well, at least the charming Mr. Hooker will be happy with the vote."

Christine glanced at her, quickly. "What do you mean? What has all this got to do with him?"

"Leave it to old Detective Ben, the master checker. Truman Hooker, my dear, is a fraud. He is not a handyman, nor is he a farmer. Truman Hooker is an entrepreneur. I shall give you one guess as to who recently bought up most of the land around here. Prospective Cabot Inn golf-course land, you-name-it land. And the rich shall get richer. Overalls, yet." Amanda shook her head, smiling ruefully.

Christine's eyes narrowed. She had always been puzzled by Hooker's attitude toward her. Was that it? The committee threatening his investments? Or was there more? His antagonism had always seemed so personal, so close to hatred. Well, either way, she told herself, to hell with Truman Hooker. I've got my own problems. She clenched her teeth and honked the horn at a slowly climbing bus in front of her.

The crowds around the base lodge were huge. After vainly trying to see some of the ski events near the finish line, the three women retreated to the deck, Joey having disappeared the moment they arrived. Everywhere around them the snow melted in the late-afternoon sun, the constant dripping sounding like falling rain.

"Good afternoon, ladies." The accented voice of Eric Teiler brought Christine's face upward. Framed in the fading rays of the sun, his tall figure loomed above Christine, a dark silhouette against the sky.

Henrietta raised her third bourbon and soda. "Hello, tiger," she murmured.

Christine squinted up into the blue eyes. "Good afternoon, Mr. Teiler. Have you seen Joey? Is he, is everybody ready?" She tried to put some enthusiasm in her voice.

"Everything is ready. And waiting." His smile, as it always did, held secrets. "May I say again, your son is an excellent pupil, Mrs. Marino. He learns . . . so quickly. I shall make of him . . . a champion." He paused, his head to one side, regarding Christine. "Since I last saw you, Mrs. Marino, I have thought about you . . . so much. About your . . . lessons. I feel that there is so much I can do for you. So much. Have you reconsidered?"

"Good-bye, tiger," Henrietta said firmly.

Teiler's eyes never wavered. "Have you?" he repeated.

Looking up into the pale, arrogant eyes, Christine's face grew tense with impatience. With everything that's going on, she thought, I have to fend off this Nordic sun god. No, it's too much. She was about to reply unpleasantly when she noticed the Landaus walking toward them across the crowded deck. She waved them over and glanced back up at Teiler. "No, I haven't," she said, trying to put some finality into her voice. "Not at all."

Teiler smiled and shrugged his wide shoulders. "Then I shall join your son at the top of the mountain." His smile disappeared. "It is, perhaps, less chilly up there."

Unconcerned, Christine watched him walk away as the Landaus approached.

"Ladies," Dr. Landau said, bowing slightly. "We came for one purpose only. To watch your son ski, Mrs. Marino. He told me he was going to lead the torchbearers. We could not miss it. Where is Nicholas, my dear?"

"He's working, I'm afraid." Christine tried to smile.

"*Na*, that is a shame. Terrible business, this restaurant business."

Within half an hour the sun had set behind the darkening mountains. Looking up, Christine saw the mists of night forming on the top of Mad Mountain, obscuring it from view. Streaks of orange rimmed the horizon, fading even as she watched.

Dr. Landau rose with an effort. "Ladies," he said. "I believe it is time. Shall we go and find a good place to watch?"

Walking toward the base of the ski runs, they discovered that the crowd had already formed. They finally found a place to observe the skiers next to the huge, clanking wheel of the chair lift. The noise ground on Christine's frayed nerves, but she tried to disregard it as she waited to see her son.

Standing next to Dr. Landau, slightly apart from the others, Christine looked down at the little man. "Emile," she said, "I'm sorry about the other day. Calling you, putting you on the spot like that. It's just that . . . we're so concerned about Joey, the way he's been acting lately, that I—"

"My dear Mrs. Marino, you don't have to—"

Dr. Landau was interrupted by a voice from behind them. "Mrs. Marino."

Turning, Christine saw the thin, dark face of the man who had spoken to her in the tavern. His features were grim, and his voice was low and intense. "I thought you should know," he continued. "I buried my brother yesterday, Mrs. Marino. I don't know yet exactly what happened to him, but I'll find out. You can be sure of that. And if I find that anybody's responsible, in any way . . ." He paused. His voice grew flat. "Why, hell, lady, I'm gonna shoot somebody."

Dr. Landau stared up at the tall man in alarm. "What are you saying, young man? You can't speak to Mrs. Marino like that. Talk of shooting! I forbid it! You must go away now."

The man did not look at Landau. He was about to speak again, when a voice from the chair lift called to him. "Hey, Gillespie! Get your butt up there and bring that snow caterpillar down here. I want to close up. I ain't got all night."

Gillespie gave the man a long hard look before returning his gaze to Christine. He stared at her for several seconds and then walked to a waiting lift chair, his head turned, his eyes still glaring at her. They remained on Christine as he lurched forward and was borne up the mountain toward the fogbound summit.

Dr. Landau shook his head angrily. "That man is a bad one. Why does he do this, Christine? I think you should tell the police."

Still in shock, Christine managed to speak. "No! It's . . . it's all right, Emile. It's all right."

Still shaking his head, Landau walked over to his wife and spoke to her quietly.

He's telling her what happened, Christine thought. Oh god. Amanda, the Landaus, everyone everywhere, whispering, turning against us. I don't think I can take much more. We'll move again, we'll—

Her thoughts were interrupted by a cry from the crowd. Looking up, she saw the first bright torches weaving their way down the highest trails of the mountain. Emanating out of the mist, like a monstrous fiery snake twisting its way toward the people below, the skiers glided across the blue-gleaming snow, soundless, lighting the night.

She don't know Gillespie, the man thought, his narrowed eyes watching the torchbearing skiers streaming below him. Thorne was right, he decided. That woman brought some maniac killer up here after her. Only he got Jeffrey instead. She's guilty as hell. See it on her face plain as day. He was looking straight ahead now, pounding a fist methodically into his other hand. His thoughts still on the blond woman below, Gillespie felt the first tingling droplets on his face as his ascending chair rose into the fog. The farther up he went, the harder it became to see. He could barely make out the trees that bordered the ski runs now. As he rose, the damp cold hit him, made him shiver. Damn woman made me forget my damn parka, he thought. A long string of mumbled curses broke the white silence and then was gone.

Suddenly, out of the night, soft thunder rolled down to him from the landing above. His face pinched in puzzlement and fear, Gillespie peered upward, trying to see into the misted air above him. He leaned back in his chair in a futile effort to halt his upward motion, but the chair creaked onward, forward and forward, toward the landing above him. When, at last, he could see who was waiting for him there, his body slumped with relief. He almost smiled. He was about to say something, when his eyes suddenly widened in disbelief. An exhalation of fright escaped his open mouth. The figure above him had grown two more heads, each with its own countenance of feral menace. Its hands reached for him now in longing. The lips rippling with desire, the three mouths slowly opened. The sounds that issued forth stunned the man in the chair, flinging him backward in a spasm of fear. It began as a howling blast of arctic winds. It ended in a snarl that filled the night with terrors too profound for the human mind to bear.

Gliding as in nightmare toward the creature above him, Gillespie pressed against the back of the chair as his hands scrabbled weakly to raise the release bar in front of him. After several seconds he finally lifted it above him, but it was too late. He had reached the landing platform and hands of hell were upon him.

As the creature's bestial snarl followed the skiers down the mountain, the eyes of the onlookers lifted toward the mountaintop in puzzled apprehension. Children huddled close to their parents. Several families walked quickly and silently toward their cars. After several minutes of consternation and talk, the attention of the crowd gradually returned to the skiers, the hubbub of voices slowly dying down, all heads turned once again toward the downward-winding torches.

All heads but one. Her body unmoving, alone in her horror, Christine's eyes remained riveted toward the peak. That sound, that cry of the beast, echoed relentlessly in her ears, bringing remembrance, bringing the huge reptilian heads of nightmare sliding from the dark burrows of her brain. She stood unmoving, her features frozen in a mask of terror, as she stared upward.

"Look, Chris, there's Joey!" Amanda's voice rose above the shouts of the crowd, above the grinding noise of the chair-lift gears.

For a moment, Christine's gaze lowered. She saw Joey, the first in a long winding line of skiers, coming down the final wide ski run. Then, very slowly, as if it were against her will, her head lifted and her eyes returned again to the shrouded summit.

Christine did not know how long she stood there, the light from the passing skiers flickering on her face, on the great horizontal wheel that whirred powerfully above her. She was not aware of who it was that screamed first. Perhaps it was a child; she could not tell. As the cries of the crowd around her rose in a chorus of horror, Christine beheld the object of their fear. She began to gasp, unable to breathe. She sat down heavily in the snow, her mouth open in soundless shrieks, her face wrenched in an agony close to death. Out of the mist, the seated figure of a man appeared. Headless, covered with blood, it descended slowly downward, its arms and legs jiggling and dangling in lifeless abandon.

36

I WANT TO get *out!* I want to *leave*." The fatigue in Christine's voice made it unsteady. She sat down among the suitcases she had strewn about the bed, her hands covering her eyes.

"Chris, I've told you twenty times tonight. It's no good. We can't run. It's no good." Nick spoke quietly, but impatience had begun to edge his words. "They'll find us again. If it's them, let's be done with it, one way or another. Here. Now."

Christine's head jerked up. "If, Nick? If? Nick, I heard it. That man's head was taken off. If, dammit? If?" Her eyes narrowed. "You *know* they're here, Nick. You've known it all along, haven't you?"

"I suspected."

"Suspected!" Christine's voice rose. "You *knew*, damn you. You *knew* it. I'm leaving, Nick. And I'm taking Joey."

Nick's eyes flashed. He spoke with a soft finality. "No you're not. Joey and you stay with Nick and the gun. We stay together. You got that, Christine?"

Covering her eyes once again, Christine began to cry silently. "Joey, Nick," she said softly. "Joey. Joey."

As he watched his wife's shoulders rise and fall, a tender sadness began to melt the hardness in Nick's eyes. He walked over and placed his hand on her blond hair, barely touching it.

"Chris," he said, "it's three o'clock in the morning. Can we try to get some sleep and talk about this in the morning?"

Underneath his hand, Christine shook her head, the sobbing still shaking her body.

Nick closed his eyes and sighed. It was a long time before he spoke. "O.K.," he said. "O.K. You win. We'll leave. At least until they catch the bastards. We'll leave, honey."

Christine did not look up. "Now? Can we leave now?"

Nodding his head, Nick almost smiled at her determination. "O.K., baby."

"Nick." Christine's voice was barely audible. "I'm sorry. The way I spoke before. I'm terrified, Nick. I'm so terrified. I just want to leave."

Nick lifted his eyes from the top of his wife's head. Murder glinted from them as he stared at nothing. "I know, baby," he murmured. "I know."

Several minutes later, Joey walked into the living room rubbing his eyes sleepily. "O.K. I'm dressed. Are you going to tell me why, now?"

"Sit down, son," Nick said quietly.

Joey shook his head once. "What's going on?"

As always, Nick was torn between his love and his disapproval of his son's tone and attitude. He walked over to a window and looked out into the night, his hands in his pockets. "We're leaving, Joey," he said, his back to his son. "We've got to leave Mountaincrest for a while. I don't know for how long."

Behind Nick's back, Joey's eyes widened slowly. His whole body tensed.

"We have to do it, son," Christine added. "We have no choice." Joey's head snapped toward her in a movement so swift, Christine was momentarily startled. "It's them, Joey," she continued. "Those people, those . . . things. They've found us. They want to hurt us because of what happened on Long Island. I'm so afraid, Joey. I'm afraid for you." Something rippled behind Joey's eyes. "I know how tough it is, sweetheart. Leaving your school, your friends. But we have to leave, for now. We . . ." Christine stopped. She was staring at her son's face. Slowly, one hand rose to her mouth.

Joey returned his mother's gaze, his eyes alien and wild. The semblance of a smile drew his lips back, showing his teeth. For the brief moment that their eyes locked together, something howled in Chaos, no flowers grew. When he spoke it was with a voice she had never heard. "Friends?" he said. "School? Yes. I shall miss them so much, I cannot go. No, I shall not go. My school and my friends are here."

Standing at the window, Nick's features froze in attention as he listened to his son's voice. He stared out the window as if watching something glide in the darkness.

"Joey, you don't understand," Christine went on uncertainly. "These things are murderers. They kill, they're after us, and they—"

"Things!" Joey's voice tore into the air. "Can you not say it? Give them a name, whore."

At this last word, Nick turned around, his face stricken, his eyes fastened on his son. "Joey!" he shouted hoarsely. "Joey!"

Joey's whole body turned toward him like a cobra facing a second adversary. "You know the name, don't you, Father." He was whispering now. He cocked his head to one side. "My father has been to Oz. He has met the wizard. You know the sweet name, Nicholas. Why don't you tell the whore?"

"Joey!" At Nick's scream, Christine stared up at her husband in terror.

His head still to one side, Joey's smile broadened. "Such pain. Such devotion. It leaves you speechless, my father. Very well. Slut, I shall tell you what the worm cannot. I have left you, my mother. I have left you for the land of rapture. I have left you for the red regions, I have left you. I belong now to the ice princes that dwell behind the frozen waterfalls of Sogne. I shall go home to Sogne fjord to learn. And to hunt." His eyes drilled into Christine's. "I am, Mother, what I am."

Wheeling blindly in his agony, Nick uttered a wordless scream. Drawing his fist back, he plunged it through the window in front of him, shattering the frame and the glass, the sound blending with his own.

Nick stood that way for several long moments, breathing heavily. When at last he turned, his face was pale, lifeless. Except for his eyes. "Who is it, Joey?" It was the way a corpse would speak. "Who is it?" he repeated.

Joey watched without emotion as his father walked into the bedroom, reached into the night table, and withdrew his gun.

"Who is it?" Nick intoned dully when he came back. "Who is it? Who is it, Joey?"

Raising his eyes from the gun to his father's face, Joey spoke mockingly. "Why, it's the trolls, Father. They are among us. It's the trolls." With a swift, sudden movement, he was out the door, slamming it behind him.

As Nick leaped to follow him, his gun in his hand, Christine cried out, "Nick! What are you doing? Nick!"

Nick stopped and faced his wife. The desperate look in his eyes was that of a man who had lost all hope. "It's all right, Chris," he said. "It's all right. I'll bring him back. Stay here. I'll bring him back." And then he was gone.

Christine lay back on the couch, shocked, unable even to cry. Her clenched fist was in her mouth, and her eyes stared in disbelief at the ceiling as loss, and then horror, slowly dawned within her.

37

THE SNOWFLAKES FILTERED down through the pale blue morning sky, falling in silence through the mountain air, covering the chill ground with a thin, powdery mantle. For the past two hours Christine had watched as it delicately enveloped the deck in front of her. She had stopped crying now. She had no more tears to shed. It was her mind that would not stop. Over and over, in an endless cycle of unendurable pain, she heard the words that Joey had said, that Nick had said. I have left you, my mother. Who is it? Who is it? It's the trolls, it's the trolls, it's the trolls. I am, Mother, what I am. What-I-am.

Twice she had run out the front door and walked about aimlessly, not knowing where to look, where to go. Several times she had heard a low moaning, startled each time to realize that it was herself. I am, Mother, what I am.

The ringing of the front doorbell jarred her back to reality. Joey! Christine's mind screamed. She jumped up, ran to the door, and opened it. Standing in front of her was Dr. Landau.

"Good morning, Mrs. Mar—"

"Dr. Landau!" Christine cried. "Joey! Have you seen Joey?"

Landau smiled. "Why, yes. He's at my place this very moment. With Berta."

Christine's hand covered her heart. "Oh, thank God, thank God. You'll never know what we've been through this morning."

The smile on Landau's face deepened. "I know, Mrs. Marino. May I come in?"

"Of course," Christine followed him into the living room. "You can't know, Doctor." She shook her head. "It's so terrible. It's so terrible."

Landau turned. "Mrs. Marino, it would be impossible for me not to know Joey's condition. Have you forgotten that I am his therapist?"

"But you can't know, Doctor. You can never understand. It's them! It's them! They've taken Joey just like they took Nick. Oh god, Doctor, help him, you've got to help him."

Landau was staring intently at her face, at the frantic movements of her hands. After a moment, his head went back, his eyes closed. "You are in pain, Mrs. Marino." He spoke quietly, his eyes still shut. "I have never seen so much pain. It sears you, burns through you like a fire." He sighed deeply.

"I don't care about me, Doctor. Joey. Help him. Do something!"

After a pause, the little man's eyes stared into Christine's. "But I already have, Mrs. Marino." He nodded his head. "Oh, I have."

Christine stared at him uncomprehendingly. "What are you talking about? What have you done?"

The eyes in front of her seemed to light from within. "Why . . . I've made him one of us."

Christine gasped. She sat down on the couch, her eyes wide, trying to understand what the man in front of her was saying.

"Oh, I admit I had some help," Landau continued, watching the lines of horror begin to form on Christine's face with

bright eagerness. "My sister. Your baby-sitter. But mostly
. . . it was me."

"No!" The cry escaped Christine's lips. "No, no, no, no,"
she repeated.

Landau drank in each word. "Do you know, murderess,
how long I've waited to see that terror, that comprehension in
your eyes? That sweetness?" He sat down in a chair in front of
her. "I am going to tell you a story, murderess, and I want you
to listen very carefully."

"No," Christine whispered through her pain. "I won't listen
to you. I'm going to my son, I'm going to my son."

Landau looked at her with the eyes of a hunting cat. He
shook his head patiently. "Have you forgotten, whore? I have
the strength of fifty men. Shall we fight? I can outrun the
wind. Shall you flee from me? Be still, Christine Marino, and
listen. Listen." The word sibilated through the room, a command spoken like a caress.

"I am Hyrmgar, son of Bestla, whom you murdered. My
mother was one of the last of the frost trolls. Not the pale
mutant that was my brother, that is my sister and myself. She
was reality, she was beauty. And you killed her. When you
did that, you brought death unto yourself. He is called
Hyrmgar. I speak not of love, nor honor, nor justice. Frail
mortal mechanics. I speak of the preservation of the clan. I
speak of revenge: sweet, sustaining, and pure." Landau sat
back and clasped his hands. "Revenge needs participants,
Mrs. Marino. The victims must be found. How, oh how to
find you, hidden away so snugly in your little worm burrows.
How clever it was of me to kill the worm father. How quickly
Nicholas wriggled out."

"You . . . you killed Loreto?"

"Let us say I helped him to die. Naturally. No suspicions
aroused. But I shall not dwell on my genius. For now came

my real problem. Hyrmgar, oh, Hyrmgar, what shall you do? What manner of retribution, Hyrmgar? Killing? Of course. But a slow murder, Hyrmgar, a thorough murder, a murder complete. A slaying of the mind and the soul. And only then the body. And it came to Hyrmgar. Such inspiration. The son. The beloved son. Yes, murderess, I have taken him. Oh, such a face. The discovery of loss. The culmination of my efforts. At long last, murderess, such a face."

Christine regarded the round little man, hardly able to breathe. Fighting through her shock and pain, she felt as if she were speaking with the last vestige of her strength. "You bastard. I'll get my son back, I'll get him back. And when my husband gets here, he'll shoot you, he'll kill you, he'll kill you."

Landau's eyes feasted on her face, on the tenor of her voice. "Such a rash statement, murderess. And so untrue. Let us dissect it. First, Nicholas and the gun. I don't like loud noises, a troll idiosyncrasy. And I don't like bullets, a dictate of common sense. That's why I removed the firing pin from his gun while you were serving us dinner three nights ago. You do remember that long phone call I made from your bedroom. Obliging Nicholas, leaving it in the night table, not wanting to scare his guests. Did I forget to thank him? Absurd Nicholas, running about out there now with a harmless toy. Poor, miserable, searching Nicholas. He should thank me for what I shall do to him this morning. What I shall do." After a pause, he continued. "Do not feel slighted, Christine Marino. You are not forgotten. It is all arranged. You are mine. My wicked red sister, she shall have Nicholas. And then, alas, the hunt shall be over. A pity. A termination of delights." Landau sighed and shrugged his shoulders. "Oh, I have not been without my morning pleasure. Visions of Nicholas. His face upon hearing what has happened. The look that must be in his eyes at this moment as he runs about, prying here, prying there, for his son. Yes, a truly joyous dawn." Landau stopped. His eyes roamed along Christine's body. "And the best is yet to come."

With an exhalation of horror, Christine flew off the couch toward the front door. Before she had taken a second step, she was flung back onto it with tremendous force. A guttural snarl reverberated through the room, doubly terrifying coming from the round-shouldered little man in suit and tie who now stood before her.

Landau collected himself carefully, tugging at his vest, adjusting his jacket. Patting his hair, he waved a forefinger at Christine. "You interrupted me," he said. "Do not do that again, whore. Or I shall have to thoroughly shake you." He sat down again. "To continue. You mentioned getting your son back. I'm afraid I shall have to disappoint you on this matter. My brother, Jotunn, in his haste for your . . . favors, left imperfections in his transformation of worm Nicholas. Not Hyrmgar. Not slow, methodical Hyrmgar. Ah, the beauty of it. Songs of perfection. A symphony of thoroughness. From the moment I spoke after you at that first meeting, from the moment you asked my sister to keep Joey company—company!—until now—perfection. What do you suppose they spoke about during those long winter evenings? Baseball and things? Cabbages and kings? Or the ice palaces of home, the Master who sings in the wind, the darkness that lies behind the stars. Oh, the tales that were told on those long winter evenings."

Christine's mind reeled. *The bastards were in my home! With Joey! With my Joey!*

The voice in front of her went on smoothly, filled with pleasure. "On this day of my days, let us reflect on the fruits of my planning, the clockwork precision of my vengeance. My sister, baby-sitter from the north, brings the worm to the young ear. It enters, with whispers of ecstasy. The young man becomes restless, disturbed. Enter therapist Hyrmgar. Yes, he will take on one last patient. Do you have any conception, whore of whores, of the pleasure it gave me to *charge* you for . . . my lessons? And what lessons they were?" Landau rose and stood in front of the fireplace. Christine stared at his back, unable to move. "It is not easy to change the human soul," he continued, looking down into the cold gray ashes. "The conscience dies uneasily, thrashing to the end. Although I've done it before, this one was . . . special. Perfection is a cruel master. I was taxed, I tell you. The ancient arts my brother must have used on your husband—the pulling of the limbs, the howling, the application of ointments—were not applicable here. Too impermanent. Witness Nicholas No. A good therapist is patient. He must change the worm in the ear to a black and feral wolf that ravens its way to the heart, and beyond, to the core of being. Ah, what hours we spent. Sessions of blood, sessions of joy. A transvaluation of values, values that you cannot even conceive. We explored the ways of a troll, your son and I. Together, we studied the black pleasures of night, the red pleasures of the hunt, the silver pleasures of the fjords that shall be his home."

In a blinding fury that obliterated every thought from her mind, Christine sprang from the couch, fingers bent like talons on her outstretched hand. With a swift motion, Landau struck her in the chest, flinging her lunging form backward, but not before one of her fingernails had scratched him just above the eye that had been her target. The breath knocked out of her, her chest racked with pain, Christine lay back on the couch staring up at her tormentor with hatred.

"I'll kill you," she managed to whisper. "I'll kill you. You did that to my son? I'll kill both of you, I'll kill you."

Landau took out a handkerchief and pressed it to his brow. His eyes were glowing red now. The look on his face was triumphant.

"No, Christine Marino, you are incorrect. You have the participants right, but the outcome wrong. It is my sister and I who shall kill you. And your husband. It shall be the final scene in this long, crimson drama. Animals for effect—how I loved watching the dawn of terror on your face—then Marinos, close of curtain." He shook his head. "That impatient man at the ski lift. Almost ruined my scenario. Imagine! Threatening to shoot you. Robber! Reflect on my consternation at his words. Shooting *my* victim! A word to my swift sister put an end to all that. Can you picture her eager face as she flew up the mountain to await the thief! It was, all in all, a fitting touch. I almost cried with joy when I saw your face upon his return."

Landau sat down once again in the chair opposite Christine, his eyes burning into hers. "Look at me, whore." His malefic whisper filled the room. "Look at Hyrmgar. He shall be your lover before you meet your death."

Christine glared in defiant hatred into the scarlet maelstroms that were his eyes. She could hear her own heart pounding within her. As the sound grew in volume, Christine was unaware of the slow cessation of horror, the gradual disappearance of her rage. Louder and louder and louder, the drumbeat filled the room now, sweeping away everything in her brain but its own steady insistence. Christine blinked. The air in the room seemed to redden, as if lighted by the rays of a blinding sunset. Neither the steady throbbing nor the scarlet room frightened her. She felt suddenly relaxed. The beginnings of a strange excitement stirred deep within her body. Closing her eyes, she leaned back on the couch languidly, inhaling the red miasma as if it were some secret incense. Rolling her head from side to side, she felt her entire being pulse in unison with the thunder that now flowed around her. Strange new sounds came to her out of the mists of her mind, frightening sounds that did not frighten her. The shrieking bellow of a creature of madness, half man, half bull, tore through her brain. It was joined by the roarings and howlings of nightmarish creatures. Other forms of terror hissed and cackled her name out of black and bestial maws. And then, above the cacophony of horror, a single voice came to her, permeating her consciousness with a piercing, shining beauty, filling her with an unutterably passionate longing. Her eyes still closed, Christine's arms rose slowly upward in a gesture of love.

The man in the chair stared at her outstretched hands with bright, feral intensity, his features drawn suddenly into a terrifying carnal mask. Between his legs, his sexual organ, like a frenzied snake, began to writhe and lunge against his pants. From his open mouth, a voluminous reptilian hiss issued into the silent room.

At the sound of speeding tires churning to a halt on the pavement outside, Landau's head turned quickly, his burning eyes mad with eagerness. Inward and downward, his body shrank in readiness, his hands clutching the armrests of the chair.

Christine's eyes fluttered open as the heartbeat sounds suddenly ebbed and disappeared. Deep within the thrall that still enveloped her, something whispered in a voice too faint to be heard. She lowered her arms, her fists clenched. She wanted to hear that voice, she wanted to. She had to remember something, to remember. To warn. At the sound of the key in the lock, two words, like oncoming trains, rushed into her brain.

Nick! Joey!

Her mind clear now, Christine turned her head toward the

door. As Nick and Ben Kiley stepped through it, she raised her voice in a scream. "Nick! Ben! Look out!"

An unearthly snarl filled the room. As the two men looked at Landau's face, their eyes betrayed what they saw there.

"My god!" Kiley whispered. "Oh my god!"

His gun pointed at Landau, his eyes never leaving the eyes of horror in front of him, Nick spoke to Christine. "Chris, are you all right? Where's Joey?"

Christine was unaware that she was still screaming. "She's got him, Nick! She's got him! His wife! It's him, Nick! It's him!"

Nick looked at the transformed, bestial face of the little man in front of him. A murderous hatred came into his eyes. "You bastard," he muttered. "Oh, you bastard." Sighting at the red eyes in front of him, he pressed the trigger.

The gun did not fire.

"Nick!" Christine was sobbing now. "It doesn't work! He ruined your gun. It doesn't work!"

With a swift motion, Ben Kiley's hand went in back of him. He brought his revolver out and held it with both hands. "Mine does," he said.

In the next instant the room was filled with an ear-shattering roar as Landau sprang toward Kiley. In that same instant Detective Ben Kiley fired his gun twice at the onrushing figure. A deafening squeal of pain out of the caves of hell came from Landau's set mouth. Instantly, red blotches appeared on his thigh and knee. The force of the bullets thrusting him off his course, Landau lurched past Kiley and crashed through the frame of the door, splintering it into fragments. Once outside, he whirled and faced Nick and Kiley as they ran after him. As he crouched awkwardly on his bullet-shattered leg, the look on Landau's face was so heinous, so profoundly savage, that the two men could only stare, transfixed in fear. His teeth snapping in unbounded rage, Landau advanced on the man with the gun. When Kiley raised his left hand in an effort to ward off the little man, his outstretched hand was seized in a grip of iron and his arm was ripped effortlessly out of its socket. Falling to one knee, Kiley managed to fire again, hitting his attacker in the shoulder. White-faced, his arm dangling uselessly at his side, Kiley prepared to fire again, but Landau was no longer there. With incredible quickness, he had turned and was running toward the adjoining meadow. Nothing that the detective had ever felt compared with the alien terror he now experienced as he watched the familiar little figure race with a horrible, wounded gait across the sunlit, white expanse at a speed that could not be believed.

Several people were running down the walk toward the two men. In the lead was Turk Brandon.

"What is it, Ben?" Turk's eyes were on Kiley's gun. "What the hell is going on? Where's Christine?"

"She's . . . she's . . ." As the pain in his shoulder overcame him, Kiley's voice faltered.

Turning to Ben Kiley, Nick answered Turk without looking at him. "She's inside. She's all right. Ben, give me your gun. I'm going to get my son. Stay near Chris. Call the police. There's a shotgun in the bedroom closet. If Landau comes back, kill him. Kill him, Ben. I'm going to get Joey. I've got to get my son." Kiley nodded, his face drawn in intolerable pain.

Turk was staring at Nick, his face a mixture of compassion and enmity. "I'll go with you, Marino," he said quietly.

Nick turned around. He saw the fierce eyes, the scarred eagle's face. His head nodded once. "Suit yourself, Brandon." His voice was flat. Without another word, the two men began to run down the steps toward the Landaus' condominium.

It took three hard kicks for Turk to break the lock on the Landaus' front door. Nick stepped through it, the gun held in front of him. He ran into the living room and stopped. Seated on the couch in front of him was Berta Landau. On a chair to her right was Joey. It was Joey who brought the slow look of dawning anguish to Nick's face. Glaring at him in unblinking menace from his lowered head, Joey stared at him in hatred. Nick did not recognize his son. It was some strange, malignant boy seated in front of him, not Joey. Not Joey.

Berta Landau's ruby eyes feasted on Nick's face for a long moment. "Welcome, Nicholas." The powerful whisper hissed through the room. "Here is your son, Nicholas."

Nick realized he was close to breaking. He wanted to run, to emit one long scream of agony. He barely heard Turk's voice behind him.

"Joey! Get out of here. Go home. Go home, Joey."

The woman's gloating eyes remained on Nick. "Yes, Joey. Go to your home. Sogne calls. Go."

Joey did not move. His alien eyes remained on his father, gleaming in sly malevolence.

"Go!" The woman's thunderous voice shook the walls of the room.

At the sound of her command, Joey rose and walked through the doorway without a backward glance.

Nick's gaze never left the woman in front of him. In the lower perimeter of his vision, he noticed that his gun hand was shaking uncontrollably.

"So, Nicholas." The voice flowed toward the two men like black electricity. "You have come to me on the day of death. Bearing gifts." The red eyes swung toward Turk for a moment. "How convenient. Put away your broken toy, Nicholas. It is the day of blood. For Nicholas and Christine. And you, Nicholas—you shall be mine."

At the mention of Christine, Turk's eyes narrowed dangerously. "What the hell's this all about, Marino?" His voice was hard. He stared at the old woman in front of him.

Nick did not answer. Instead, he pressed his finger against the trigger.

As the explosion filled the room, the woman grasped her left shoulder where the bullet had grazed her. She stared at the gun in evil wonder, as if it were someone who had betrayed her. Then her burning eyes flashed up at Nick. "You would shoot one of your own, Nicholas!"

Nick shook his head once. "I am not one of you." He was still trying to stop his hand from trembling. "I am not one of you," he repeated, his voice an agonized whisper.

The woman's eyes grew brighter at the tone of his voice. A slow, knowing smile creased her mouth. "The secret songs are never forgotten, Nicholas. Listen. And remember."

A voice. In the dark recesses of his mind Nick heard a voice, singing enchantment, singing desire. Louder and louder, a melody of unbearable sweetness filled his mind with tones of rapture. Nick's eyes fluttered. His outstretched hand slowly lowered. He listened.

The woman's head nodded in covert eagerness as she watched the gun point gradually downward. "Ah-h-h, Nicholas," she said softly, each word spoken like a caress. "You do remember. Ancient, oh ancient. Dreams beyond dreams. Listen. Oh, listen."

His mind reeling with the wild beauty of the siren voice within it, Nick stared in dull horror at the figure seated in front of him. Berta Landau's face and body were quickly disappearing. Emerging, as from an insect chrysalis, a new figure began to form.

The wrinkled skin palpitated and stretched, growing with the enlarging body. The bones, as if suddenly unbound, seemed to elongate as the muscles that held them in relaxed and expanded. Within a minute, a tall white-haired woman was seated on the couch in front of the two stunned men. Nick did not move. Turk Brandon took one step backward, his mouth open in disbelief and horror.

The woman stretched one arm out toward Nick, her eyes still on the gun. The other hand quickly ripped the blouse she was wearing, revealing the breasts and red nipples beneath. "Look, Nicholas, oh, look. The day of consummation. Nicholas." Her voice remained low, magical. "Remembered desires, Nicholas. Unbounded, unbounded." She cupped a breast in her hand and slowly raised it toward Nick. "Place your lips upon me, Nicholas. Come."

The voice within Nick's brain, joined by others now, rose to a crescendo of ecstasy, filling him with a blinding passion. His hand fell to his side, his lips parted in expectancy.

"Nick!" Turk Brandon's voice knifed through the air. He stared at Nick for another instant and then he was at his side, wresting the gun from his fallen hand.

The face of the woman on the couch turned to an atrocity. Her body slumped down, coiling on itself in preparation to strike. "You!" she hissed. "I do not deal with you."

Brandon raised the gun, leveling it at her head. "You're doing it, bitch," he said evenly. "Nick, get out of here. Get the police. Stay with Chris. I'll keep this—"

A voluminous scream of rage filled the room. The woman's body glided through the air like a grim reptile, the bared teeth aiming at Turk's neck.

Sidestepping instinctively, Turk fired. The bullet struck the oncoming troll in the eye. As she lunged past him, an immediate howling roar erupted from her throat, a roar that shattered light bulbs, mirrors, and windows in a single, splintering second. It sent Turk staggering back against the far wall, his eyes glazed with shock. Unable to move, he watched in horror as the troll raced madly along the walls of the room, roaring her pain and rage. She did not run. She used her entire body, writhing and undulating around and around at a speed that he could barely follow. Every few moments she would slither up a wall in her blind torment, only to fall back again to continue her circling, bellowing insanely.

Staring in disbelief at the madness in front of him, Turk raised his hand and fired a bullet into the troll as she circled past him. A change in her voice told him he had hit her, but she did not stop. She continued until she came to the glass door that led to the deck. Without pause she crashed through it, broke through the wooden deck railing, and fell down to the sharp rocks below.

With the cessation of the unendurable noise, reality came back to Turk. Grabbing Nick's arm, the two men raced out past the broken front door and around to the back of the building. Sprawled below them, the body of the troll lay unmoving, her head at an awkward angle among the rocks, a red bullet wound seeping blood above her heart. In death, her mouth was open in a snarl of hate.

Turk waited above her, the gun held in readiness, but the troll was not breathing. She was dead.

The two men gazed down at the figure beneath them. It was Nick who spoke first. "Turk, I . . . I don't know what happened. I couldn't . . . I couldn't . . ."

Too many things were behind Turk's eyes. "Forget it, Nick. She's dead, whatever the hell she was. It's over."

Nick shook his head. "No. No, it's not. Not yet. Give me the gun, Turk. I'm going to finish it." Silently, the two men climbed back up the rocks toward the buildings above.

38

THE MOMENT NICK and Turk walked through the doorway, Christine was on her feet.

"Nick, did you find Joey? Did you find him?" Christine's voice was weak with fear.

Nick looked at the pale face of his wife. Behind her, Henrietta was tying a sling behind Ben Kiley's neck. "Yes, I found him." Nick tried to hide his emotion. "Is he here? Did he come home?"

"No, Nick, he didn't. Where is he? What happened?"

"You were right, Chris. Berta Landau. She was one of them. I've called for an ambulance. And the police."

"My god," Christine exclaimed. "Do you know what they tried to do with Joey? Do you know? I hope you shot her."

Before Nick could answer, Turk Brandon spoke quietly. "She's dead, Christine. She won't bother anybody anymore."

Nick shot a long glance at Brandon before looking back at Christine. "I'm going after the other one, Chris. I'm going to get him. Now."

Christine shook her head too many times. "Don't, Nick. To hell with him. Find Joey. Bring Joey back."

Nick's eyes bore deep into Christine's. When he spoke, it was with a sad finality. "I've got to go after him now, Chris. I can follow him in the snow. He's bleeding badly. We saw it on the way back here. Ben hit him. Ben hit him good. He can't go far. I'm going to finish him, damn him. He's dead. I've got to do it, Chris. If I don't get him now, he'll come back. He'll kill us all. You know them. You know them."

As her eyes searched her husband's face, Christine felt a sudden premonitory rush of fear. "Nick!" she said abruptly, her eyes wide. "Don't go! Stay here! Don't go!"

Henrietta glanced up at Christine sharply. She turned to Nick. "Chris is right. Stay here, Nick. Find Joey. Let the bastard bleed to death. Stay here. Stay here."

Nick shook his head, his eyes never leaving Christine's. "The bastards don't die, Hen. You've got to kill them. I can't let him get away. Not now. I just can't."

"They're right, Nick." Ben Kiley spoke with difficulty, his mouth drawn in pain. "Let the police get him. He's too much for you, Nick. I put three slugs in him and he ran, Nick. He ran. You saw him. What in the name of God is he, Nick? What is he?"

"He's dead," Nick said. "That's what he is."

Turk Brandon was staring at Nick, the look in his eyes unreadable. "I'll go with you, Marino," he said.

Nick turned his head toward Turk, his eyes bright with excitement. Something passed between the two men, unseen by the others. "No, Brandon," Nick said evenly. "I'll handle it. This one is mine." The eyes of the two men were locked together now. "Find Joey, Brandon. Get Joey. Find my Joey."

Christine ran to her husband and grasped him tightly in her arms. "Please, Nick," she whispered. "Please and please, Nick. Don't go."

Trying to smile, Nick kissed his wife's blond hair. "Now don't get dramatic on me, baby," he said. "I'll be right back." He kissed her hair again, smelling its fragrance. He spoke softly. "I love you, pally. My pally." He pulled himself out of Christine's grasp, turned, and walked swiftly through the front door.

Landau's footprints were easy to follow in the newly fallen snow. As Nick crossed the neighboring field and entered a pine forest, he could see the small red spots that mingled with the prints below him. He half ran, half walked, looking warily in front of him. Bleeding like that, the bastard beast can't last long, he decided. He'll die, or turn and wait, but he can't last. He gripped the gun firmly, his finger held in readiness on the trigger.

A half hour later, panting heavily, Nick found himself at the base of Mad Mountain. Looking up, his eyes followed the tracks as they led through the silent forest toward the summit. This was the side that the skiers did not use. It was laden with steep cliffs, sharp boulders, and piles of fallen rock. Without hesitation, he continued his pursuit, his face set in determination.

Toiling upward, Nick swore to himself. The telltale signs of blood had stopped. What the hell are you doing, bastard? he thought. You should be dead by now. What the hell are you doing? And then he noticed something else that sent an eerie shock of fear through him. The footprints below him had suddenly become farther apart, as if Landau were taking huge, leaping strides. Nick stopped for a moment as the realization hit him. There was no more Landau. It was him and the troll on the mountain now. He looked up, almost in longing. His mouth formed the words "I'm coming, beast, I'm coming." He scanned the rock face above him with predator eyes before beginning his ascent once again.

After another hour of slipping and sliding on the loose rocks, Nick was near the summit. He found himself on a small plateau of deep, unmelted snow surrounded by huge boulders. As he leaned against one of them to catch his breath, a powerful, guttural whisper came from behind a boulder directly in front of him.

"Worm Nicholas." The words slid through the air, a deadly malignancy. "I am Hyrmgar, your death. Before I slake my vengeance with your blood, I would share information with you. How I long to tell you. Do you listen? Worm Nicholas. Your son. He is ours. He is one of us, forever unto forever." There was a pause, and then the voice continued. "Do you sigh, Nicholas? Do you sigh? I tremble to see your face. But not yet. Not yet. Your father, Nicholas. I slew him. In my fashion. Do you cry, Nicholas? Do you cry?"

Only Nick's eyes showed the depths of his agony as the troll continued to speak. His mouth was set in a rigid grimace of hate. The revolver in front of him, he took a step on the soft snow toward the voice.

"Be still, Nicholas." The sibilation rose in volume. "Do not be impatient for death. We have not yet discussed your wife. I shall have her, Nicholas. Only today her arms stretched toward Hyrmgar. In longing, Nicholas. Such longing. Do you die, Nicholas? Do you die?"

Beyond feeling now, Nick answered with a deadly calm. "Come to me, bastard. Come to me."

"Oh, yes. Oh, yes. The mouse calls to the cat. Nature in chaos. Superb. But the mouse has a problem. He knows how fast his death can move. So fast. Does retribution come from the right, Nicholas, or the left?"

Nick glanced at both sides of the boulder, the gun waving slowly in his hand. Again the voice came to him, low, mocking.

"The right, Nicholas, here I come, or the left, here I come. Right or left. Right or . . ."

With an ear-shattering bellow of rage, a three-headed figure came sailing over the top of the boulder, its arms outstretched, its eyes bright suns of madness.

Paralyzed in hideous nightmare for a moment, Nick reacted instinctually. He rolled forward, passing under the hurtling figure by inches. Lying prone on the ground, Nick turned. The troll was already on his feet. Nick stared in horror at the apparition in front of him. He screamed. He screamed at the black wolf's head ravening in blood lust. He screamed at the white-maned, hoary head of winter, shrieking its madness at him from its black and steaming mouth. Still screaming, Nick raised his gun and fired.

A horrendous sound erupted from the troll as a wound appeared in the side of his neck. Squealing his agony, he backed away toward the edge of the precipice behind him. In a paroxysm of pain, the ice-rimmed, maniacal face beside it clamped its teeth on the profusely bleeding wound, screeching its fury. Lost in terror, Nick pressed the trigger of his revolver repeatedly. The sharp clicks came to him like the tolling of his own death. At the sound, the troll's heads were suddenly stilled. All else forgotten, three pairs of eyes glared at him now in fiery triumph. In the sudden stillness, Nick leaped to his feet. No more bullets, he thought calmly. Good-bye, my love. Good-bye, my son. He drew his arm back and threw his gun at the monster in front of him. He waited.

Looking skyward, the troll slowly raised his arms in victory, in sacrificial offering to his ancient gods of terror.

It was a mistake. Instant logic tensed Nick's body. Blind hatred, and something deep inside his soul that he could no longer endure, drove him forward. His charging figure caught the troll in the midsection. Locked together, they flew out over the cliff, soaring above the jagged rocks far below, a man-beast that could not fly, drifting in fatal embrace, beyond enmity, beyond purpose, toward distant, secret realms of silence.

Norway
Spring, Present

39

MBER EVENING CLOTHED the land in beauty. The final
gift of the departing sun had been a cloak of gold.
Gold emblazoned the rippling surface of the fjord. It
sifted and glittered through the gently swaying pine branches,
and turned the high mountain cliffs into gilded parapets. The
burnished stillness was broken only by the magic laughter of
the melting snow wending its way down to the gleaming waters below.

As Christine strode along the narrow path, she stared upward at the sunset precipices in wonder. Although she had
seen them before she was still awed by the gray austerity of
the bare crags, the icy, misted waterfalls. She glanced in
shy longing at the huge, tumbled boulders and the cavelike
darknesses beneath, afraid to climb toward them, not able to
leave them.

Joey. Sweet, sad bell, tolling, Joey. In the six years since
Nick's death and the disappearance of her son, Christine had
come each year to Sogne fjord, driven only by the same remembered sentences: ". . . the frozen waterfalls of Sogne. I
shall go home to Sogne fjord to learn." "The silver pleasures of
the fjords that shall be his home." "Sogne calls." She had not
found her son, but Christine knew she would be back again
and again. Joey was here. Somehow she knew it. Joey was
here, he was here.

The path wound upward, deeper and deeper into the snow-patched cliffs. Above her, water trickled downward onto a frozen cataract of ice, its thick stalactites forming a cave of blue darkness behind it. She glanced about her, not moving. She listened. There was the sound of falling water, nothing more. Christine closed her eyes, unable to move.

High on the rock face above her, a figure stepped out from behind the frozen waterfall. With the swift stealth of a stalking predator, he advanced downward, his eyes fixed brightly on the immobile woman below him.

Moments later, at the sound of quick footsteps on the path behind her, Christine's eyes opened. She knew who was there. She turned to face her son. She did not see the beard, the ragged furs, the wild eyes. Seeing only Joey, she raised her arms and called out his name in love.

The onrushing figure stopped. The shaggy head went to one side as the piercing eyes rose to meet Christine's. Dim recognition changed his features, but the eyes remained alert and fierce. With a hollow, bestial voice, a voice unused to words, the figure spoke.

"Hello, Mother," he said.

Shaking with joy, Christine walked toward her son and embraced him, her hands clinging to his neck, his long hair, in a grip of love. She did not feel his body tense; she did not see his head turn away in awkward disdain. She only clung to him, her face in repose, her head resting on his chest.

"Joey," she murmured. "Oh, Joey. My Joey."

In another moment, Joey had grasped her shoulders and pushed her roughly away. "Mother," he said. "Why are you here?"

Christine heard the faint tone of the beast in his voice now, but she did not care. "Come home with me, Joey," she said. "I've found you, my son. Come home."

Joey's eyes widened in surprise. "But I am home, my

mother. This is my kingdom." He looked around with glaring eyes. "My kingdom of ice, my realm of darkness. You do not belong here. You are an intruder here. You must leave." His voice grew low, his eyes cunning, strange. "It is dangerous for you here, Mother. No one walks these mountains after sunset. I am not alone. You must go away. Go away."

The back of Christine's hand rose to her mouth in disbelief, in torment. "Joey!" She could barely speak. "Come with me. I can't let you go, I can't. Come with me." She tried to touch him, but he moved away too quickly. "I'll get you help, Joey. You can be cured, you can be cured."

The wild eyes flared. "Cured? Of what, my mother? Cured of rapture? Of desires that are my being? I know things that you cannot know. I can hear him whom you cannot hear. Would you cure me? Would you deny me joy? Have I not told you, my mother? I am what I am."

Christine looked at him in agony, her eyes filled with tears. "No, Joey! No!"

Joey's head rolled toward her. His voice pealed like thunder. "What I am! Go home! If you look for me again, now or ever, you shall not find me. Go home!"

Christine stood there sobbing, her arms at her sides. "I love you, Joey," she whispered. "I love you, my son."

Joey stared with curiosity at the tears that streamed down her face. Deep within his eyes, something glimmered. "I am happy, Mother," he said, his voice softer now. "Go home."

And then he was gone.

Christine slumped in anguish. She could not move.

Above her, the ice became fire in the setting sun. Deep in the valley below, the glistening pathway on the fjord turned a deeper gold, gleaming inland toward the shadowed mists of evening.

Night. Silver and silent. Under a silver moon, drifting on silver rivers of starlight, the boat wound its way down the fjord.

Beyond tears, beyond sadness, Christine looked down at the ship's wake below, her hands folded carefully in front of her. After five futile days of looking for Joey, even though she knew he would not appear again, of sobbing herself to sleep, she had entered into calmness, a serenity born of knowing. I do not know if I shall come back again, she thought. I must limit my pain, or perish. Slowly, she raised her eyes to the dim, receding mountains. But whatever the future holds, she thought, I am alone no longer. The faint trace of a sad smile touched her lips. I have seen my son. He is alive and I have touched him. I have held him in my arms.

She lifted her gaze to the countless stars. How beautiful. Splendid white embers. She closed her eyes, her face bathed in the gentle night radiance. Faces, echoes of voices, like quicksilver dreams, filled her mind.

She thought of Henrietta, safely ensconced in bed in a cabin below her, and the look on her face when Christine had asked her to live with her permanently. And the Henrietta answer: "If I have to."

She thought of Turk's eyes in that wonderful, ruined face when he had asked her to marry him, to give up her job in Manhattan for the oil fields of Texas. When the ghosts are gone, she had told him. Dear, unlovely Turk would do it, bring her peace, an end to sorrow. For it was Turk who knew all the answers, which, he had begun to teach her, was only one answer. When the ghosts are gone, she had said.

She thought of Ben and Amanda, married now, her closest friends. Ben's torn arm had never healed; it was useless. Ben was quieter now, but he was content with Amanda, deeply in love with her.

A shadow of pain passed across her features. She thought of Nick. Oh, Nick. My Nicky. Tonight I miss you still. After so long, you will forgive me. I have no more tears. I am out of tears. But I miss you, my love. I shall forever.

The expression on Christine's face changed. She thought of the trolls. Her eyes opened, shining as fiercely as the stars. Her mouth drew down in a hatred that would not die.

Damned beasts, she thought. I know you, damned thieves. Her head nodded. You took from me everything that I loved, damned dread beasts.

The hatred slowly drained from her face, leaving only sadness.

Oh, thieves, oh, ye dreadful. Our wars became our destinies. Joined in battle too ungentle for survivors, feral soldiers, we are, all of us, slain.

Yes, ogres, I, too, am killed. A murder of the mind. For there is a sadness that is unassuaged by time. There is a loneliness that does not end.

Christine looked for the last time at the distant, night-shrouded mountains.

Good-bye, my son. Good-bye, my heart. I leave you to the dark hills. I leave you to the violent night. I leave you.

Good-bye, and again. Good-bye.